QUESTUS

SHAWN WILLIAMSON

This edition published by CFI Books 2022

ShawnWilliamson.com

First published in the United Kingdom in 2022 by CFI Books

CFI R&D Limited trading as CFI Books
27 John Smeaton Court, Manchester, M1 2NR

ISBN 978 1 7391019 1 6

Edited by Anthony Johnson
Editorial Assistance by Lois Stevenson
Typeset by Anthony Johnson
Cover Illustration by Jordan Haynes
Graphic Design by Martin Smith
Book Cover Design by Nathan Newman

SPECIAL THANKS

ACKNOWLEDGEMENTS

With special thanks to our first Questers

Nicky Linas
Karl Sinclair
Gill Harbach
Elaine Griffiths
Lois Stevenson
Jo Stevenson
Nathan Newman
Mikki Lewis
Wayne Murphy
James Gavin
Vicki Dilley
Ken Keeser
William Roberts
Marcia Stephens
William Richardson
Carl Whitwell
Jane Mashburn
Elizabeth Lee
Mary E. Glenn
Giorgiana Newman
Anthony Johnson
Ryan Parker
Nicholas Connor
Craig Travis
Christian Turford
General Lee
Freud Houdini Newman
Alan Scott
Alan Lingwood
Peter Williamson
The Zackarelli Family

Mark Riley
Toby Webster
Christine Cole
Chris Ross
Beatrice Cassetta
Sean Cullen
Wendy Mitchell
Roxanne Newton
Maisie Fenner
Ruby Alexandra Beloz
Graham Gardner

CONTENTS

Prologue 3

1. Truth in stone and words 6
2. Questers versus New Babylonians 8
3. DNA History 11
4. The Grail Revealed 13
5. How Angus and Vanessa discovered the key one week earlier 26
6. Angus Falls 30
7. Angus tells the secret 43
8. Sacred Love in Santiago, Chile 48
9. The Journey begins 49
10. Plato and Atlantis 55
11. Sacred Lovers 61
12. The Research begins 66
13. Looking back at the Sinclair Castle and Lighthouse, 2015 70
14. The Feast of the Knights and Pirates 74
15. Sea Legend, Chiloe, Chile 75
16. Rodrigo Bermodes, Special Forces, Chile 77
17. The Templar Tombstone 79
18. The missing statues of Rosslyn Chapel 80
19. The search for the carved codes resumes in Scotland 83
20. Hotel 'Highland Dirk', Rosslyn Village 89
21. A night visit to Rosslyn 96
22. Isobel arrives in Edinburgh 102
23. Castro, Chiloe, South America 108
24. The Island of Sailing Souls 109
25. Vanessa and her Island of Sailing Souls 113
26. The Spada Peninsula – Mr and Mrs Poole 124
27. Sacred Love on the Island 137

28. What really happened at the Calbunco Volcano 1320 AD 152
29. Native Chilean Mapuche 154
30. The lost Templar fleet re-appears 2020 157
31. Angus discovers his sword in the lost Templar fleet 164
32. The Quester address against the New Babylonians 175
33. Ye shall know them by their works 180
34. The Ark is revealed 185
35. Angus's test to Seize the day 189
36. Questus report from Andrew Sinclair 196
37. Angus becomes a Knight Leader 201
38. The Locust Pit 206
39. The New Babylonians cometh 212
40. The attack of the mice and rats 216
41. The drone Assets of Babylon 218
42. El Nino leads the stray dogs 222
43. The Battle of the Mosquitoes 228
44. The Deluge comes 231
45. The Last Tango dance 233
46. A promised Tango 234

QUESTUS

BY SHAWN WILLIAMSON

'When you are young and strong and full of hope, sit down one day and think about the world. Decide what you would like to do above all else and then go and do it. Follow your star to the bitter end no matter the hazards or the perils; no matter even if the star proves to be a false guide and you die in the attempt. You will have lived life to the full, you will have enjoyed yourself, and even if you leave behind no material treasure, you will leave riches in the hearts of those who have drawn strength from your strength and who will cherish your memory until their day is done."

-FA Mitchell Hedges

This book is dedicated to the writer Dr Andrew Sinclair, "that's all I am saying".

Prologue

Ackergill Towers, Scotland 2018

The Sword and the Grail

"You found something under Rosslyn didn't you?" Angus MacWilliam asked the writer.

The old writer continued to scribble. He wore lines on his face like intellectual battle scars of knowing things, better left unknown. It was going to be difficult for him to avoid answering the question under his Quester Oath.

"But we are here to talk about your discovery Angus? Questers are pledged to honour and honesty regarding their discoveries."

"Aye Andrew, I know, but there's been many developments lad!" Angus MacWilliam replied urgently.

The morning was cold and calm over Sinclair Bay, where Ackergill Towers, the hereditary home of Clan Keith stands stretching its stone fingered battlements to the sky. Here the sea can be raised to a furious storm by the punishing winds. But there was also a sense of ominous change which went deeper than the weather. Already much had changed in the country and seemingly not for the better.

Angus looked, through the narrow slit window from Ackergill Towers, over to the ruins of the mysterious Sinclair sea fortress plaited into the rocks across the bay. A beam of light from the lighthouse flashed on and off further up the coast. Once it was the headquarters of the modern-day Templar Order known as Questus to which both Andrew and Angus belonged. It was a place where a person received enlightenment and education which changed their perception about the nature of the world. In one form or another, the Quester School had been in these parts since the dawn of time. From this tower of light shining into the Pentland Firth, the Questers had planned to make the world a better place. The Quester School was forced to operate underground.

"What did ya' discover in the vaults at Rosslyn Chapel?" Angus asked again.

"You'll know all you need to know, remember you were not a Quester when I began my excavations and you were not quite ready for the truth," Andrew said, grimacing. "And as we know things are changing in the world." Angus buried his head in the sand, ignoring Andrew's words.

Angus reflected on how he'd met the famous writer and Grail Quester back in 1994, after his book '**The Sword and the Grail**', had been published. He'd received a copy of Sinclair's book from his outlawed father. Inside the book, Mike MacWilliam had written, 'seek this man out' in the spidery writing of a tortured genius.

In 2005 the most popular fiction book ever published had been written by Dan Brown, called '**The Da Vinci Code**'. Back then the obscure Rosslyn Chapel, had been highlighted as the possible tomb of Mary Magdalene; many had asserted she'd been the wife of Jesus Christ. The implications of this reverberated across the world as his book sales rocketed. But this fantastic statement paled into insignificance before the truth. Only the writer Andrew Sinclair had dug down into the vaults of Rosslyn and by chance, the event was filmed. Andrew had been sponsored to try and find the 'Holy Grail' and 'The Ark of the Covenant' there. But those who knew him were aware of something else going on in the background, something he pledged to keep secret with his life.

Angus walked over to the window where Andrew was sitting on an armchair upholstered in Clan Keith tartan. He reached out and their two hands locked together in the secret sign of eternal bond reflected in the Quester's grip. Thumb to small finger, small finger to thumb, the alpha and the omega, the beginning and the end.

Truth in stone and words

Angus walked over and warmed himself by the glowing coals of the fire. Andrew lurched forward from the tartan armchair where he waited, warming himself next to its glow. The fire spat out flames into the blackness. The old writer beckoned Angus to sit in the chair opposite him.

"It's been a long time Angus, but as soon as I heard of your discovery I came right away," he said, reaching for his glass of wine. And saying "Stop pacing around and sit down, we don't have much time!"

Angus glanced at the wine. "Och', looks like our brand ?"

"Yes, it's a 'Châteauneuf-du-Pape Reserve', rather a hypocritical choice, some might say, based on my demolition of the Papal Inquisition," Andrew replied. Angus glanced at the medieval sword displayed on two metal brackets above the fireplace. The sword triggered him to have a memory from when he'd been a Grail Knight.

"Aye, you were the man who rectified the Inquisition back in the day," Angus said.

Andrew reflected over his medieval legal battles on behalf of the Templars. "My legal challenge against the King of France back in 1310 was nearly upheld. As we know the enemy did all they could to destroy us back then, yet failed." Andrew slammed his fist down on some notes he'd been writing. "Furthermore, those insidious servants of evil are back again, today we call them by their true name though, the New Babylonians, those who put profit before God." This was consistent with Angus's vision of the ancient Babylonian Kings and officials who once wore golden threaded garments but now wore plain suits for their work of corruption in the halls of governance worldwide. Now humanity faced the greatest emergency ever, as events were once again turning biblical.

Often Andrew, through time, had confronted dictatorial organisations that were oppressing the people. He travelled the world, appearing phantom-like in areas of political upheaval challenging tyrants and documenting his missions. But it was never quite clear if there was any other organisation behind him since the Quester School had gone underground.

"You know in my early days, I thought the Holy Grail was not real, but more like a body of sacred enlightenment." He fumbled inside his writer's case for something. "I've since changed my mind on that."

There was something on Angus's mind. "When you dug down into the vaults at Rosslyn, you must have felt the sacred energy of vibration or power?"

"I was the only person ever to dig down into the vaults. And yes! I did feel something booming through the ground, like a sacred note of music. But now is not the time to talk about it! We are pressed by a great danger."

Angus persisted with his questions thinking about the Rosslyn Chapel excavation film where Andrew broke through the stone slabs on the chapel floor.

"And you found something, didn't you?" Angus repeated.

"I came here to talk about what you found Angus, not to go down more rabbit holes!" Andrew responded.

Angus had concerns, which he couldn't explain directly. As much as he admired Andrew, he was being elusive about something.

"Och' Andrew, now it all makes sense. I knew some months ago that the best way to conceal a secret in plain sight would be to promote a film of you discovering an old wooden Grail at Rosslyn. But I know you found something else didn't ya'?" Angus asked, smiling.

Awkwardly Andrew walked over to a large oil painting of a 17th Century beautiful fair-haired lady. He held his hands behind his back as if ready to address a hall of academics when really he was about to change the subject.

Having dealt with some of Angus's character deficiencies as well as being aware of his own, Andrew smiled the all suffering look of a martyr.

"Angus you still have much to learn. I've always valued your technical skill and knowledge about stone and its properties during our investigations of sacred buildings and tombs. Now is the time to use your gift of intuition to protect yourself in this world of jackals and hyenas".

"Aye,' you're right Andrew lad," Angus replied mellowing. "The world has gone insane. Some might say evil."

"You know as well as me, that the New Babylonians are ramping up their world control agenda in various malignant ways. And as always they must be stopped!"

Questers versus New Babylonians

Angus drifted elsewhere. He thought back to the Quester School of enlightenment, where he'd learnt about the real problems of the planet and the projects being driven against the interests of humanity. The driving force behind this was a malignant scientific plan to attempt to change people's DNA. Once the people were disconnected from their spiritual source, they would live as mere zombies, herded around like compliant slaves. Those perpetrating this infernal regime on humanity had already reverted to worshipping the gods of biblical Babylon. Yet they thought of themselves as augmented or enhanced in some way because they'd altered their own DNA by removing the God gene. Now those malignant adepts wore silk suits and drove elite cars and did diabolical things by their willingness to do anything which brought in money and power. God had warned humanity about them in the Bible.

The New Babylonians were engineering world chaos through enmity linked to political control by bribing politicians. And if people had ideas contrary to their plan they were outed, and cast out from their jobs and sometimes jailed and worse. These poor souls included better-qualified scientists, medical professionals, and politicians with integrity. Most of the information which the New Babylonians and their agents used against the people, came from artificial intelligence in the form of fake statistics and computerised human model planning. Running parallel with this, were increased occurrences of famine, volcanic destruction, plagues and fake wars all linked to their war against God. Humanity was living yoked to fear as the world's animal species became extinct. People talked about global warming, remaining unaware that the real apocalypse was coming.

Those who could see the truth became Questers. The Quester School at the Lighthouse study centre had enlightened many. And all of them would at some point stand shoulder to shoulder against the New Babylonians.

"The Quest is to save all humanity, Angus. And don't think you can't become a New Babylonian just because you are a Quester! We make those choices in our hearts by the way we think and behave in our little lives; like making a corrupt deal or not speaking out against injustice or crimes against humanity and the natural planet. To be compliant with the New Babylonians is as bad as being one of their leaders." Andrew looked very serious and continued.

"You see we've discovered that the changes which occur in a person when he starts to become a New Babylonian, first begins in their blood. It starts as soon as a person doesn't speak out about corruption or darkness or essentially wicked things. And it gets worse the longer a person says nothing. Then people become pacified to the idea of having their DNA further changed through many different processes, including medical procedures. But for Questers we have a chance to change the world for the better, because for us, what is born of the blood can never be driven from the bone."

"Aye yer' right Andrew. I see being a New Babylonian, not as a state or country, but more like the condition of ya' soul." It was a conversation that could have gone on forever, but the clock was ticking. "Aye Andrew lad, it has gotta' stop before we all get consigned to the coming apocalypse."

"You see, that is the problem, Angus. We know the New Babylonians by their blood. And actually, so does all of nature. Dogs can scent their difference. Ever heard of the saying 'if a dog doesn't like you, it's because of a good cause?' Even Insects avoid those with New Babylonian blood in the same way they swerve away from margarine. Birds through some unknown sense, steer clear of them. Crows are curiously able to discern them from a great height. Animals are so much closer to the source we know as God. For as in the Bible and ancient texts the New Babylonians are God's enemy in all they are and do."

Andrew wanted to continue to tell Angus about what he'd sworn to keep secret. But he thought Angus wasn't ready. But he was wrong; he had no idea of what Angus had discovered and how far he'd gone on his own Quest. He'd quested inside himself to find the truth, enabling him to make an incredible discovery.

"Och' Andrew, man alive, we all know they're pissing on our backs and telling us it's snowing!"

Andrew smiled again. "Always to the point Angus."

DNA History

Outside Ackergill Towers gusts of wind buffeted the battlements. Below attached to the huge roof beams, moth-eaten silk flags wafted in the breeze. Meanwhile, Andrew traced his thumb over the beautiful portrait of the lady in the gold picture frame, as if he'd painted her himself.

"I digress. Look at this beautiful work of art. People die for love or the lack of it, which never ceases to amaze me." He turned around on his heel, facing the sea. Light emanated from behind the grey clouds scudding across the bay, casting shadows and highlighting every divot and thought scar on his face.

Aye Andrew, ya' always changing the subject!"

"And what about that lady you brought up here? She thought she'd been connected to your own people, Clan Gunn for God's sake, and from another life? And you unknowingly brought her here to Ackergill where she discovered this portrait painted 300 years ago, looking exactly like her, which by the way was not a coincidence!"

"Och' man! Andrew don't be so hard. I was in love with her."

"My point is Angus, sometimes previous lives are not always good for us. Yes, your gut feeling was she was descended from Clan Gunn, a correct intuition as her DNA test proved. But because you're a romantic fool, you'd imagined that somehow from a previous life, she'd been your bride." Andrew was in full swing. "But the reality was, she'd been dragged here to this castle to be the reluctant bride to the Chief of Clan Keith. Don't you see it's all about synchronicity?"

"Och', Andrew, you know how it works in love." Angus looked around awkwardly, searching for Vanessa.

"You thought that it was all about you, but in fact, you were merely part of her synchronicity!" Turning to the window, he raised his hand like a stage presenter introducing the next act. "But I'll tell you what happened to her, back then in 1620. Did you realise I checked out her history?" Andrew looked down again at his notes. "And not on the bloody internet, I am talking first source information from the British Library, the good old way of research."

"Och, I did na' know you'd studied all that Andrew."

"All I am saying is, that your lady friend was so repulsed by the ugly Clan Chief, that in her other life, she threw herself onto the rocks below, spilling her lovely blood into the sea!" Scowling, he looked down onto the rocks where the sea was frothing with anger. "Maybe you had been her original suitor, but then you lost her to the richer, more powerful, yet repugnant Chief of the Keiths. But what really happened was that she was remembering her previous life, but needed you, to help her release her from that event. You were just part of her release from an unfulfilled past life". Angus was demoralised by Andrew's words. But it was the truth.

"Aye, that'll be right then," Angus admitted reluctantly.

There had always been alliances and wars between the clans in northern Scotland. Clan Sinclair was stronger than the others because they were better connected to the establishment since they'd become **Guardians of Sacred Relics and Treasure**. The Sinclairs also held a secret alliance with the Templars written in the blood of their souls. In fact, it was they who rescued the refugee Templars that fled from France.

Angus looked up into the castle roof. Moths floated on the warm air rising from the fire. They feasted on the silken banners as they had always done over the years.

The Grail Revealed

"Now Andrew, come on man. Tell me about your discovery first?"

"Ok, I will show you, but remember, if I tell you the secret of what I discovered, then you will be eternally responsible for it?" He took off his reading glasses and looked directly at Angus. "I hope to be sure that you are not a treasure seeker? And that you are aware of the grave responsibility of knowing things which should not be known?" Andrew sighed. "And in any case, we're both still Agents of God. But through the Quest, we will solve the problem of the New Babylonians and the danger they represent to the Earth."

Mysteriously a raven flapped prophetically past the slit window cawing and screeching around the battlements. Angus watched it like a schoolboy admiring his favourite model car.

"Ravens Andrew ma' man, ravens. They brought food for the prophet Elijah when he was hiding from his enemies. Then God sent him to destroy the Baal worshippers."

"Exactly Angus, people still think the Bible is a work of fiction. Because they've been conditioned to watch TV propaganda like it was real life, made that way by the New Babylonians, who are now preparing to usher in a wicked form of control over the entire planet. A control which will force people to take an electronic mark under their skin if they want to buy food."

Angus's mind was back in the swashbuckling past. "But Andrew ma' man, the greatest mantra of all time was that of the Pirate Brethren. I know there's more than a passing connection with them, and the Templars and the Hospitallers." Sometimes Angus said things that seemed like they were not related but were later linked to the unfolding truth.

"I know it well," Andrew replied, but before he'd chance to recite it, Angus began saying their mantra.

"***We the Pirate Brethren of the coast are enemies of the world, but friends of God.***"

This somehow spurred Andrew to tell his secret.

"Meanwhile, I found something outside the vaults of Rosslyn, which was not only significant but also extraordinarily beautiful."

"Och' come on man, tell me, tell me everything!" Angus replied excitedly.

"I found a Grail bowl in an oblong cavity with skull and crossbones carved into it, next to the main vaults. It was impossible to get into the main vaults directly as they've been walled up in some cunning way and backfilled with silica sand. Which I might add, we discovered came from Egypt. The walls down there are like a jigsaw, each stone interlocking together. They were impossible to get through."

"Aye, I'd heard all about the interlocking stones. I studied similar building techniques from ancient cities in Peru. But the sand question is interesting. There's a lot of silica sand down on the beach of the Firth of Forth. So why would they bring it from Egypt?" Angus asked.

"I'll get to the sand question later," he said without any intention of mentioning it again. "All around me underground stood the sacred beautiful carvings of the Templars. The Lamb of God, St John the Baptist, Mary Magdalene, Mary Mother of God. Many other statues and works of art were down there also. The problem is that the surrounding stonework was designed to collapse in on itself or onto anyone attempting to break through its sealed stone walls."

Angus had a curious feeling about the 'other statues' Andrew mentioned and wondered if he'd seen the statue of Admiral Piri Reis in the vaults when he was down there.

"The Grail bowl was compacted with frankincense oil and sheep fleece. Inside it was the Urim stone, wrapped in the wool," he said, turning to Angus, "I think you know about the Urim stone don't you Angus?"

"Aye, that resonates. Ya' wily ol' fox," Angus replied, remembering.

"Did you recall in my film, that I found it rather difficult to hide my joy, as I scrambled back through the Rosslyn crypt passage from the vaults? Of course, the cameras were still rolling and my discovery was not expected as we simply couldn't dig deep enough. I found other things there, like bits of armour and a medieval-style knight's helm. And the ring you wear, with the Clan Gunn crest. Thus proving the Gunns, also known as the Ancient Sea Kings, in some capacity had also been down there." Angus had no idea that Andrew had recovered his ring from the vaults of Rosslyn.

Andrew reached into his briefcase and brought out a leather pouch with the small wooden Grail bowl in it. Finally, he presented it, holding it up. Inside the bowl was a gold clasp with a turquoise stone.

"Here is something more powerful and precious than anything else!"

Angus reached over to touch it. Andrew pulled it away quickly. "No, don't touch it! Don't touch it! I haven't even touched it yet! I only handle it by the stone's gold frame, protected with sheep's fleece, as was the real-life Shamir." Andrew gazed transfixed by the stone. "When Aaron the High Priest attended 'The Holy Ark of the Covenant', he wore a vest of stones just like these." He pointed at the gold surround and handed it to Angus. "Just look at the inscription in the gold."

Angus held the carved gold snake surrounded with flames belching out of the fanged mouth, being careful not to touch the stone between his fingers. They were both captivated by the weird lambent light emanating from it. Engraved around it was an illustration of the Holy Ark of God. It was like drawings of the Holy Ark seen in ancient texts where the Holy Ark was drawn as an oblong box with carrying poles, with two naive style angels sat on top leaning towards each other as if in conversation.

"Och, it's a beautiful thing. But something puzzles me?"Angus questioned.

"I know what you're going to say, you're going say what about the fire breathing snake?" Andrew sat back. "Because you know exactly what it is Angus, because you damn well discovered it for the Templars. You really must start to remember about your past!"

"Aye, true man, I know the gold clasp represents the Shamir. It's the tool the ancients used to cut stone with light, illustrated as a fire breathing serpent."

Silently Andrew pondered Angus's self-doubt, wanting him to remember.

"Come on Angus you know exactly what it is. Otherwise, I've failed as your teacher? You need to start believing in your abilities. It's time for you to start believing again. The New Babylonians are the enemies of God."

"Aye, that is the truth," said Angus.

Andrew scowled. "Realise that we walk a different path and in the opposite direction to them. That's the way it is. And thank God we had time to awaken you in our incredible Quester School over at the lighthouse. Otherwise, all would have been lost. Because we've always known who you are."

Angus thought back to his days as the last keeper of the Sinclair Study Centre at the Lighthouse, a few years earlier. It was the time everything came back for him and he began to remember the shadows of his previous life as a Grail Knight. Angus gave the stone back to Andrew in the beautiful snake clasp. He carefully re-wrapped the sacred relic in the sheep fleece, putting it back into the briefcase with his writings. Angus looked at the Gunn clan ring on his own finger. It reflected an orange aura coming from the fire.

"We know you were there as part of the original excavation team who retrieved 'The Ark of the Covenant' from the Temple." Angus shivered. "Do you remember anything else, Angus? Did the Urim stone help you remember ?" It was a loaded question.

"Aye there is something man, there's something else to all of this." But the truth was Angus suddenly felt sick. "One knight amongst a hundred Templars was a Grail Knight. And I know I was the Grail Knight."

"Good Angus you are remembering at last!" Andrew proclaimed.

"But how can that help the Earth now?" Angus replied. But Andrew had more to say about the wooden Grail bowl.

"In the film, it appears that all I found was a medieval wooden drinking bowl belonging to some overworked stonemason. The fact is, that humble bowl is made of acacia cedars of Lebanon. We know this wood is sacred, used in the Holy Ark to protect it." Andrew closed his eyes and began to recite ancient texts about the building of the Temple of Solomon.

"For the house, while it was in the building, was built of stone made ready at the quarry; and there was neither hammer nor axe nor any tool of iron heard in the house while it was being built. "

'Hell fire Andrew what are we getting ourselves into."

"The Midrash tells humanity that the stones of the Temple flew and rose up by themselves, setting themselves in the wall of the Temple and building it." Andrew was very knowledgeable when it came to sound and how the ancient civilisations used it to levitate stones.

"Aye, sometimes I am out of ma' depth bonnie lad, that much is true."

"Now you will know Angus. The Ark is activated by the sacred stones on the breastplate of Aaron. The Urim and Thummin stones, activate the Shamir or fire breathing lance, bringing it to life. You have no idea how powerful it is. What we have here, is advanced technology. As such, it is desired by the New Babylonians now destroying the planet." Andrew clenched his jaw. "Angus where is the other stone, where is the Thummin stone, we need it now!"

"Och' Andrew I canna' remember."

Andrew raised his eyebrows. "Oh yes, you can Angus for the sake of humanity you must remember!"

Angus changed the subject. "I am no scientist, but that little wooden Grail you discovered has got to be supernatural."

"I took the liberty of having the Grail bowl carbon dated. And although they thought it was medieval, I can confirm that it was in fact, far older. In fact from around the time when 'The Ark of the Covenant' was active. You see the natural fibres of Acacia cedars of Lebanon protect humans from the invincible power of the Ark. This very special wood also protected all the other treasures in it. Only those accepted by God can handle them directly. But we must never touch the stones."

Angus was curious about the sheep fleece. "What about the sheep fleece? Why is the stone wrapped in sheep's fleece?"

"Sheep fleece has supernatural qualities and a high resonating hertz value associated with protection. Remember the Golden Fleece which the Greek hero Jason and his Argonauts searched for? Let's not forget the mass of sheep fleece used to stabilise the beach around the Nova Scotia Oak Island money pit."

"Is it true Andrew? I read that there was a great magus called Michael Scott involved in planning the money pit treasure shaft in Nova Scotia."

"Yes, Michael Scott was Fibonacci's teacher. Early wireless radios needed a cat's whisker and a crystal to enable it to function. It's a kind of alchemy because when natural molecules of flesh or fur interact with certain elements from the planet, like stones or crystals, supernatural things tend to happen, some call it Alchemy."

"Aye, that'll be right, I learnt about sonic vibration in the Quester School of Enlightenment. We need that school back right now!" Angus looked dejected. "Och' but I know I was na' the best scholar."

"No, you were more interested in singing your bloody Hibernian football songs! I will never forgive that period of your distraction, from our very important works."

"Come on man ya' know what happened to me," Angus replied. Then he started mumbling the Hibernian anthem made famous. ***"The sun shines on Leith. My heart was broken, my heart was broken sorrow, sorrow."***

"Stop Angus! Look, we are at battle stations now. The school will return back into the open, once we've thrown off the yoke of the enemy. And there's a more important spiritual dimension to this." Andrew spared Angus the full scientific explanation. "The Grail bowl was miraculously hidden away on a ledge when I found it and inside was the Urim stone. It shined with some supernatural light, yet there was no light down there in the darkness of the vaults, apart from the light from my tiny torch. The Urim stone inside the wooden Grail comes from the breastplate of the High Priest Aaron, who attended the Holy Ark." He looked down at his briefcase.

Angus watched intently. "Aye make sure it's safe, Andrew for God's sake."

"You might remember from your bible studies that Aaron was the brother of Moses. I am telling you this because you are now a modern-day Quester. But we all know that once you were a Grail Knight. You were the one knight in every hundred who attained the status of 'Grail Knight'. And I know you've been having dreams about the dreadful magnificent light, the flaming sword, and the red meteorite stone in the crypt at Rosslyn because we all do. You've also been feeling ill or depressed or both. It's a hard path, but enlightenment has come to you, as it's coming for all of humanity. All of us who Quest, experience the same visions and illness during our evolution. So I know who you are, I've always known. But it's up to you now to remember."

Angus walked over to the table and poured himself a glass of wine from the house of the Pope, 'Châteauneuf-du-Pape', still mumbling the Hibernian soccer anthem.

"Aye, the Urim stone you found in the Grail bowl, must be connected to the greater treasure in the vaults under Rosslyn?" Angus replied fishing for more information. He was also intuitive enough to know there was another story about the Holy Ark, a story which he knew Andrew was holding back. A story so outlandish and supernatural a standard type of person or 'normie' would label the tale-teller, a conspiracy theorist. It was a title both Andrew and Angus were proud of wearing, like a badge of honour.

"Truly, there's more than one treasure in the vaults. As you are aware Angus, I carried out, the only major ground scan of Rosslyn when I was writing my book, ***The Sword and the Grail.*** And I know you've studied the Rosslyn ground plan map."

Andrew pointed down to the information on the map next to the wine on the table. On the Rosslyn ground plan there were other vaults or chambers marked in red.

"The land which Rosslyn Chapel is built on belonged to the Templars and in a way it still does. The mystery starts in the forbidden caves below the chapel, already a sacred site. As you are aware they only built Temples like Rosslyn on geo-physically important ancient sites linked to specific magnetic power points." Something else was on Andrew's mind though. He looked intently at Angus. "We have been patient with you Angus, because you know where the other stone is, you know where the Thummin stone is don't you? It was you who discovered the Grail bowl with the stones inside it in the Temple of Solomon!"

"Just gi' me a break Andrew," Angus clawed at his shirt. Suddenly it felt tight like a noose again. He felt like he was suffocating. He saw himself in the Hibernian football crowd singing 'The Grace'. It stopped the panic attack. It was clear that somehow Angus had been avoiding remembering his Grail Knight purpose by distracting himself in various ways, including drinking too much whisky sometimes known to lower a person's vibrational frequency. Angus needed to increase his vibrational frequency to help him remember.

Andrew rocked forward stiffly, hissing out words. "You see, nobody knows exactly what's in those metal containers, down in caves below Rosslyn," Andrew said looking distant.

"Aye, I bet you'd like to know though?" Angus questioned.

"All I found, in reality, was the Urim stone in the Grail bowl, carbon-dated back to the time when 'The Ark of the Covenant' was active. But the steel containers?" Andrew stopped mid-sentence looking up into Ackergill's vaulted ceiling. "The world would be a very different place if the contents of those containers were brought out, perhaps a much better place than it is now." Angus could not be perfectly sure of what he was saying but he had the distinct impression that Andrew knew what was in them.

"Perhaps 'The Ark of the Covenant' is somewhere else?" Angus replied digging deeper.

"You must remember your past life experience and what you discovered when you were part of the exploration party of Templars who excavated the Temple of Solomon. Because we the Questers know you found the Thummin stone."

"It's coming back, a little at a time," Angus replied, but with the impression that when Andrew mentioned 'we' he wasn't talking about just Questers. Angus felt there was another organisation looming in the background which Andrew was obscuring.

"But it is not just about the Ark, it's also about the Shamir the famous fire breathing lance, they used to cut the stone! It was the Shamir that they used to cut the great two hundred ton blocks for the Temple under the Mount in Jerusalem. It is a forbidden city in stone under there," Andrew reminded Angus.

"I need to know more about the New Babylonians," Angus replied, sliding away from the questions.

"And yes, we know the New Babylonians are tightening their net. All they do is against humanity, written in the blood of mankind. The truth is a new version of their cult has rooted itself once again over the entire planet, strangling it with greed. They come with false gods and their greed for more than their portion. They are a race which puts profit before everything else."

Angus sat back with heartfelt resistance against them. "Aye God will only let them get so far though, ye' can see that."

"Now the New Babylonians control most of the world's governments. And many have joined their infernal ranks paid off with fifty pieces of silver. Perhaps many of them who were once the same as you Angus? I hope you realise the New Babylonians are really just like us, gone bad through a process which changes their blood by their negative actions. And that's how we know them. Their blood is different from ours."

"Jesus Christ save us, och' man they are horrible bastards," Angus replied.

Andrew stood up again. It was his final address.

"There are two stones the Urim and Thummin required to activate 'The Ark of the Covenant'. I rediscovered the Urim stone as you now know. If the Ark is activated it could be a great weapon to the detriment of mankind if the wrong people get hold of it. And those who try to use it for the wrong reasons may well become the Ark's victims. This was a fate which destroyed the Philistines who stole it from the Israelites. The Ark destroyed the Philistine army, both burning them and covering them in horrific sores."

Angus sat there holding his brow, his fingers tracing the scars of a past battle in the desert around Jerusalem, although obscured by hundreds of years, layering back like onion skins to the medieval times, when his wounds had been stitched by catgut. Those past wounds began to mysteriously reappear back on his skin. Even Andrew could see them.

"Nasty wounds you got back then Angus."

"You can see them then?"

"Yes, I see them from several battles of your past."

"Aye Andrew I am remembering."

"But now your role in this Quest despite your faltering enlightenment is to apply yourself to getting your purpose back. On that day of blood back then when you rescued the Grail, by yourself you killed thirteen warriors from the Sultan's special guard, whilst the Templars prepared their escape. Your head had been cut to the bone with their curved swords, but you healed unnaturally overnight. You should have been a dead man!"

Andrew dare not mention the Thummin stone again. He knew there was a mental block stopping Angus from remembering his purpose. He suspected it might be the fact that Angus had discovered something else by default. He began to suspect Angus had already discovered the key to something equally great.

"Now Angus, you'd better get back to your South American lady and start trying to remember who the hell you are! You've had too much time trying to learn how to bloody dance Milonga Tango and you're too clumsy for that malarkey! That and your damn football songs!"

Just then Vanessa walked in looking up at the rugged splendour of the castle. She marched across the stone flags like she was on a mission, as always she moved panther like.

"Sorry to break in darlin', just realised that I got the times of the flights back to Chile wrong. If we go now we'll just make it," she said with her Chilean Spanish accent.

Andrew stood to attention creaking like an old hussar. He was shocked as soon as Vanessa had mentioned Chile, South America.

"Oh dear, I didn't realise you were here with Angus?" Andrew went crimson with embarrassment. "Angus, you buffoon why didn't you say?"

Angus smiled to himself. Andrew and Vanessa shook hands cordially. Vanessa had a feeling that somehow they'd meet again. Andrew tried to place Vanessa and how she fitted into the situation.

"My dear, Angus tells me that you've invented a programme that can convert ancient symbols of navigation into Latitude and Longitude?"

Vanessa prickled with anger. She didn't know exactly why but she knew that Andrew was playing Angus like a violin. But, how did Andrew know about the Ancient Symbol's App she'd invented?

"Firstly, Mr Andrew Sinclair, I am not Angus MacWilliam, and I don't have to tell you anything!"

Andrew sat back astonished. "My dear, forgive me, I've asked a question too many!"

"I am Vanessa Bermodes here in this mysterious country to find information about my brother Rodrigo." She had a peculiar way of appearing erotically charged when she was on a mission. Her lips tightened with determination. At last, Andrew knew that Angus was on the path God had provided for him.

How Angus and Vanessa discovered the key one week earlier

Angus had a feeling the world was going to end. He staggered again overwhelmed by the site of the famous chapel springing from its foundation mound, overlooking the Vale of Rosslyn. He'd prepared accordingly for the face recognition technology he was bound to encounter.

Around 1480 Rosslyn Chapel had been ornately carved out of the local sandstone well after the supposed demise of the Knights Templar. He'd spent years trying to discover the secrets. Finally, using his uncanny ability to find hidden things he was on the verge of knowing the truth. Still, something was causing him to black out from time to time. He'd been checked out by the doctors who reported they had found a neurological problem in him. Angus knew that the world was going wrong and that he was going to play a part in making it better. Many folk were feeling the same emotion in their hearts, they knew they had to change the world.

They say some animals can sense earthquakes and tidal waves and other geophysical catastrophes coming. Often the animals escape to safer ground. This is how Angus explained his ominous feelings. He felt all the signs around him were predicting another earth deluge on its way and he needed to escape. Angus had discovered the real evidence which led him to the source of this apocalyptic premonition with divine timing.

He had been forced to split from his wife and daughter, and his remaining friends were worried about his future. Later a priest explained that there was nothing wrong with him and that he was on a mission for God to conclude unfinished business from the past. Angus laughed into his whisky. But there was a ring of truth to what the old priest said. Angus was aware he was evolving through a passage of enlightenment to discover the true nature of the world and perhaps himself. Whisky numbed his intense premonitions rendering them tolerable. Meanwhile, his curious research concerning the Knights Templar and their curious role in history kept his mind focused as the world fell from God's Grace.

Angus's enlightenment had started inside Rosslyn Chapel a few years earlier. He'd been doing restoration work there, after he resigned from his role as an archaeologist, returning to his trade of stonemason. After tests for epilepsy it turned out that he had an abnormal brain function. One day his boss had left the building to get chisels sharpened. Angus decided to take a rest and went to sit in one of the pews looking towards the high altar. All-day long he'd felt the curious feeling of being watched. He could hear breathing behind him. It was like the breathing of an army, all breathing together. Naturally, he turned around. And sat in rows behind him, were Templar Knights. There were at least fifty bearded knights in their cloaks with the red cross on their mantles, stained with grime. They leaned forward, staring at the altar. Angus pinched himself and looked again. They were all still there, sat in the same positions. Then they just disappeared.

Scottish history was at the forefront of Angus's mind. He was forever researching books and exploring the ancient ruins around him. After the dissolution of the Templars, some of the surviving refugee knights entered into other Holy Orders including the Knights Hospitallers. The refugee Templars in Scotland pledged allegiance to King Robert the Bruce and his fight for freedom, because, like the Templars, Robert the Bruce King of Scotland had also been excommunicated. Then on the feast day of St John the Baptist, the Templars helped the Bruce at the Battle of Bannockburn, when the Scottish army destroyed the larger army of Edward 11 of England. Thus the cry of liberty echoed back through the ages, carried forward by the voice of Scotland aided by the Templars. It was known that the Templars were tasked with protecting

'The Ark of the Covenant' in Scotland before it joined the rest of the refugee Templars and where they went. And where they had gone, was where Angus and Vanessa were going. They just didn't know where yet.

Rosslyn Chapel was the same as the inner sanctum of the Temple of Solomon, where, according to the Bible, God dwelt. It had been designed by its Architect Sir William Sinclair to hide precious secrets and treasures not meant to be known. These included predictions of earth cataclysms and deluges, disguised in the ornate carving in Rosslyn's stone ceiling. Many recognised that geophysical and astronomical information, discovered in the Temple of Solomon, had been encoded into the stonework of Rosslyn, carved by the remaining Templars and their descendants.

The Templars had astrolabes and rare maps and other navigational instruments inherited from the Phoenicians and used by the Templar Viking master mariners. All these advancements were known to have come from the lost civilisation of Atlantis. This is why an illustration from 1700 which Angus had seen, showed the missing statues of Rosslyn Chapel. One statue in particular, stood out from the others. It was the famous statue of Admiral Piri Reis, holding out an astrolabe. The statues had been sculpted by Templar stonemasons to commemorate sacred knowledge. And Angus suspected that it was the secret Templar descendants who had removed the statues for safekeeping. But it went much deeper than this. Angus had thought that there was another far older Templar Order.

Clan Sinclair historians declared that some of the stonemasons who carved and built Rosslyn were descended from stonemasons who had built the Temple of Solomon. Furthermore, the chapel was sculpted with the power of nature, illustrated by healing plants and herbs aided by biblical scenes of wisdom and the spiritual symbols of the Templars.

St Bernard of Clairvaux the founder of the Templars formulated a brotherhood of warrior monks, enlisting a Cistercian monk called

Archard, to train stonemasons to build cathedrals and other sacred temples. Aided by the secret Templars amongst them, they encoded apocalyptic information about planetary alignments, carving this information as symbols into Rosslyn Chapel. This was the last building where this happened. Rosslyn Chapel was a warning in stone to the world.

Angus falls

In the numbing cold, Angus was in danger of getting hypothermia. Even so, he felt unnatural warmth flowing from Rosslyn Chapel. He held his hands over his ears trying to dull down the incessant humming as bright lights flashed behind his eyelids. His legs buckled and he fell forward, down to the frosty ground as the blackness returned. His breathing became less laboured, as he lay there with his face pushed into the damp earth. It was impossible now for him to get medical treatment since he was out of the system. However, he intended to heal himself in other ways using holistic treatments. Furthermore, he operated on the periphery of society to avoid many of the medical procedures being forced onto the world population as the world entered a modern-day 'dark age' set in motion by the New Babylonian plan to control human beings like sheep.

Angus was aware of looking down on himself, like an out of body experience. From above it appeared like he was sleeping peacefully with his arm around a frozen mound of mud as if it were a pillow. He knew changes were occurring in his body. He was committed to what side he was on, as God and the planet picked its champions for the coming conflict. Clouds scudded across the crescent moon illuminating the ancient tombstones behind him. It was the second time he'd collapsed that year. Still, he could see his Gunn clan ring on his left index finger glinting in the moonlight giving him hope. Perhaps all was not lost.

Angus had another vision. He was standing amongst a group of knights in Rosslyn's crypt. One of them lay in full armour on top of the famous meteorite stone where a giant radiating sword appeared. The fallen red meteorite stone in the crypt had always been there. Augustinian monks built over the caves where the meteorite lay before Rosslyn was constructed. The meteorite acted as both transmitter and receiver of information to and from the universe. The meteorite inside the spire tower of Chartres Cathedral performed the same task.

Angus realised his 'blackouts' signified a remembrance of a previous life where his rational mind conflicted with his strong subconscious urge to recall something important for humanity. As a child, he'd experienced problems concentrating. He was always daydreaming about being in other worlds. He'd been taught to block the occurrences, discounting them as fantasy. But it was time to start believing in himself as he remembered back to his former life as a Grail Knight. He'd done his duty back then. Now it was time again to do his duty once more.

Curiously Angus was being looked after in some way. For he was being watched from Rosslyn's perimeter wall by a South American woman. She was a mapmaker called Vanessa Bermodes. God had sent her, it was that simple. Dressed in Patagonian expedition gear and military-grade boots she'd been given by her brother Rodrigo Bermodes before he went missing, presumed dead, she moved jaguar-like over the ground towards him. Her life's work concerned the mapping out of strange geophysical information, alluding to the phenomenon that there was a hidden land under Antarctica's ice cap previously occupied by another civilisation. The landmass had shifted after the Earth had spun out of axial alignment causing the last ice age. Deep thinkers thought that these cataclysms were linked to the state of humanity's fall from God's Grace. And there was something else happening on the planet now, something abysmal.

Vanessa Bermodes' family had fled to Chile from Spain in 1700. They were a cultured family in many ways. Half of them had been Spanish Imperialists with the other half sympathising with the Mapuche natives of South Chile causing friction in her family. In the South of Chile, especially Chiloe, the Spanish had maintained dominance over the emerging Chilean Republicans. But that didn't last long and war with the Mapuche natives began.

Although Vanessa had never met Angus she'd been experiencing similar unexplainable visions about Rosslyn, compelling her to travel there from Chile. She saw Angus moving in the mud in front of the wall and moved quickly towards his fallen body. She bent over him rubbing his wrist. As she rubbed she began to feel connected to him as their skin transmitted some kind of electric remembering. She gave him sweet tea from her flask. Angus moaned and began to wake. To start with she thought he'd been disfigured. His face was contorted horribly. Then she saw sellotape glinting in the moonlight stuck to his face. And she knew right away he'd been trying to avoid facial recognition technology by contorting his face with sellotape. She started to pull the sellotape off his face. Angus winced as she pulled off the tape, she smiled as she did it.

"You know my friend I discovered that this facial recognition technology has not been installed here yet." As she removed it, his real face sprang back. Vanessa was taken by him. "Mio Dios" she whispered.

"Och lassie be careful ya' pulling ma' skin off ma' face!"

One of the triggers which helped Angus feel happy was a smiling feminine face looking at him. It was as though he was a child waiting for the face of his mother. He'd fought long and hard to retain his dignity after taking his Quester Code Oath, endeavouring to know the truth of the world. Angus's opportunity to attend the Quester School had been his rights of passage and his enlightenment began.

He didn't want to be monitored by the New Babylonians and their plan to control world populations through their criminal levels of surveillance. In many ways, he'd been a covert activist against the so-called 'new normal' draconian measures all countries were living under. Many people still denied this was about the accursed installation of the New Babylonian World Government, assisted by false computer programmed predictions, carried out by their agents in all countries.

Another happiness trigger was listening to beautiful music. Or being near the sea or becoming lost in his work as a stonemason. In these places, his subconscious mind worked; unchained from the mundane directives he needed for his day to day survival. When Angus came round to the face of Vanessa Bermodes, everything started to make sense. It was like she was the key to helping him remember. He felt much deeper about Vanessa's face than anything else because in his past medieval life she had been his wife.

"This place is terrible!" Vanessa said in her lilting Spanish voice.

"Aye, terrible because it tells the truth to your soul."

She was unaware, she was quoting the carved words from an engraved stone slab in the crypt laying inside Rosslyn Chapel which Angus had discovered a few years back. The carved slab showed a sculpted child standing on a globe next to a sand timer. The child walked over a hollow Earth to another child sitting on a throne supported by books. Behind them was the grim reaper holding a scythe. The prophetic stone's carved message explained in symbols that humanity must remember mortality and that death may come at any time. Yet some of us will return to complete unfinished business. Angus and Vanessa were two such people who had returned.

Many medieval scholars still thought the Earth was flat when the prophetic death stone Angus had restored had been carved. The freethinker Giordano Bruno had been burnt at the stake for thinking that the Earth was not flat; and that as a sphere, it circled the sun in processional trajectory. A couple of symbol scholars had remarked that the carved stones of Rosslyn Chapel predicted the next cataclysm. Angus decided to risk everything in search of rediscovering his purpose whilst there was still time.

The trouble on the planet had already begun with mass riots over the political changes occurring, progressing to plagues of various kinds.

Even giant grasshoppers decimated the crops of Africa and South America, devouring their way through valuable food supplies.

There was continuous volcanic and seismic activity, never properly reported by those in power and who controlled the media. Angus felt that somehow life as he knew it was re-entering biblical times. He was not the only person thinking that these emergencies described by the media as 'new normal' had been contrived in a kind of warfare against humanity. All those good people who remained on the planet felt the grip of evil tightening and squeezing around them. Although they didn't want to acknowledge it, deep down, they knew in their hearts who was responsible.

Angus's previous career as an archaeologist failed because he'd gone against standard-compliant patterns of behaviour to get ahead. He'd struggled to maintain a false front in the world of archaeology spurred on by Caroline Agostini his social-climbing wife because he'd never been enough for her. Yes, she liked his personality and adventurous out of the box approach to life, but in the end, it was all about the money and she'd left him for Max Rothman, who owned a management provision company in New York. Angus hated the idea he'd been abandoned for this type of man. It would have been easier for him to accept if Max had been a lion tamer or a deep-sea diver. Max still has copper mining interests in South America along with another group of secret investors with political connections to Argentina. These investors were also supplying cash for controversial genetic engineering programmes described as the worst of sins, because of the hateful hybrid monsters they cobbled together.

Now Max Rothman and associates were on the way to Buenos Aires, to meet another Oligarch destroying the land through the unrestrained mining of other minerals used for computer hardware, mobile phones and electric car batteries. By chance, if one could call it that, it was near where Vanessa Bermodes had inherited the mysterious Island of Sailing

Souls. But the fact was Don Miguel Monte, the man they were expecting to meet, had been kidnapped. Vanessa's brother Rodrigo had been involved in that situation in a security capacity.

Max Rothman had lots of blood money, but that was it. To make matters worse Caroline Agostini, Angus's ex-wife had won custody of their beautiful daughter Isobel because of Angus's so-called psychological problems. He'd been crushed after losing his family in a world gone wrong. Recently he'd experienced flashbacks of those dreadful Manhattan parties congregated by cardboard cut-out people, trying to get their noses into the feeding trough being controlled by Max. It was where Angus witnessed his wife's hand in the hand of Max Rothman as they gazed at each other. Angus flipped out at the party and punched Max over his minimalist Augustus Rodin sofa, then the New York Police arrived. That was the end of his life as he knew it. The worst thing was, it was his own wife, who had called the cops on him. Angus had been bundled into the back of the police car shouting "ya' bastard Rothman, I'll be back for you, ya' fanny!" But, this memory only strengthened his resolve to keep on his Quest as a deeper version of events began unfolding. Vanessa looked at Angus, searching deeper for answers.

"Scottish man, tell me how you met your ex-wife. I'd be interested to know?"

"Och' yes, lassie, I'll try to remember that broken life, but da' na' press me!"

Angus didn't want to talk about it. But from the mud outside Rosslyn, he figured he should explain some of the strange connections to his wife to Vanessa who had probably saved his life. Angus, could also spot an opportunity when it was emerging. It made him feel like one of those wading birds treading frantically to dredge up food from the sand. Angus thought it would also give him a chance to assess the possibility of giving his daughter Isobel a chance to spend some time in

South America, especially if everything worked out with Vanessa and by the hand of fate it seemed like that was happening. Besides, Isobel was not wanted by Max Rothman or her mother. She was misplaced with nowhere else to go.

Vanessa started to remember Angus as he lay panting in the frost on the ground. She roused him and he lurched awkwardly onto his knees. A beam from a security light shone into the graveyard. Luckily, it was a remote camera, scanning for large profile movement near Rosslyn's perimeter wall, which they could easily avoid. The strange thing was that Vanessa could see the truth right away. Because she saw him laying there like a fallen knight, his right hand and arm was stretched out like he should be holding a sword. She knew then Angus was the Grail Knight returned because she knew in the depths of her mind, that she had been his wife back then.

In the 17th Century, Father Haye from nearby Rosslyn Castle carried treasures and books down the secret tunnel connecting the castle and chapel like an umbilical cord between mother and baby. Many of the books were about astronomy and the use of advanced navigational instruments and forbidden maps. These books had originally been rescued from the burning library of Alexandria. Father Haye saved many sacred books from the all-consuming fire raging through Rosslyn castle and hiding them in the forbidden vaults of Rosslyn along with many other treasures.

The Priest had stated he'd seen many Sinclair knights in their golden armour laid out on stone slabs in the vaults. One dead knight which he examined, turned immediately to dust after he'd opened the visor of the dead knight's helm.

"Come on Scottish man, we have to move. They have private security here now."

"Aye, that bloody sellotape, I wrapped around ma' face was useless, didn't even need it. Fancy Rosslyn Chapel not having face recognition technology." Vanessa had trouble not laughing.

Coming to his senses, Angus's steel coloured hair stood out in the moonlight. "But you're a lovely sight to behold! I am coming with you, I am coming!"

Although Vanessa was much smaller than Angus, she pulled in close to him holding his arm around her shoulder to support his body. Her work as a mapmaker often took her on extreme expeditions, strengthening her physique.

"Come on lassie there's no need for that. Och' I can walk, right enough now," Angus said as another torch beam scanned across the ground. "We can go back to the camper van over there, beyond that field. It's ma' operations office."

"Speak a little slower Scottish man, your accent is difficult to understand?"

Vanessa was cold and didn't need convincing about going to Angus's camper van. She was anticipating the next security torch beam, yet she felt chemistry awakening between them.

"Dios nos protegerá y Nuestra mission," she replied. Strangely, Angus understood her Spanish, but why? The light of the security torch beam scanned the graveyard on a second sweep, as they staggered back over the frosty turf towards the stonewalled perimeter. He muttered under his breath the exact translation of what Vanessa had said in Spanish. "May God protect this mission." Because of her, he was remembering.

Angus switched on the heater in the camper van. He hadn't felt the grip of attraction to a woman for some time, at least a woman who'd similar interests and passions. He wanted to tell Vanessa about what had happened with his wife Caroline Agostini and the breakup of his little family and conventional life.

"What's ya' story lassie, why are you here on this terrible evening?" He didn't want to seem opportunistic, but he liked her, he liked her a lot despite his opportunistic thoughts.

Then Vanessa introduced herself. "My name is Vanessa Bermodes and my work is making maps and exploring and charting our lands in South America." But that was only half the truth.

For Angus, visions came faster than his ability to think of the words to describe them. He visualised Vanessa dressed in an Islamic silk dress next to a beautiful marble fountain set in a courtyard. A peacock was calling out, presenting its huge tail feathers like a fan. Vanessa was shaking her hair out so that it cascaded onto her shoulders, creating a beautiful frame for her high cheek boned face. Synchronistically Vanessa pulled down her hood and began to shake out her wild black hair. Angus watched intensely.

"Tell me what you are doing here?" she said confidently.

"Aye and I wull' and I could ask the same of you?"

"You first, then!"

"Once upon a time, I was an archaeologist, but I decided to carve stone instead. I kinda' got lost in it, like it was a mantra."

"You mean to say you were working as a stonemason here?"

"Some time ago, I was doing restoration work at Rosslyn Chapel, you know, before it became Dan Brown, Da Vinci Code famous." Angus was reluctant to say anymore. He was curious as to why Vanessa was so far from home.

"Anyways, here ya' are bonnie lassie!"

"This place is very mystical," Vanessa shivered. "Something was calling me here from Chile connected to my work and my brother Rodrigo. I can't explain it. I was just compelled to come here with a sense of mission. My spirit guides were telling me to come here."

Angus loved her Spanish pronunciation of English words. It was different from the pure Spanish from Spain. Her accent had a South American lilt but unlike Cuban or Bolivian Spanish. "Did you find anything during your work restoring the carvings in Rosslyn?"

"Aye, we did," Angus replied.

Vanessa was seeing visions of knights and ships with huge hawsers, flaming angels and skulls and crossbones. Carved stone ropes had been found at other sites where the Templars had been, thought to represent their sea power. Ropes had been carved on Rosslyn's famous apprentice pillar spiralling up to heaven or descending to the underworld in helical curves, held in the mouths of serpents with membranous wings. He'd studied the enigmatic pillar at Rosslyn when he worked there as a stonemason. And then there was his discovery of the stone carving, which depicted a globe, the child, and the angel of death with a scythe. Perhaps it was time to explain his work as an archaeologist to Vanessa as well, even though the memories were still raw.

Vanessa spoke the words she was seeing in her mind's eye.

"Wine is strong, the king is strong, women are stronger, but truth conquers all. "

"Och' lassie, those very words are carved on the sacred stone lintels along with biblical illustrations carved inside the Chapel. I once worked on them. I know they are the words of Zerubbabel a leader of the Hebrews who rebuilt the Second Temple. I was originally hired by

Rosslyn because I was the sculptor to the Clan Sinclair. The work came to me after my troubles when I'd been an archaeologist. But the money was shite. Caroline ma' wife wanted more money; she always wanted more of everything. And I could na' get on with the people around me. They were such phoney bastards, with their speciality trowels and bullshit degrees. And most of 'em sold out to the highest bidder anyway." Vanessa suddenly scowled.

"But it's the way of the world, perhaps it was your own fault. Maybe you were controversial with your rude words?"

"Aye, maybe lassie. Tell the truth and shame the devil, as we say in Scotland. I'll always say it like it is."

Vanessa's scowl turned to a look of admiration. "Well, I guess I can live with that!"

Angus was determined to tell her something else she might consider weird about himself. "The madness started for me a few years back, in Edinburgh on Princess Street, whilst walking to the watchtower over at the ancient graveyard. I'd been involved in restoring the stones on that as well. The tower housed soldiers and was built to protect the dead from body snatchers like Burke and Hare."

"Yes, darlin' I heard that they sold the corpses to medical schools for big money, disgusting !"

"Well lassie, I went berserk because I couldn't get through to my place of solitude in the graveyard, because of all the people looking at their phones like zombies, walking like the living dead. And I started to slap their phones out of their hands. I could hear them smashing on the flagstones and in the road. And the police came pretty quickly, but they dare not follow me into the graveyard. And none of them communicated properly because they'd got the Government masks on to show their compliance and they just kept walking looking at where their phones should have been, when they were holding them. It was scary!"

"My God darlin' you went insane."

"Aye, something happened to me, it was another blip out."

"Well, darlin' something similar happened to me as well, when they tried to stop me researching the truth about Antarctica and how it was linked to Atlantis. I did similar to you. I smashed up their laboratory. I don't know what happened. I knew I'd be sacked, so I thought it was time to buy the company out."

Angus understood her frustration, he was happy to hear this information as it placed them firmly on the right side of history.

"Aye, you'll know by now, it's never the best people who make it in any profession. It's always those who conform the most to the paymaster's agenda, leaving everyone else with a bloody complex. And it's the same in any research organisation. There's always an underlying agenda."

Vanessa knew exactly what he meant. She felt a sense of dread. She also knew that results of archaeological research were often manipulated to fit the agenda of those paying for it. In fact, that was another reason why she'd set up her own research and exploration company. She watched Angus carefully. It was clear something else was going on with him.

"Why are you here at the same time as me? Tell me everything."

"I can't answer exactly lassie. It's just that I found something, that's all. I found something to do with the great mystery of Rosslyn Chapel. A bit like the Da Vinci code novel, but the real stuff, the real secrets," Angus avoided eye contact with her. They were both still testing each other out.

"Maybe we are here together for a reason?" Vanessa asked.

"I discovered the main clue to these mysteries when I was the last keeper of the Sinclair Lighthouse in Scotland. I'd like to call that place a refuge of mercy." Angus didn't know why he was telling her, the things he'd kept secret for a long time.

The lighthouse at the tip of Scotland had provided a home for him during the modern-day flooding which displaced thousands of people on the Scottish borders including himself.

"Tell me about your secrets?" Vanessa asked tired of jumping over his hoops.

And then the inevitable happened. He reached out and touched her hair. He'd wanted to do it ever since he set eyes on her. Now he could feel its silkiness over the knuckles of his brawny hand. Vanessa winced a little, but it was a wince of the expectation of romance. Angus hadn't thought about anything carnal at the time, there was no lust involved with his gesture. It was more of an emotional cry for help. He recognised and embraced a kindred spirit after the pain he'd gone through. Vanessa turned her cheek into Angus's hand, enabling him to stroke her with his fingers. Both of them knew there was nothing more exciting than this first touch of flesh upon flesh. It was like their life force cried out for it. Then he decided to tell her everything.

Angus tells the secret

"I found some information when I was the keeper of the Sinclair Lighthouse. I found an old book with Rosslyn Chapel's missing statues illustrated in it. Mysteriously, all the statues disappeared sometime around 1700. The niches where the statues once stood have remained empty because the statues were purposefully removed," Angus said.

Vanessa wanted to explain about her work studying the great map makers.

"You know, you should try to study Charles Hapgood's book ***Maps of the Ancient Sea Kings***!" It seemed they were both on the same page.

"Aye, for God's sake! It was me who identified that one of the missing statues here at Rosslyn was Admiral Piri Reis, the famous explorer and map-maker. On his early map, Piri Reis had identified the landmass under the ice in Antarctica."

Vanessa interrupted, she couldn't help it. "I know all about the map maker Piri Reis! Through my Chilean company, 'Geophysical Data.com'. I've been studying his maps and discoveries, since the last major volcanic eruptions in Chile in 1963. I worked for the company originally and then bought that company out as well. It was the only way to cut out the government's interference. You see they only wanted the oil and the natural resources there anyway."

"Och' lassie, there's been ice over Antarctica for thirty thousand bloody years. Originally the landmass under the ice, according to advanced thinkers was from another part of the earth's shifting crust. A catastrophic event caused a malfunction of the axial alignment of the spinning planet on its processional cycle around the sun and the earth tilted causing a polar shift. Then the earth's crust, including the continents, slid around the inner molten core. Contrary to popular belief, it wasn't a meteorite that caused the problem, it was a default explosion inside the planet. The land under the ice had previously existed in a warmer region on the surface of the earth sliding round, to where it is now."

Vanessa was impressed. "Continue darlin', you know nearly as much as me!" Vanessa said.

"Aye, a few years ago, scientists discovered the frozen body of a woolly mammoth in Antarctica. Everyone thought the frozen mammoth must have lived in Antarctica. But that wasn't the case, it was actually from a much warmer part of the world. Yellow buttercups and other warm-climate plants had been discovered in its mouth, suggesting its area of origin was likely to be somewhere like Madagascar. The mammoth had been spontaneously frozen after the cataclysm causing the ice age to happen within hours, turning the planet into a giant iceberg overnight."

Vanessa squeezed his hand encouragingly. Angus felt calm, caused by the lovely aroma of her hair, which shone like Obsidian. He realised she knew as much as he did, perhaps even a little more.

"Aye, well, we don't know everything. But do ya' know if there weren't these wonders to behold on this beautiful planet for me, it would na' be worth living here, the way this mad world is going." Angus reflected how the world control mechanisms set in place by the New Babylonians had started to inflict casualties in various ways.

"There remains an advanced civilisation under the ice, I think it's Atlantis," Vanessa added.

"Aye' I hear ya', I have some interesting information which nobody has seen yet."

"Come on tell me, stop being intriguing!" Vanessa said smiling.

"There's a corbel on the exterior of Rosslyn, which I've seen several times. A corbel, by the way, is a feature carved in stone to support something much bigger, like a statue."

Yes, I know, I studied history of Architecture at the University de Catholica Santos in Santiago!" Vanessa said impatiently.

"There was a plaster copy of the corbel at the Sinclair Lighthouse Library in Caithness, where I was the last keeper. It was on the top shelf in the library where nobody ever saw it. The replicated plaster corbel depicted what many considered to be a ceremonial Templar initiation scene carved at least one hundred and fifty years after they'd been outlawed. So obviously, they were still operational well after their so-called demise. Lassie, I've got a feeling they might still be operating now. I am talking about the secret inner-wheel Templar Order that persisted after the main Order was obliterated."

Vanessa knew about the anomalous stone carvings thought to be Templar in Patagonia, where stones had been found with Templar carved symbols on them.

"Come to the point darlin'!"

"You'll not be surprised to know, I discovered something else carved on the top of the corbel."

Then Vanessa said something completely out of character.

"Look, I am falling in love with you." It was as though those words drifted back from their other lifetime.

Angus wasn't surprised as he was feeling the same exhilarating emotion. It can happen that fast, everyone knows that. They embraced, holding each other tightly. It was as if the molecules of their bodies were exchanging information via their beating hearts. Finally, Vanessa asked the question Angus had been waiting for.

"Come back to Chile with me, we can then plan properly? We can work together. You can't stay here without any resources. The winter here is so very cold and you are not very well. You need to rest. You've been here at this terrible place too long!"

She didn't know exactly why she'd offered him this opportunity, but it felt right to her because Angus had also confirmed his interest in Admiral Piri Reis, whom she'd spent years studying. But the truth was, they simply couldn't resist each other.

"Now it's your turn, why are you here?" Angus asked, overcome with emotion.

"I am here because of my brother Rodrigo first and foremost! He's been missing in South Chile, near where I inherited a small island, where I look after the graveyard."

"Aye lassie you mentioned that."

Angus was lost for words, but the fact she looked after a graveyard intrigued him, because he knew she'd be a thinker. Most people around the dead seem to think a lot. It had been the same for Angus when he'd gone off to sleep in the Edinburgh Princess Street graveyard when he'd needed peace. Strangely, he felt those long-dead people were advising him from beyond the grave. It was a further connection to the sacred chain of the living and the dead.

"Och, lassie watching over a graveyard of dead people on an island, that's a strange pastime?"

"I will explain later about that. The important thing is that I've been having dreams and visions of Rosslyn Chapel. I can't explain it. But I know my brother still lives. I just had to come to see what's happening here for myself. And I found you!"

Angus didn't see the connection right away, he'd never been to Chile. But recently, he'd developed a strange fascination for South America. And what were the chances of meeting a South American lady on a cold winter's night outside Rosslyn Chapel in Scotland?

Sacred Love in Santiago, Chile

With Vanessa's help, Angus summoned enough strength to lay up the camper van in the yard of a friendly farmer whose stone walls he'd once rebuilt. His search for truth had taken him onto another path, causing him blackouts and physical illness. He understood he was on a sacred journey and this meant knowing the painful reality of a past life, a life most would want to forget.

The Journey begins

The journey to South America was straightforward. Angus instinctively trusted Vanessa, now they were in love. She'd booked their tickets for a next day flight back to Chile. They would be leaving the mystical early winter of Scotland for the spring warmth of South America. For the first time in three years Angus, although unwell, was excited.

On the flight to Chile, Vanessa held Angus's hand like a big baby. She sat next to him listening to his mumbling dreams. She wanted to ask about his ex-wife whilst he was exhausted. She knew he would not put up any resistance. She was trying to see the bigger picture of why they'd met. She would wait till the aircraft had taken off and they'd loosened their seat belts. If she was going to be part of this synchronistic adventure, she wanted to know where it was going.

"Darlin' you said you'd tell me something about Caroline Agostini and your father?" She asked expectantly.

"Aye lassie, I'll tell ya about ma' ol' man first." It was as though he'd got a script ready to read from his mind. "I went to a school in northern Scotland near a place called Thurso. It was a normal kind of comprehensive school, where it seemed to me even at the young age of fourteen, most of us attending could make a real difference to the community around us when we grew up. You know, they were really smart, caring kids."

Vanessa knew in which direction the conversation was going. She called over the stewardess and asked for another couple of mini whiskies. Angus crunched the screw tops off and drank them. She would let him sleep soon enough.

Angus continued. "It seemed that the cold dedicated kids got singled out for special treatment, they became like the favourites of tha' teachers. We could see how compliant they were, or 'arse kissers', as we called them. Even back then I started to think that the school situation was like a sorting house, to sort out the bad clever kids from the good clever kids. Then they sent the bad ones off to boarding school like they favoured them and called it a scholarship. That's how they made them ready for the world. Like there was a special group of world dominators who favoured certain traits in compliant mean kids. I never believed the teachers. I never trusted them, they tried to brainwash us into being like them. They said I'd some kind of mental disorder because I didn't comply and was awkward. I admit I looked out of the window a lot, thinking about the world, rather than applying myself to learn about the natural resources of other countries on boring pie charts. No wonder kids got depressed. Who wants to know how much copper there is in Peru unless you wanted to steal it for something?" Vanessa nodded in agreement.

"Yes, darlin' there was always a lot of trouble in North Chile above the Atacama desert where our copper mines were. The British mining companies were there exploiting the natives. It's the House of Babylon education system, they who put profit before the Earth."

"How do you know about them?"

"I know more than you think Angus MacWilliam!"

Angus continued his story. "So I spent more time learning away from school, learning how to fish and row boats and living a hard life by the sea in the Pentland Firth. It was at that point my dad called for me. My mother wasn't very well. She'd written to him and asked if there was any work for me in Canada." He sighed and took another gulp from the miniature bottle of whisky finishing it. "Well, I didn't know much about my father, only that he was a sea Captain on the Great Lakes. I attended an Archaeology Academy in Toronto as planned, and met my

American girlfriend Caroline Agostini there, later we were married and pretty young at that. And it just so happened that my father had been reading Andrew Sinclair's book ***The Sword and the Grail.*** Just before my father died a weird thing happened in a bank in downtown Toronto."

Vanessa squeezed Angus's hand again.

"Ok darlin' just tell me what happened in the bank?"

Angus smiled sickly. "Aye ya' should know, they say I'm a conspiracy nut or the like. And 'am fuckin' proud of it."

"No! It might surprise you to learn, I know what's going on with the New Babylonians." He knew she was awake to what was happening in the world.

"I'd gone to the Toronto Dominion to get a bank account sorted when I arrived in Canada from Scotland. My father introduced me to his bank manager friend at the bank in some plaza nearby. I remember it well. We were standing between two plastic neo-fifties palm trees near the main entrance. I saw a bank clerk lady and she started asking a million questions. I gave her my downtown address where my father and his second wife were living in a large apartment. She started asking obtuse questions about me and my situation and wrote notes down as I spoke. You know, as they do, maybe more so. And then my father appeared like he'd overheard the conversation. He was a pretty formidable person almost like a nasty Captain Haddock out of Tin Tin."

Vanessa smiled. "Go on darlin' carry on," she said.

"Hey, you!" my father shouted, "Where's that bloody information you've been writing down?" The poor lady was just doing her job. He watched her eyes drift over to the desk where she'd put the information for further processing. Angus was reluctant to go on.

"Come on darlin' what happened? Its ok, you can tell me."

"So then he just crashed through the security gate and snatched the paper, he looked at it, and then ripped it to shreds. The bank manager who knew him calmed him down."

"Maybe he was working for an intelligence agency," Vanessa said smiling.

"I don't know, it was weird, a bit far-fetched, but he worked a lot around the gulf of Arabia. And later he died in strange circumstances. I didn't know much about him. My mother divorced him when I was twelve. And then later I got married to Caroline Agostini. And the rest is history. Well, the problem was she was already developing into being one of them, she was turning New Babylonian before my eyes through her greed alone."

"Yes love, it seems like the choice of being a horrible New Babylonian is easily fallen for. The system we live in grades us to join them or not, just like your school near Thurso which tried to groom you to turn Babylonian."

Angus had more to say, but Vanessa backed off knowing he was exhausted. Angus slept with his head braced against the plane's window on a pillow. She could see his eyes flickering behind his eyelids. Vanessa thought that Angus's father was an unusual man with an instinct, even back then, not to want his information recording well before the culture of mass surveillance. Back then only a few people would be aware of the New Babylonian plan to monitor everyone to protect themselves from being accountable for the things they were doing to the planet and humanity.

Meanwhile, Vanessa carried on with her research about the Argentinian industrialist Don Miguel de Monte who'd disappeared aboard his superyacht in the same Archipelago where her Island was. She was convinced her brother had been taken prisoner by those involved in the suspected kidnapping of the New Babylonian linked Industrialist. Her recent enquiries had been met with silence, yet her gut feeling was that Rodrigo lived. She knew that an operative from the special forces would be more than capable of surviving in the strange seas around her island. She had an idea that despite the wall of silence, Rodrigo had gone missing as a result of his security duties on the superyacht. She knew Angus was the key to helping her find out more. But the very fact that they felt they'd been lovers in a past life was more than a curveball.

After arriving at the airport of Santiago, Chile, Angus was searched twice clearing customs. It was a good job that Vanessa was carrying Angus's papers through customs. Soon they would be on the way to her family estate in the foothill of the Andes on the outermost limits of the metropolis of Santiago. Dangerous in the wrong hands, Angus's research papers were his most precious possessions. Strangely, he felt at home with the Chilean Spanish being spoken around him. Yet he struggled to speak the language himself as if somehow he was still resisting knowing his past life in Spain as a Grail Knight where Spanish had been his first language. Soon he would have to confront his own death, back in his medieval life, after he'd been taken prisoner by his enemies. He would have to remember it properly and face up to the consequences of his life now and his continued mission.

They collected their baggage from the humid terminus where world travellers were going about their business in the bright sunlight. Outside on the airport entrance, Angus thought how pale his skin looked next to the honey brown locals. Stray dogs waited for treats as travellers emerged to continue their journeys over land in the heat.

The old taxi drove Angus and Vanessa away from the airport. All around box structures towered above, ingeniously built by working people to live in. There was a mix of different cultures here now. Chile like many other nations had opened borders to other countries. Angus had his own opinions as to why this was happening. It felt like the ruling elite were exerting more control by impoverishing the masses. Angus was perceptive enough to see patterns of social engineering emerging around him. It was something he'd first thought about when he was a boy in Scotland. For some reason, he'd developed an ability to see patterns of engineered behaviour all around. Yet many people felt they'd been born to help change the way the Earth had been ruled over the centuries. There was a feeling of enlightenment and ascension amongst them.

There hadn't been any trouble in Chile since the Pinochet coup d'état in 1973. It seemed that the people had accepted the status quo. The New Babylonians had been controlling governments like puppets from their underground bunkers and skyscrapers all over the world.

But who exactly were the New Babylonians? This was a question that Angus had pondered for many years. It was very difficult to put names to the faces as their leaders operated in the shadows. Often they would pay people off to do their bidding. So they remained untouchable for their actions. Angus knew that something was drastically wrong with the way the world worked. It was a feeling many people had but remained silent. Indeed, it seemed that the world malfunctioned against the common good but people didn't want to know. It was too much for them.

Plato and Atlantis

Nobody studied Plato anymore. Nobody cared about his words about the disappearance of Atlantis, and if they dared, they were branded conspiracy theorists. The system demanded that people be brainwashed to the mainstream narrative sponsored by the New Babylonians. It was ironic that many universities taught Plato's philosophical knowledge, but not his theories on the lost continent of Atlantis. This aspect of Plato's genius didn't fit well with the world plan the New Babylonians were enforcing. Angus figured it was because Plato recognised a physical connection between God and the Earth. And when that connection was negatively interrupted, a massive geophysical event was unleashed. And it was not by chance that the information about the great earth deluges and cataclysms had been encoded in the stonework of temples and edifices, for those who had eyes to see. These records in stone survived the cataclysms because they had been carved in the living rock for as long as humanity remained to see them.

Naturally, paper or papyrus records would be destroyed. Even records kept in the hearts and minds of humanity, recited in the oral tradition would be lost in the 'raging torments of the world in cataclysm' as Plato had called it. And so it was in Angus's understanding that Rosslyn Chapel was the last great temple on the planet where such geophysical information was also encoded into the elaborate stonework. Astute writers had deduced that the ornately carved stone ceiling in Rosslyn was an apocalyptic prediction of what would happen to the planet, once the delicate balance of its axial alignment as it circled the sun went wrong. It was a phenomenon caused by humanity turning away from God. It was clear mankind was in a cycle of negativity caused by their actions on the planet. Indeed, it was a situation being fuelled by the New Babylonians.

It was also apparent to Angus, that something else was going on. It was clear, all the political machinery in all free countries were melding together to create one mechanism of control. Under this infernal regime, their corporations formed the thrust of the earth's destruction. If this system was drawn as an illustration it would appear as a vast tentacled monster reaching into every country in the world like a hydra. The New Babylonians denied there was a symbiosis between humanity, the Earth and God. For they worshipped evil false gods and glorified all that was bad. God was angry and even the masses were waking up to know everything was interrelated. The people were slowly becoming enlightened, and the New Babylonians knew it. Part of their infernal plan was to cull the world population to a figure they'd chosen from their shopping list of actions to save themselves from what in reality they'd created through their drive for power and money.

"Darlin' you must not keep re-thinking over the same information, you look terrible." Angus snapped out of it, shielding his eyes from the bright sunlight in the taxi. The road trip to Vanessa's estate was further into the foothills of the Andes near San Marino.

In November around Santiago, the temperatures are humid running at 26 degrees. The main highway through the city was packed with cars. Street vendors wandered dangerously amongst the speeding traffic selling drinks and melons. Everywhere Chileans were coming and going smiling and talking. And encamped on the Central Boulevard of the Plaza De Italia under the monuments of previous governments lived recently arrived refugees from Haiti and more recently Venezuela. It seemed like Chile was carrying out its social responsibility to help the victims of other South American countries in economic peril created by the New Babylonian system.

After a bumpy ride through the avenues of grapevines, the taxi pulled up outside Vanessa's small estate. Further up the track next to naturally flowing irrigation dykes, four large dobermans waited by the electric gate for Vanessa's arrival in that supernatural way dogs wait when they know their owners are returning. The taxi driver left them at the gate with their bags and sped off back down the track followed by plumes of dust. Seeing their mistress the dogs wailed frantically. They wailed, even more, when Angus appeared blinking in the bright sun with his pale Scottish skin and gringo scent. The electric gate to Vanessa's hacienda cranked open.

Her home was a South American style ranch set in a sprawling semi-tropical garden faithfully watered and tended by her caretaker Don Carlos. He claimed descent from one of the soldiers serving the infamous Spanish Conquistador Cortez, the evangelising force in Mexico, who ruthlessly defeated the even more famous Aztec Emperor Montezuma. It was a contentious matter whenever it was mentioned. Vanessa was a spiritual supporter of the defiant Mapuche natives in her native Chile and they hadn't been conquered by the Conquistadors. Don Carlos, although old was surprisingly light on his feet on account of his expertise in Latino dancing. When he wasn't dancing, he was riding the dusty tracks on his motorcycle. He came over to assist with the baggage from the taxi. Vanessa walked over to him, he was standing next to a watering trough like an elegant old bandit. She gave him a hug and said "aquí está Angus de Escocia. Le gusta beber whisky. Y él estará aquí por algún tiempo ... tenemos que hacer una investigación".

She explained that Angus was in Chile, researching and that he liked to drink whisky. Don Carlos nodded, grinning at Angus as if he'd passed an unseen test. He sauntered over and shook hands, exclaiming, "Johnnie Walker ah, you Johnnie Walker?" Don Carlos moved his feet deftly with perfect poise, beckoning Angus.

Vanessa explained. "He wants to teach you to dance Milonga Tango."

Angus smiled, "aye, right then!" grateful that something colourful and fun might enter his life. He looked at his luggage on the red-coloured earth. "Don Carlos here's a little gift from Scotland." Bending down, he opened the bag and brought out a dark blue Scotland Rugby shirt. "Here ya' are man, it's a Scotland Rugby shirt." Don Carlos took it smiling.

"Mucho gracias Johnnie Walker," he replied beaming. And like many other peoples of the world, he always wanted Scotland to beat England at the rugby. It was like Scotland had become the voice of freedom for all the world as a result of the declaration of Arbroath, and those famous words:

"As long as but a hundred of us remain alive, never will we on any conditions be brought under English rule. It is in truth not for glory, nor riches, nor honours, that we are fighting, but for freedom - for that alone, which no honest man gives up but with life itself."

It was true that Angus as a Grail Knight had known some of the Sinclairs, who'd signed the declaration of Arbroath. But that was in another life a long time ago. Yet their chain mail still glinted in the sepulchre of his mind.

Under the waning sun, the three of them walked across the lawn to the house with its terracotta roof tiles followed by the attentive dobermans. The ranchero was a natural haven, where small birds of every description lived amongst the trees and bushes and where hummingbirds drank the sweet nectar from the abundant flowers. Angus was still muzzy from the flight, unable to process the change of scenery. Small brown rats appeared from amongst the vines where the grapes were growing over the porch. They were almost tame, unlike the common grey rat he'd seen skulking amongst the ruins of damp castles in Scotland. Vanessa watched Angus's strained inquisitiveness as a brown rat head poked out from behind vine branches. She knew he was burnt out.

"Don't worry about the rats, I have an agreement with them. They don't harm me, if I let them live under the roof of the house." She pointed to three rats scurrying up the roof, clutching grapes in their mouths.

"Ya' joking hen," Angus felt like saying more but didn't. He felt it might be a sensitive subject and perhaps none of his business. The rats went under the pantile tiles. The last one looked back cheekily into the garden of bliss. It was clear, she had some kind of influence over them.

"Don't call me hen please," Vanessa said.

"Och lassie hen is a term of affection in Scotland." But it was clear she didn't see it like that.

"Darlin' please stay in the smaller bedroom tonight until you've recovered from the journey, we've been travelling for eighteen hours and you are still sick."

Vanessa decided to put Angus in a study bedroom in the main house, rather than in her bed. Jet-lagged Angus was too tired to complain. There were artefacts, papers and old maps bundled around a scale model of a volcano next to the bed. Angus needed to recover from his exhaustion. Distracted by the lack of proper sleep, he couldn't resist. As he shuffled towards the bed, he saw old maps on the wall from Southern Chile illustrated with pirate ships, sea serpents, and strange occult symbols around the islands in the archipelago known as Chiloe, where Vanessa's island was. There was a large black question mark on top of the Volcano called Calbunco, set in the area called Lagos.

He put his case by the window which looked over the main part of the garden estate. The window was open and the curtains moved gently in the softer light under the ragged vines clustered above. He could see the shadows of the four dobermans pacing about outside through the satin curtains. Vanessa helped him into the bed after removing his clothes. He wanted to pull her into bed with him. It was an instinct to want her warmth, to know her more. But the fact was he was physically and mentally beat, and she knew it. As his head touched the pillow he couldn't stop the gentle bliss of oblivious sleep soothed on by the clicking of singing insects outside. Then he saw her face looking down at him in the mellow light coming in through the window. She kissed him on the mouth.

"Sleep well darlin' ".

Sacred Lovers

In the early morning in the rising warmth of spring in Chile, Angus could hear the soft whimpering of the dobermans outside the window. He got out of bed feeling like he'd been run over by a locomotive. He opened the curtains where the dogs sat gargoyle-like wagging their stumpy tails. Across from the window, there was a small swimming pool. Something spooked the dogs and they thundered away across the lawn.

Standing in his shorts Angus looked at the pool from the window of his bedroom. A swim would wake him up properly, he thought. The window was not high. He opened it and climbed out onto the stone tiles under the vines which twisted across the beams of the veranda. The white limestone paving was already warm underfoot. He walked across the damp grass of the lawn and stood on the edge of the pool. A few insects were floating about on the surface and the hummingbirds nearby were busy hovering about clusters of flowers, gathering nectar.

Stepping into the pool he was shocked by how cold the water was. He surfaced blowing out like a whale spouting. It brought back memories of swimming in Sinclair Bay in Scotland when he was the caretaker of the famous lighthouse there. Angus stretched his muscles in the water feeling life coming back into them. He was naturally a well-made man without exaggerated muscle tone. Years of working and lifting stones had developed his body subtly, somehow increasing his vitality. Yet lines of trauma were etched around his eyes scoring his flesh like tributaries on a desert landscape where whisky flowed rather than water.

He floated a while in the pool on his back looking up at the magenta blue tones of the sky. With a sideways glance from the pool, he noticed Vanessa's face at her bedroom window. She was watching him and it excited him. The force of feeling love was back. His heart rate increased and he felt alive again. Vanessa came out of the patio door in a bathrobe. She was beaming a big ripe smile of desire, which caused Angus to imagine aromas of Frankincense and opulent bath oils from his past life. She subtly arranged her black tangled hair around her face like an erotic shawl and looked down at him in the pool. Her white robe, loosened as if her receptiveness was expanding out of it. If ever you have felt this magnetic attraction to a lover, you will know that when it comes, it is unquenchable. It fills the body with a superhuman desire to be next to that person, to feel their skin. Angus lifted himself out of the pool and stood ready to receive her in his dripping wet shorts. "Ya beauty," Angus whispered.

Without thinking Vanessa picked up a towel. Angus held the curve of her waist. She began to dry him whilst staring up into his eyes. She was prey and huntress at the same time. They say that many reunited lovers describe this feeling of somehow being connected from the past. As if this love can be relived through genetic memory as a conduit of time travel or something immortal. Angus held the back of her neck, pushing her lips towards his mouth. Then it came, the return of the supernatural moment of vision from Moorish Spain. He stood with her again back in that time, next to a marble fountain amongst minarets and prayer towers. Back then they had gazed into each other's eyes before the point of death. He'd let his sword slip clattering on the marble tiles. It was all so clear. He took her brown-skinned hand lifting it to his face to feel her softness. She smiled her white teeth at him, framed by cherry red lips. Just visible was the tip of her tongue, he wanted to grip it with his lips. He did, and to his surprise, she pushed it further into his mouth. In the background, Moorish soldiers strode about carrying the curved scimitars of Islam, somewhere a melodic harp was playing as water cascaded down the marble fountain.

"What do you see darlin' what can you imagine in my eyes?" Vanessa was as curious as Angus to discover more about this supernatural love.

"I can see the castle in Moorish Spain near the sea. Like a vision out of the history of the Templars."

Angus was uncomfortable and disorientated when he imagined the tombstones he'd seen on the Balantrodoch ground scan which had been the HQ for the Templars in Scotland. It was the other end of the spectrum, first his love for Vanessa, and then the death symbols carved on the tombstones to which he was intimately connected. Yet to know what was coming after death was to understand that a Quest could continue until resolved, that was the purpose irrespective of the limited life span of human beings.

"There are always the two symbols, the skull and crossbones, and the Templar cross. We are standing together next to a stone window looking out onto azure seas. Behind, the skyline is made up of Islamic minarets. You are in a satin dress with your jet hair cascading onto your shoulders. The faithful are called to prayer. You are as beautiful then as you are now."

Vanessa supported Angus as he staggered from the vision. Her scent was all-pervasive. It combined with the aroma of Argan oil, which she'd stroked into her hair. He held her close next to the pool hoping not to be drawn further into their awakening genetic memory. He began to kiss her neck near her main artery, she flushed pleasantly. His hand slid down her chest, caressing her breasts. The touch and firmness of her nipples glided over the tough skin on his hand. Her bathrobe slipped easily down over her soft skin, down onto the tiles. She pressed up against him. She stroked his face and jaw almost like he was an animal. He liked it, he liked it a lot. He was comfortable with the natural love she could give him. He held her close in a tight embrace as if to stop her from returning to the vision of the courtyard and the marble fountain in Seville. He saw himself gathering her up and carrying her towards the stone vaulted room where he'd been held a prisoner back then. The vision merged with the present, becoming one. Now blood was dripping onto the white marble stones beneath him, as it had in the genetic memory vision from Seville, Spain.

"Darlin', you've cut your foot, you're bleeding!" Cloudy red swirls ran into the pool water anchoring them both in the present.

He carried Vanessa back to the hacienda bedroom door from where she'd been watching him. The sun reflected off the glass, forming a halo around it. That moment floated between the two worlds with the dripping blood symbolically linking both ages.

"I am dying, I don't want to go, and I am carrying you to my deathbed," Angus said. Vanessa tried to pull away from him as if she knew what was coming next.

"Angus, it's hauntingly beautiful, you are bringing your sword, leaving it next to the bed. It's a medieval knight's sword with a Templar style cross on the handle and that Viking writing engraved on the blade. You get onto the bed with me and we wrap in a wonderful embrace, your legs are wet with your warm blood. I see a tombstone with a skull and crossbones carved into it, at the bottom of the bed. There are other symbols carved into the stone. There's an hourglass and there's a Grail like a medieval wooden goblet," Vanessa was struggling. "Darlin', I can see so clearly. I can see your body lying on the bed under the castle window. We are surrounded by Islamic warriors with their curved swords. They're knights of the crescent moon, paying respects to you in their Islamic way and I know what they are saying."

Angus watched Vanessa's face tighten with fear and then release into tranquillity all in a moment, as he carried her through the window door.

"What's wrong lassie? What is it? What happened?" Angus blurted out.

"Darlin', they have a dagger!" Vanessa screamed. Gently, Angus put his hand over her mouth and stopped her screaming again. "They killed me and laid out my body next to yours."

Angus was confused, there was a suggestion in her tone that he'd been responsible.

"We are lying in our own pooling blood covering the white silken sheets, our faces white with death."

Neither of them could continue to make love in light of this genetic memory.

The Research begins

After the death-bed vision of themselves, Angus and Vanessa found an increased appetite to discover the truth of their situation. They began to combine their research into ancient manuscripts. It was not by chance that the first books and papers on the list began with the history of the famous Clan Sinclair, the builders of Rosslyn.

Vanessa sometimes felt compromised when it came to discussing Scottish history with Angus. But then she equalled the situation with her ancient map-making knowledge which left Angus wanting. Since her dreams about Rosslyn, she'd been studying Rosslyn's history intensively. Angus had gone a little bit further, delving into a Templar legend. He'd been researching the curious historical links with the Pirate Brethren of the coast, and the Knights Hospitallers and the Templars, whose sworn oath involved saluting pirates and corsairs. Indeed Angus found this very strange.

"One of the rules of the Templars was that a newly admitted knight must pledge allegiance to brother and sister pirates," Vanessa said smiling, straightening her dress provocatively. "Yes, darlin' in 1700 in desperation, the Captain of the merchant ship 'Oak' gave the Templar sign of distress on the deck of his ship before he was about to be hung from the yardarm. He was then spared by the pirates and given back his goods. Even his dog was returned with a special ribbon and a bone still kept to this day in a museum in Poole, Dorset."

"Och lassie, you know your stuff!"

"The Templar pirate Captain was Jacques Le Bon. His ancestors were from a Templar family." Angus listened and then rolled his eyes in mock defeat. There was healthy competition between them.

"The original Templar ships which escaped La Rochelle in 1307 with a supernatural treasure were already in alliance with the pirates and the Knights of St John of Malta. Both Orders used the flag with the skull and crossbones, also carved onto the tombstones of long-dead knights. Together they continued the battle against their enemies on the high seas. And we know who their main enemy was! Because the Templars and pirates are on the same side, and still fighting their old enemies, the New Babylonians." It was no mistake that Angus had used the present tense in describing the pirate and Templar alliance. It was an inadvertent slip of the tongue of truth. He just didn't know it yet.

"But what happened to them?" she replied.

Vanessa discovered that the Vikings had sailed to South America before 1500, well before Columbus's so-called voyages of discovery.

"It's obvious the Templars fought back with their formidable fleet aided by their pirate allies. The Templars made it to the Americas before 1400. We know that Prince Henry Sinclair sailed to Nova Scotia and Newport, Rhode Island in 1398. And it was his grandson who built Rosslyn Chapel. Don't you see the chain linking the living and the dead?" Angus finally questioned.

Vanessa and Angus had been discussing the theories of ancient global exploration. He maintained the Vikings travelled worldwide in their fabulous dragon-headed longboats. Greenland was like a motorway service station for viking ships to replenish supplies on their world voyages. Angus believed they'd inherited special maps and advanced ancient navigational instruments, allowing them to travel anywhere over the seas.

"Nobody talks about those incredible navigational instruments in the early middle ages; they'd have been reported, hunted down and burned by the Papal and Spanish inquisition! The Vikings were using loadstones and magnetic needles floating in brine pointing the way to true North. The Inquisition branded them as black magicians. No one was supposed to know that the Earth wasn't flat," Vanessa said.

"Aye lassie it's still the same today, with them bullying folk to watch TV. And if anyone decides on another path they become heretics just like in the medieval days, a sure sign that the New Babylonians are still exerting their evil influence over humanity."

"Yes Angus, it is just the same today. The Kings and Queens back then who paid in gold for voyages of exploration were still targeted and influenced by the Inquisition. I mean even all-powerful King Edward 1 and his son Edward 11 became pressured to allow the Papal inquisition torturers into Britain to hunt down refugee Templars. They wanted the Templar's knowledge of their explorations and their power. And remember they'd already burnt to death at least fifty Templars and their last Grand Master Jacques de Molay. Although I don't believe they did burn him. I don't have any proof, just yet." Angus was astounded at her knowledge.

He thought about the implications of the escaping Templar fleet which left La Rochelle with all the sacred treasure.

"The Templar fleet fled to an unknown destination?" Vanessa replied, flashing a suspicious scowl.

"Aye, there's something supernatural happening, like there's another version of historical events. Yet people are blind to it. Back then, the Templars continued their battle against their enemies, perhaps disguised as Pirates and Corsairs?"

Vanessa listened patiently, she'd done plenty of interesting investigation herself.

"What about that eighteenth-century Pirate Lord. Lord Stroma, also descended from the Architect William Sinclair of Rosslyn Chapel?"

Angus had discovered information describing how Lord Stroma in 1700 described as a 'firebrand' had offered hospitality and lodgings to pirates. Something wasn't right! Vanessa had been researching into the Sinclairs and she wanted to know why Lord Stroma had been entertaining pirates.

It was no shock to know that the rugged coastline of maritime Chile was a safe place for pirates and refugees escaping persecution, including criminals and those persecuted. But there was much more to the history of the pirates than previously known and their connections to the Templars. It was something that had always motivated Angus's research after he'd identified the controversial Rosslyn Chapel Knight Templar, initiation scene carved onto a corbel which had previously supported the enigmatic lost statue of the Turkish Admiral Piri Reis who discovered the lost maps of Atlantis.

A secret alliance of formidable strength had existed which was still in existence today. It was just a matter of time before the truth was discovered.

Looking back at the Sinclair Castle and Lighthouse, 2015

Looking back to Scotland from the hacienda paradise in the foothills of the Andes, Angus had often thought about alternative world history when locking the gates of the ruined Sinclair Castle on dark winter evenings. His heart longed for them again. He was having a strange nostalgic feeling most Scottish people experience who travel the world to better climates. Because when they think back to the Scottish winter gloom they miss the melancholy. The Welsh had a very good name for it. They call it Hiraeth.

Back then Angus's duties included patrolling the castle ruins, where the original Lord Stroma had lived in 1700. He who was the friend of pirates and corsairs alike. Sinclair Castle was much more than another fortification situated on a remote headland. The castle was barely accessible to those who owned it, let alone its enemies. This remote castle was a sea fortress provisioned from Sinclair Bay through its sea gates.

From 1400, the Sinclairs were supplying and building ships from their castle well after the Templars were supposedly finished. It was like the Cape Canaveral of the medieval world where boats and galleys were built and flat packed and then transported for clandestine explorations and other matters. Many secret contracts had been honoured to build pirate ships bound for the Americas, from Sinclair Castle. These vessels had been crafted for attacking and robbing the enemies of the Templars. The Sinclairs had invested their energy into assisting Templar sea power.

Outside in the heat, Don Carlos was busy watering the plants under the plum trees. From time to time he burst into some antiquated Milonga tango love song, amusing Vanessa.

"Darlin' I want you to learn Milonga Tango with Don Carlos, because I will expect you to dance it with me when all this has finished," she said beaming a smile.

Angus stopped thinking about his wanderings around Sinclair Castle. He began to tap his feet as Don Carlos sang out his Milonga. Angus was happy with Vanessa's dancing proposition. He just hoped they wouldn't be killed before then. Then she found something else in their research papers. She looked intensely at her laptop.

"I am scrolling down to see the Royal Navy records. It seems the British Navy was observing their pirate enemies."

"You mean those enemies, who were friends of the Templars?" Angus replied smiling. Vanessa knew what she meant. She went into investigative mode, putting on her reading glasses.

"This transcript is intriguing as it concerns the voyage of the Frigate Trinity, a known pirate vessel operating from the Orkney Islands, Scotland. It's important as the vessel was also provisioned at Sinclair Castle by Lord Stroma the friend of pirates. Both Pirates and the Templars always had one common enemy. And they retaliated attacking the ships and agents of the Vatican, particularly in South America." Vanessa had much more to say. Perhaps more than Angus expected.

"Angus! When the Templar fleet left La Rochelle in France they were not flying Templar flags, they were flying black pirate flags with the Skull and Crossbones on them. We will discover that this specific group of Templars within the Order carried on the fight and still do to this day. Such Templars are buried beneath Wheel Cross tombstones symbolically coded to represent Templar global and maritime mapping knowledge. For they were an inner sanctum of International Templars, predominately active on the high seas and allied with the pirates."

Angus stared open-mouthed, he was astounded that she knew this, for it was information only known to a few.

"As we know lassie, when I say the friends of the enemy, I am talking about the friends of the New Babylonians. Those who put profit before God," Angus grimaced. By now, Angus and Vanessa knew the New Babylonians planned to dominate and destroy the Earth by casting humanity in chains both spiritually and physically. And you're right about the secret inner wheel of the Templars, that's the Order which continues to this day."

"Yes, darlin', I know, please read the report. I think it's the work of an 18th Century British Government informant."

"Och lassie ya' mean a filthy grass," Angus replied, drawing his finger across his throat.

British Navy reports 1700 Sinclair Bay, North Scotland

Our agent in the North of Scotland informs us of the departure of a vessel of 200 tons in April year of our Lord 1700. It is a sloop with 30 guns named the Trinity from Sinclair Castle. This vessel I learnt was provisioned by the Earl of Stroma, who supposedly paid for the expedition. I was also informed that the vessel was carrying armaments, arms, gunpowder and victuals, also saddles and other leather and bridles for horses. Also taken on board the Trinity were blacksmithing equipment and mason's tools. The swords which were brought from Italy, I am further informed were forged by Farrar. I find that matter intolerable when our arms are much inferior.

Cost of information. 10 Guineas paid in Inverness April 2, 1700, AD to the agent of King George known as Mr Crab.

Vanessa drew her olive-skinned hand across her throat in a mock execution.

Angus was in his element, explaining Scottish history.

"At Sinclair Castle, ships were custom-built, bound for the new world. The strength of these clans, particularly the Sinclairs and Gunns was in their sea power. And for this reason, they bore the name of the Ancient Sea Kings. They lived by the same symbols with a shared code of brotherhood. Their age-old enemy was the Spanish, formerly Papal, Inquisitions now taken over by the New Babylonians."

Vanessa had abandoned her faith, resorting to new-age worship of the trees and nature. She'd been part of a spiritual rebellion happening all over South America.

The Feast of the Knights and Pirates

Angus thought back to the discovery at Sinclair Castle of pirate cutlasses. It appeared that Clan Sinclair's Gypsy armourers were making weapons for the pirates as well. The local legend tells about the great Knight and Pirate Feast held every year at the Castle as a theatrical event. Here the locals hoisted skull and crossbones flags and attended it dressed as corsairs bearing flaming torches. Each year, nearly one thousand people attended. It was traditional for costumed pirates to serve about a hundred men and women dressed as Templars. The event had gone on for as long as people could remember. But most people were not aware of why it happened.

"Aye lassie I'll say it again, there's no smoke without fire," Angus said.

"Yes, so true darlin', and I can feel us getting closer to the truth, my spirit guides are telling me the same."

"Och da' na' be silly lassie."

Sea Legend, Chiloe, Chile

Vanessa scrolled further down the laptop clicking another file named newspaper clippings. She clicked them and they appeared in sepia tones. Some went back as far as 1780. She translated from Spanish reading from a pamphlet produced by the local Jesuit newspaper discovered in 1800.

The main Island of Chiloe in southern Chile had first been colonised by the Spanish. The only conventionally literate people at the time were Jesuit and Salesian priests working to convert the Mapuche forest peoples there. The state of Chiloe remained entirely a Spanish hybrid as the rest of Chile was becoming a Republic. Vanessa snarled staring at the pages opening the screen. She was fiercely loyal to the native Mapuche in the area where she'd turned her back on the church.

Missing Vessel the Eagle with Jesuit brothers 1780

Around the beginning of spring, Father Pedro and Father Felipe Jesuits along with several assistants from our Castro mission settlement Chiloe Islands went missing. These brave map makers, missionaries and envoys of Christ made it possible for the spreading of God's word through unknown areas of Chiloe. We call on the Holy Virgin to protect them and cry out to our Lord to return them safely.

Cardinal Castro.

Vanessa looked up from the laptop. She knew a lot about the tensions between the Catholic Church and her beloved Mapuche natives.

"The ship 'Mary Magdalena' was never seen again. There was no wreckage, no clues appeared. She wasn't the only ship to go missing, many missing ships were recorded around the Chiloe Islands. And still, those disappearances and mysteries continue to this day".

Vanessa began to cry. Not just murmuring's of sadness, but full-on wailing, embarrassing Angus.

"Nobody knows why those violent Christians couldn't keep away from our natural sanctuary, the Mapuche didn't want them around robbing their sacred forests. We never asked them to force their religion onto us. We have other ways to heal each other with our Shamans, nature and the moon cycles." Angus grimaced.

Six months earlier the Argentinian industrialist Don Miguel de Monte vanished with his super yacht manned by ex-special forces operatives. It made no difference. There had been a violent struggle and blood was found in what wreckage was left, ruling out natural phenomena such as tidal waves or lightning bolts. The blood samples were analysed and found to match genetic European blood groups. Additionally, there was also Mapuche native blood splattered with the drops from the Special Forces operatives. As usual Mapuche native insurgents had been blamed.

Rodrigo Bermodes, Special Forces, Chile

Vanessa was still angry.

"Let me say this darlin', my brother will be avenged if anything has happened to him," she said yet again. "Such operatives are trained to survive at all costs. We have to hope Rodrigo may still be alive."

Angus realised she meant business. But he also realised that her perceived enemies might not be who she thought they were. Vanessa still had a feeling that there was something phenomenal nearby. She'd experienced such feelings for years, even before her brother had gone missing presumed dead.

"My spirit guides are telling me my brother lives, Rodrigo lives, I will clear the name of the Mapuche because they did not attack this Argentinian's super yacht!"

"But then who did?" Angus replied already knowing the answer to his question.

There were several other transcripts from various newspapers and journals which they'd each collected during their research. It was a little early to know if any of their findings would help them solve the question of the disappearance of Vanessa's brother. But both knew that his military activities might never be spoken of again.

It seemed that the missing vessels over the years were linked. They both knew that a few missing smaller vessels per year would not be overly scrutinised. However, the number of vessels missing over the years, if examined together may well merit further scrutiny. It was obvious there was a cover-up. It was clear to Angus and Vanessa that the unknown blood samples found on the wood wreckage in the water around where Don Miguel's yacht went missing could well be the groups they were looking for. However, Vanessa did have access to the DNA information taken from the blood samples. But neither dare say another word.

The Templar Tombstones

Angus opened another computer file containing the pictures of the ground scan of the Templar tombstones from Templar HQ at Balantrodoch. He'd first found the ground scan report about the tombstones whilst he'd been the last caretaker of the Sinclair Study Centre in 2015. He had a supernatural feeling about them. He felt he wanted to lie down on top of one of them and sleep with his hands in the dead praying knight position and he felt morbid about it.

Every time he visualised the numerals and the symbols on the tombstones he felt they were familiar and got the shivers. Both Templar tombstones were carved with an elaborate flowering cross sat on top of the stem of Jesse with sprouting leaves. Next to this was a set of sheep shears, a symbolic reference to King David being a shepherd. Set around the carved cross were other symbols, such as the bible and a Grail and the sand timer which symbolised that human life on the Earth is limited by God. And he knew that every time he saw a Grail and sword carved into a tombstone he knew there was a Grail Knight buried under it. His hair began to prickle under his shirt making his skin crawl.

In contrast, over the coming days, their lovemaking intensified in the beautiful sanctuary of Vanessa's hacienda-style estate. Angus drank the honey of love and ate the manna of heaven growing in the garden around him. All the vegetables and fruit they ate grew in the subtropical garden. At night they drank the wine from the nearby vineyards and in the early morning after making love again, they researched their coming Quest together, relaxing amongst the hummingbirds and bees of the beauty around and they were getting closer to knowing the truth of why they'd been lovers in a past life.

The missing statues of Rosslyn Chapel

The archaeological establishment had discredited Angus and his work. This was why he'd turned to other methods of retrieving that which had been denied him. He'd improved his powers of intuition, well beyond normal. And then he'd discovered a connection between the Templars and the Islamic Admiral Piri Reis, who owned the map illustrating the landmass of Antarctica before there was any ice covering it. The Piri Reis map had revealed information about the Andes mountain range well before the great explorer Pizarro had been to Peru. How did Piri Reis know about them? There had always been the question about the illustration on the map of the South American coast before 1513, and the fact that the Turkish Admiral Piri Reis had been Muslim. But why had he been celebrated and remembered in the Christian Chapel of Rosslyn built by the last of the Knight Templars?

Just to clarify, around 1700, all one hundred and thirteen Rosslyn statues had been removed. Some said to protect them from the defilers of religious images called Iconoclasts. Or perhaps the statues were removed because they telegraphed forbidden information about the real purpose of Rosslyn? But if so, was there still a culture somehow connected to the Templar mystery somewhere? Many thought so, but dared not say.

The importance of the 'lost statues' should never be underestimated as physical illustrations of the purpose of Rosslyn. The very fact, there'd been a statue of Admiral Piri Reis on Rosslyn's exterior hinted at something much greater and a secret that had been covered up perhaps by both sides involved in the secret war.

To this day there remains a clue carved into the top surface of the corbel where the Piri Reis statue once stood. Angus had been on his way to the chapel to examine the carvings when Vanessa had rescued him responding to deep visions about the chapel which were connected to her research and desire to find her lost brother Rodrigo. More information was filtering through now, but it was Vanessa who spotted it first.

"Darlin' take a look at this picture. I just found it, taken when that protective metal frame and scaffold canopy covered the whole of Rosslyn." Vanessa pointed at the photograph enlarged on the computer screen. "The camera angle is looking down on the corbal top where the statue had been. I am sure there's something scratched into the top of the Templar corbel?" Angus moved over onto the laptop and started to enlarge the image, looking intensely at the screen.

"Correct boss, it looks like there are numbers or symbols carved into the top of the corbel, where the Admiral once stood."

"It looks like the pixel strength is low, we canna' see the full detail yet. We will have to go back there, right away. We have to return now, to do the full investigation on the stonework before the New Babylonians get to it. It's unfinished business lassie."

"What you say is the truth, and it will help me to find my brother, I just know it will."

"We must excavate at the Templar headquarters at Balantrodoch, it's not far from Rosslyn. The ground-scan information I found in the document from the Lighthouse indicates a pair of Templar type tombstones behind the wall."

"Darlin', you keep mentioning those Templar stones affectionately like they are your relatives or something."

"Och da' na' be strange lassie," Angus said smirking.

Vanessa realised that the Templar tombstones were causing Angus problems. She'd already seen the ground scan information which Angus had also found at the lighthouse. Furthermore, there was a connection between Angus and one of the tombstones. But how could she tell him, to excavate his own grave?

"It looks like the numbers carved into the stone are geophysical measurements darlin'?" Vanessa said.

She was sure with her knowledge as a cartographer that the numerals and symbols looked like they could have originated from South America. And she'd already invented a solution. Because she'd been developing a software programme able to translate ancient symbols of stars, moon cycles, numerals and navigational information into direct modern geophysical coordinates of Latitude and Longitude. She was aware that before longitude was discovered, this measurement was often measured from the horizon, partly calculated by fixing the position of stars and planets. It made sense that these symbols related to the cosmos.

Angus was right, they'd still have to study the carvings on the Templar tombstone at Balantrodoch and also carved on top of the corbel at Rosslyn.

It was time now for Vanessa to download that information through her ***Ancient Symbols and Navigation Translation App*** she'd invented. Soon they'd know the inevitable truth.

They said their goodbyes to Vanessa's Santiago hacienda estate for now. They'd had one month of love, recovery and research. Don Carlos assisted them both into the taxi placing their luggage in the boot. He was familiar with waving Vanessa off on her constant adventures.

"Buenos dias Johnnie Walker!" he called out. He once again branded Angus after the most popular whisky available in Chile. Angus laughed. Vanessa hugged Don Carlos as the dogs gambled excitedly.

"Darlin' Don Carlos expects you to dance the Milonga Tango with me when all this is finished."

The search for the carved codes resumes in Scotland

Temple Balantrodoch, south-east of Rosslyn.
Balantrodoch is a Gaelic word meaning 'stead of the warriors'

In the cold grey, Angus MacWilliam with his steel coloured hair was down in a shallow pit digging in the ground at Balantrodoch. There was a look of Doc Savage about him. Vanessa had helped him read his ground scan information and find the place where the tombstones were. Two huge tombstones now lay in the clay soil. He bent down and touched one of them and got a jolt. He stood up, knocking over his tools. Another vision came and he saw himself and Vanessa on a silk bed covered in blood. Then he was back in the reality of the pit doing what he did best. Moving stone and digging in the ground and examining carvings.

"Jesus Christ and Saints protect us och' man these stones are conclusive proof!"

"Darlin' are you ok?" Vanessa asked.

From down in the pit Angus looked over the ground at the ruined Templar Church, over the way.

"Come on, it's time to leave," Vanessa added.

"Aye, I am coming, alright! Who hid these tombstones away from the world?" He wrestled one, lifting it and standing it up against the pit side. He swivelled it around on its base. It must have weighed 500 pounds. The tool marks on the back of it were rough and jagged, never meant to be seen. There was an oblong box section carved to hide something. But he passed over it. He turned it round to the front, to see a sequence of symbols and numerals carved into the stone's surface. But he should have recognised the slot carving in the back. It was very well hidden in the years of mud and plant growth. He'd glazed over it, transfixed by the emerging aroma of roses and honey, a sickly morbid smell, strangely familiar coming out from where the stone had been.

Vanessa with her wild black hair climbed down the ladder into the shallow pit to try to settle him down. "Darlin', hush people are here. They're coming over," she said.

Try as he might he couldn't keep his eyes off her. Vanessa felt his desire and it excited her. The hairs on her arms and neck pricked up responsively under her waterproofs. Her feeling seemed to be linked to the newly emerging scent of roses and honey. It conjured up scenes of medieval Seville in Spain in the flower garden by the pool where they'd both once died in their past life. The simple things of the feeling of love and the smell of flowers are in fact keys to our previous lives, but most of humanity had forgotten this under the onslaught of New Babylonian materialism and the denial of God.

"Darlin' I am going to distract the men." Angus knew what she was going to do and didn't like it.

She clambered back up the ladder. She was no stranger to trouble. Vanessa walked over in front of the men batting her eyelashes, to distract them from seeing the newly made investigation pit where Angus was digging.

"Thank God you came, my truck is over there. It won't work, it won't start," she said with her broken Spanish accent, acting anxious.

Meanwhile, the heritage officer presented a false yellow card bearing his picture ID, hanging about his neck.

"Do you understand the English language lady? We are not the rescue service. But we'll see what we can do. We are investigating heritage crimes shall we say. Have you seen anything?" He looked over to his colleague rearranging his ID card. Vanessa knew they were lying.

"Take this lady over to her vehicle, it's getting dark and I wouldn't like anything to happen to her. She might want to be thinking about hiring a small electric car. A diesel truck's a big job for a wee lassie."

"You're are so right!"

Vanessa had heard what they said and played their antiquated chauvinism accordingly.

In the early winter gloom of Temple Balantrodoch, Vanessa had a question for the fake heritage officers. "I've heard that this was the headquarters of the Templars." She nodded her head towards the ruined church nearby hoping to distract them. The outline of the little chapel stood out against the darkening sky like a painting.

"For the love of William Wallace. If I'd a guinea for every time I'd heard that I'd be in the Bahamas again, sipping a coconut cocktail wi' a lot of whisky in it."

Vanessa knew their game though. "With my little English, it is difficult. But I am pleased you are good people here, in this strange place."

"Och, never mind lassie, you are a tourist and tourism is important to us, and we shall do everything we can, to help you on your way," he said playing the concerned official. "Now follow my assistant Archie. We can see what the problem with your vehicle is."

People still feared the Templars perhaps not their swords anymore, but their kudos and stature which still lived on. In a world lacking in spirit and integrity, people naturally looked to Templars as an example. The truth was though, the New Babylonians were searching for the Holy

Ark of God as well and these so-called officials were merely agents of them.

From the pit, Angus whispered, "Och yes, ya' beauty! I found the other coordinate symbols".

Sure enough, the symbols and coordinates had been incised around the ring cross form of the Templar cross. Angus took photographs. He brought out his locksmith's putty and pressed it into the incised number sequence next to symbols of the planets and moon phases, to get a positive image from them. Climbing out of the pit, he saw a white-fleshed hand in the soil near the upturned tombstones with the symbols carved on them. The hand appeared like it was trying to grasp one of the pens he'd knocked off the tray. It was similar to the momentous vision of the white hand turning over the pages of a book, he'd witnessed when he was a boy. The strange thing was he wanted to touch it like it was his own.

He heard the pickup truck start-up across the road. He saw one of the heritage men over at the Templar Church walking around it like the laird of the Manor. Angus knew Vanessa would drive away drawing attention away from himself. She drove around the village whilst Angus lumbered off around the perimeter wall, keeping his head down. But in peripheral vision, he saw a figure in a hood standing in the nearby forest, although he couldn't be certain as sometimes he confused reality with his medieval visions. But often the visions were meant to be like that.

"Quickly, come on, let's go!" Vanessa shouted.

Angus jumped into the pickup with his muddy boots. He pointed to the bag with the camera in it. He was still shaking.

"I got it on the camera, all we need, we can take a look at the pictures over at the hotel, and there are a few good ones," he said breathing a sigh of relief.

"What's wrong, you look like you've seen a ghost," Vanessa asked.

"Aye, true, maybe my own ghost lassie." He would wait to tell her about the honey preserved hand. It was too much to think about right now.

"The truck started up as expected. They gave me a lesson on how to start a vehicle in the cold. You know, turning the key a couple of times, making sure the heater plugs were working in the damp," Vanessa smiled. "He asked me if I'd seen anything unusual happening, whoops a daisy."

"Och' tremendous, I didn't expect any unwanted visitors coming," Angus smiled with relief. They sat there in a lay-by talking for ages.

There had been more trouble in the village near the ancient Templar HQ. The police were there and had blocked the road to the village. There was a scene-of-crime forensic tent up, a sure sign a body had been found. By chance, the Templar tombstone which Angus had discovered was now being read on the local radio news bulletin from another area of the ancient Templar HQ. It appeared the stones had been dug up again and moved. Angus tuned in the truck's radio.

"This is Scottish F12 news, special reporting from Temple Balantrodoch made famous by the Knights Templar. Another body has been discovered near a medieval grave, illegally dug up. Bringing you the latest news within hours of it happening."

Angus remembered the hooded figure standing in the wood, which he confused with one of his medieval visions of a monk. He could not get it out of his mind.

"Och' lassie tha' police are swarming all over, we better get on wi' it."

Hotel 'Highland Dirk', Rosslyn Village

Back at the Hotel Dirk named after the Highlander's dagger, Angus and Vanessa brought in their bags, checked in, and went straight to the hotel bar for whisky to warm themselves. The hotel was decorated with Victorian Scottish paraphernalia. There was an enormous stag's head looking down the hall. There were badger skin sporrans, snuff mills made from ram's horns on the tables and an array of tartans decorating both furniture and carpets. On the wall was a glass case portraying the unlikely scene of a weasel attacking a pheasant with a badger watching like a robust spectator. There was the distinct aroma of fried breakfasts and haggis. Although dark outside, three windows remained with their curtains open. The window which looked out over Rosslyn Chapel had its tartan curtains closed. Impulsively Angus marched over and began to try to open them.

"Sir, what are you doing? We have express instructions that the view from that window should not be seen. Leave the curtains and sit yersel' down for some refreshment."

A busy whirlwind woman came out from behind the bar. She pushed in front of Angus securing the golden curtain cords.

"You'll not have heard then? It's been all over the news; one of the local heritage officers was shot dead over at the old Templar headquarters today. There's always trouble there," she said, recalling painfully how her husband had been shot inside Rosslyn Chapel but keeping it to herself. "Always there's a coincidence at Rosslyn, always so much coincidence."

Vanessa and Angus stared open-mouthed at each other. It was essential to return to Chile before they became implicated in what was happening.

"Now if its whisky ye' will be wanting, we have got some beautiful single malts from the east coast, including the Old Stroma and if you like our range here and you don't like peat overtones, then surely the Old Stroma will be to your liking."

Angus walked back to his seat. Firstly, because he knew Mrs Sinclair wouldn't tolerate the curtains open and secondly her bribe of the whisky had worked.

"A Caithness whisky you say, and why would you be wanting a Caithness whisky in particular?" asked Angus, "and if I am not mistaken, we are talking Clan Gunn, Clan Mackay, Clan Sutherland, all the original Viking Clans up there." Angus strategically left out the most controversial, Clan Sinclair from the list.

"A good observation laddie, and which one of the clans you mention, would you hold allegiance with?"

"I might ask you the very same question?"

"Then there's no harm in letting you in on a little secret!"

"Well, based on the proximity of this hotel to the famous Rosslyn Chapel, I would offer good odds on you being a Sinclair of some description."

"But anyhow, we are all Sinclair's here at Rosslyn."

Angus smiled he would have to be careful with her, she was smarter than he realised.

"Would it be possible to take a bottle of the Old Stroma and we can drink a toast to the famous Sinclairs, perhaps even one for my ancestors, the infamous Gunns of Caithness?" Angus added probing.

"I think we can make an exception for even Clan Gunn over a bottle of the Stroma whisky," she said.

She went back to the hotel bar to get the whisky. Vanessa went back to their hotel room to call her Chilean travel agent to re-book their flights, this time with the connecting flight to Castro near Vanessa's remote island, The Island of Sailing Souls, which would serve as their base during their exploration of the Chiloe Islands.

Vanessa was unhappy about taking Angus's daughter Isobel with them to Chiloe, but she never let on. Isobel was in her gap year at University. They'd discussed the situation and Vanessa had finally accepted her coming, but it was only because she didn't want to spoil the potential of using Angus to help find her brother.

Caroline Agostini, Angus's ex-wife, and her new partner Max Rothman were planning to get married in California, being billed as the elite party of the year. Isobel was not on the invite list. There was big money and family politics running in the background. Max didn't see eye to eye with Isobel in many ways. She'd been involved in an embarrassing scandal with Damon Shultz, Max's best friend. Damon was 20 years older than Isobel and the two of them had been found drinking together in the early hours of the morning at Max's plastic mansion in Hollywood. The event had been typically brushed over. Caroline, Isobel's mother was livid, rationalising the affair to Damon's inability to control himself. But she didn't want to damage inter-family relationships, especially as Max and Damon were in business together, until she could get the truth from her daughter.

Angus had been confused and helpless. All this had happened miles away in New York, away from his beloved Scotland. He just remembered the happy times of teaching his daughter about the history of Scotland. She'd developed a particular interest in the Jacobite Rebellions. He used to love her marching around brandishing a wooden coat hanger shouting, "Follow me, follow me, I am the little Bonnie Prince Charlie, like a rhyme".

Angus wanted to find out more about what had happened to Isobel. He felt she hadn't been happy for a long time. He would if necessary offer her sanctuary in Chile, that was his hope now. He was good at offering friends and family opportunities at other people's expense. He wanted to offer her an alternative path from the decadent New Babylonian life to which she'd become accustomed. He and Vanessa were about to confirm something very significant regarding their combined research, and the answer was heading towards them like a fireball of enlightenment.

Vanessa came back down from the hotel room cradling the laptop. Mrs Sinclair poured out the whisky, which she thumped down on the table.

"And who was that? I don't trust her," Vanessa said.

Angus said nothing.

Vanessa's lips tightened. "Isobel is coming soon. We're meeting her at Edinburgh airport so don't drink so much tonight."

"Nay lassie, we've got the world to conquer tomorrow," Angus said over dramatically. Both of them acted so well it was hard, to tell the truth of the situation.

"Please, no more whisky."

And Angus knew that the Sinclair sentinels would be watching, more so than ever. He took a sip, it warmed him, he followed up with a deeper glug. Mrs Sinclair watched from behind the hotel desk.

"Darlin' be careful, it's very strong," Vanessa said.

"Aye! But we deserve a drink lassie," Angus replied.

Angus gazed into Vanessa's eyes. Sometimes their eyes drew together magnetically attracted anyway.

"Your eyes are the same colour as honey made from fields of Scottish gorse."

"Green eyes darlin', you have deep green eyes like the magical sea in Chile, you are like a Merman, like the legends in my native Chile, where men and women live in the sea, frolicking like dolphins."

Embarrassed Mrs Sinclair scowled feeling like throwing up at their sickening love. She'd lost her beloved husband the previous year shedding light on why she'd always insisted that the curtains remained forever closed, for the window looked out at the famous Rosslyn Chapel. Stephen Sinclair her husband had been the curator and keeper there for thirty years. And it was his steady hand and life of leadership which had been brought to an untimely end in a callous execution type killing inside Rosslyn Chapel. Mrs Sinclair had found him slumped against the famous apprentice pillar with a bullet hole through his forehead. No one had heard the round go off.

The killing shocked the world, fuelling more conspiracy theories. Angus had always been suspicious of the hype. To him, it was merely a smokescreen hiding the fact that the real sacred treasure, 'The Ark of the Covenant' was or had been in the vaults of Rosslyn Chapel. Like many other murders around high stakes and political intrigue, nobody heard about Mrs Sinclair's husband the Rosslyn Chapel caretaker again, the event was conveniently airbrushed out of reality. But the incident had drawn the Sinclairs of Rosslyn together like nothing else.

Vanessa showed Angus the laptop from which she'd recently downloaded the pictures of the Knights Templar tombstones. She'd highlighted the navigational symbols and coordinates carved around the Templar cross. Vanessa enlarged the image of the symbols and numbers. The Roman numerals and carvings of moon symbols had been cut deeply into the Tombstone.

They prepared for a final night visit to Rosslyn to make their final investigations. It was time to examine the corbel carving in real life where the statue of Admiral Piri Reis had once stood dressed in a turban, billowing pants and Sinbad style shoes, holding an astrolabe. The statue had been immaculately carved by descendants of the Templars. Unfortunately, the Islamic Admiral statue had disappeared along with the 113 others. It did not matter in the great scheme of things because the clue still remained on the corbel. The carved inscriptions remained on top of the corbel where a Templar was leading another man blindfolded with a noose around his neck, to swear on a bible. Conventional history had hidden the fact that the Templars lived on. And now Vanessa and Angus had discovered something far more interesting which they were about to analyse and run through the sacred ***carving and navigational App*** Vanessa had also invented. Angus put his formidable knowledge of stone carving to use.

"The depth of the carved images on the top of the corbel is unusual, as they are deeper than normal. But we must see them in real life, though. Andrew always stated that first-hand observation was the best."

He copied the pictures and sent them to his phone which pinged into place. Vanessa downloaded and enlarged the important carved symbols so they'd have a portable version to help cross-reference against the other carved symbols there. He supped at the whisky, so did Vanessa.

Mrs Sinclair bustled about in the Hotel Lobby cleaning and going about her normal routines. She kept busy distracting herself from thinking about her beloved husband. She worked late to exhaust herself into sleeping like most of Scotland she was also on medication. Vanessa went over to Mrs Sinclair.

“We’re going to bed early, we’ve got some business to attend to in the morning so if we can have an early room call, we’d much appreciate it and we’ve paid the bill online.”

“Aye, thank you, that’s good then I am not one for the internet. Ma’ daughter does all that stuff.” Mrs Sinclair bustled out to do a final inspection of the area they’d been working in. She went over to the curtains again and double-checked they’d not been tampered with. As she walked by Angus, she took a glance at the whisky bottle.

“You liked that then, half the bottle finished in no time. You’ll be sleeping well tonight.” Angus got up from the sofa staggering a little. “Wisht’ laddie, you might as well take what’s left of the whisky up to the room. Waste not, want not, as they say!” Mrs Sinclair had an unfortunate way of looking contemptuously at people without being aware of it.

“And I take it you’ll be wanting the full Scottish breakfast in the morning. Do ye’ want a black pudding? It’s a great cure for the hangover. I’ll put it down on your order.”

Mrs Sinclair was intimately woven into the greater culture of the Sinclairs and their unseen network of spies, already knew ahead of time, that Vanessa and Angus wouldn’t be coming for breakfast.

A night visit to Rosslyn

In their first-floor hotel room, Vanessa peeped out of the curtains to look over at the Victorian entrance to Rosslyn Chapel. Although similar to the body of the chapel it was evident it was only a copy of Rosslyn's late medieval style at best. After fine-tuning his senses, Angus had learnt to see what others could not. It was strange but no one ever listened to his warnings, yet his premonitions about them always happened. He'd learnt to stop warning people because they never listened to him. Despite the Asperger's link, Angus had also inherited the misfortune of telling the truth. He could never lie about certain archaeological finds the establishment wanted him to keep quiet because they didn't fit their contrived version of history.

Back in their room, Angus and Vanessa sat on the bed and slipped on their balaclavas. Outside the noises of the evening activity began to diminish. The shouts and talking coming from the last of midweek revellers had subsided. An owl screeched its night hunting song, whilst beyond the full moon illuminated the grey mist over the distant fields, making them appear like there was smouldering fire underneath. Rosslyn Chapel stood in darkness covered by the surrounding trees and overshadowed by the remains of Rosslyn Castle. Angus had been told by Andrew Sinclair that there was a tunnel running from the castle to the chapel. And that there'd once been a tower of priestly learning administered by monks in purple robes, the royal colours of King David, whose son Solomon had built the Temple on which Rosslyn was fashioned. Andrew had remarked that the castle tower had been set alight. Father Haye, a priest, who served the Sinclairs of Rosslyn, had saved many of the ancient manuscripts from the Rosslyn Castle scriptorium. Those books in turn had come from the fabled library of Alexandria which had also burned down.

Mrs Sinclair bolted the mock Jacobean doors of the Highland Dirk Hotel and retired to her bed to lament the passing of her husband as she did every night. Ever vigilant of the enemy, she'd got a poacher's shotgun next to the photograph of her murdered husband. She was not a lady to be messed with.

It was a short drop to the back street. Vanessa looked out onto the deserted street and then they climbed out of the hotel window. Angus had chosen the hotel room least visible from the street. They recovered themselves and made for the chapel like a couple of car thieves. They'd already planned out their mission. It was late Autumn and mid-week, the increased footfall of other tourists spawned by Dan Brown's Da Vinci Code being much reduced. They passed the empty car park near Rosslyn. Facing them was the newly built tourist attraction with the reflection of the moon radiating through its bulletproof glass. Security lights were on complementing the flashing CCTV monitors. They veered off, striking out towards Rosslyn's graveyard positioned next to a collapsed wall.

"Over here, look the wall is down!" She'd found a place where they both could climb up and over the cemetery wall, Vanessa was a better climber than Angus. Her body had developed subtly, exaggerating her curves economically. She scaled the wall treading on the firmer stones, clambering over them easily. From the top of the wall, still holding Angus's hand, she pointed the way down. Slowly he climbed up whilst she slid down the other side. He followed her over the wall and then through the mud towards a large marble cross with an elaborate angel glowing white in the moonlight. So far they'd avoided the CCTV cameras. Aware of the danger Vanessa jumped up onto the lower chapel boundary wall. Dropping onto the other side, she saw the magnificent carved splendour of Rosslyn. Angus followed her dropping to his knees, he could hear his joints crunch.

"For pity sake ma' bloody knees!" Angus cried.

They moved across the ground past the various gravestones of long-dead aristocrats, creeping towards the restricted door in the three-foot thick walls. Next to it, was another empty niche where the statue of Admiral Piri Reis should have been. All the niches were empty now, paying silent testimony to the everlasting mystery.

The outside of the chapel had changed. Red and white safety tape covered the stonework and a framework had been set up around where the statues once stood. There was a plastic screen attached to the scaffolding to hide the intended restoration work. They'd arrived just in time. Rosslyn was on the watch list of several other countries allied with the United Kingdom. All of these countries had been infiltrated by the New Babylonian world power wanting the sacred artefacts they thought were in the vaults.

Angus and Vanessa gazed at the enigmatic stone corbel. Angus took a picture of the severely decayed stone carvings. It seemed like every time they discovered something, then the New Babylonians were close on their heels. The flash could draw attention, so they hadn't got long to get the evidence.

"Here are the numerals and the symbols, notice they're carved on top of the corbel like on the other photograph," Vanessa whispered giving the thumbs-up sign and Angus took the photos.

"I've studied the plaster cast of the corbel for a long time. And I never once looked on top of it. I was always looking up to the corbel replica at the Sinclair Lighthouse Library. Because it was placed on the top shelf above the books, no one had ever thought to examine the top," Angus said, looking like a disgruntled schoolboy.

"Look! the coordinates and symbols are here!" Vanessa had memorised the other set of symbols and numerals which Angus had discovered on the Templar tombstone at Balantrodoch. It wasn't exactly clear, but her intuition told her that the geophysical coordinates were from South

America, perhaps from the same territory where many ships went missing near her island. How could this be? But the laws of synchronicity were guided by a higher power.

"The numbers and symbols are similar to those on the Templar tombstone at Balantrodoch," Vanessa said.

"I am thinking Templar! The carving style is late medieval, this is why the numerals are more precise," Angus pushed his finger into the incised carving. "It took stonemasons a couple of hundred years to refine their tool-making skills. Aye, and much later on, their chisels were much sharper so whatever they carved, had clearer sharper lines."

All the time Angus had been talking, Vanessa had been processing her calculations on her mobile phone. She looked at Angus patiently waiting for him to finish but he carried on again.

"Balantrodoch had originally been the Scottish Templar HQ. After the battle of Bannockburn 1314, the defeated English King Edward 11 gave many Templar lands to the Knights Hospitallers. The Hospitallers were allowing the Templars to operate under the radar in Scotland." Vanessa knew something of their history. She wanted to tell Angus something, but he wouldn't shut up.

"Why?" exclaimed Vanessa.

"Because there's much evidence to suggest King Robert the Bruce who was another infamous heretic at the time, used the refuge Templars against the English at Bannockburn. As we know the huge English army was annihilated by a much smaller force of Scots. The Templars presence helped Scot's morale. The rest is history as the Scots triumphed."

"Darlin' please shut up, we've got everything. We must go!" She said losing patience.

"Just one more thing," he explained, rooting in his pocket, pulling out his locksmith's putty. And with his fat thumb, he pushed it into the incised numbers carved into the top of the corbel above the Knights Templar initiation scene. He'd done the same with the numerals on the Templar tombstone at Balantrodoch.

"Ok, we're finished, let's get the hell out of it. I'll transfer the coordinates later. We have one more trip before we can leave," Vanessa added ominously.

Since the bestseller success of Dan Brown's book, Rosslyn had become an esoteric supermarket of knowledge to such an extent it was monitored by CCTV. It was a different culture there now since Andrew Sinclair made his discoveries.

They crept back to their room at the hotel. There was still something on Vanessa's mind. Angus took another drink from the bottle of Old Stroma and fell asleep on the bed. Vanessa listened to his breathing for a while, following him to sleep with the unnerving feeling that whilst they'd been at Rosslyn someone had been watching them. Still, they got a few moments of undisturbed bliss on the bed.

Vanessa's phone alarm rang and she sat bolt upright with a shock. With his face pressed into the pillow, Angus stirred next to her. "Och' lassie my mouth feels rough as a badger's arse," he said wrinkling his nose.

Although the dawn was breaking, it was still dark enough for the street lights to be on. Angus got up, rubbed his creased eyes and lumbered over to the bathroom to wash his face. They opened the window climbing out onto the street facing Rosslyn's new car park. Vanessa was careful to switch off their room lights. They climbed into their old truck with their bags. Angus started it, and it fired up first time. Angus smiled. "So much for the heritage official as a mechanic eh?"

They pulled away into the frosty morning heading towards Ackergill Towers in the north of Scotland for their meeting with Andrew Sinclair.

Vanessa smiled, rolling her eyes, looking back at the stone Victorian hotel with its Norman Bate's psycho mansion ambience.

She couldn't be sure, but she thought she saw Mrs Sinclair looking through the curtains from her upstairs window, as they drove away down from Rosslyn Village.

Isobel arrives in Edinburgh

Although Vanessa didn't show it, she was apprehensive about meeting Angus's volatile daughter at Edinburgh airport. She knew that Angus would be happy to be reunited with Isobel after her university gap year. Yet she couldn't stand the thought of them laughing together. She couldn't stand the thought that there was another influence in his life, perhaps greater than her, now. The way things were occurring was truly supernatural. Angus was tiring after driving back from Ackergill towers. He wanted to ask Vanessa about her loss of faith in God again. He'd often pictured her sitting in a church in her traditional black Spanish dress praying with reverence as she'd once done. Then a large tri-coloured badger waddled out in front of the truck. Angus braked and the truck jolted to a halt. A large book slid onto the passenger side floor from her bag. Meanwhile, the badger recovered itself charging into the nearby brush decorated with mounds of waste paper and hamburger wrappers.

Vanessa reached down and began to push the book back into the bag, but Angus had seen it. On the book cover was written ***Navigating Ancient Oceans*** by Vivian Gonzaga. Angus's heart thumped quickly as he looked out of the window, sucking in more air. He now knew she'd got a lot further than him, but then, after all, she was a mapmaker.

"Fuck it," he whispered under his breath. "We gotta know where we are going lassie, can ye' not' do the conversion now for the symbols, just ta' give me peace of mind."

Instantly her laptop was out with the recent map of the redundant Calbunco volcanic crater near her island in Chile. They looked at both sets of coordinates they'd discovered. The numerals and symbols flashed onto the computer screen. There were tiny carvings of moons in various stages of their lunar cycles. There was a large planet nearby and another star system scratched into the top of the stone with numerals underneath. There was a number under each moon phase like on the Templar tombstone symbols. Angus shivered again when he saw the images of the tombstone.

"Calm down, darlin', look I have the conversion programme for the symbols and numerals. I created this app myself a few years back. All we need to do is input the information and it will convert it into the nearest geophysical coordinates of Latitude and Longitude." They knew exactly where the coordinates were going to lead them, truth was coming. Vanessa had booked their flights already knowing where the coordinates would take them. She just needed the direct proof carved in stone.

"Aye lassie we'd be lost without those directions and your programme. I have no idea how this happened. I mean the Longitude measurement came much later in the history of navigation," Angus felt overwhelmed. "It's hot in here, open the window, please." Angus was losing it again.

"Ok, not so angry! It's not my fault the badger ran out."

Vanessa looked at Angus. She meant business.

"Look my App is doing its job. So just shut up!"

Angus said nothing. Ping! The converted coordinates flashed up on the mac screen in blue lettering. Angus looked at Vanessa.

"I am sorry lassie, I got a bit excited."

Vanessa read out the readings in Latitude and Longitude.

"Latitude: S 41° 19' 57.9396 Longitude: W 72° 36' 39.9312."

Vanessa knew before they appeared that they were going to the Calbunco volcano near her island. She'd known for a long time. Her spirit guides had told her. But Angus called that synchronicity.

They reversed back into the first airport parking position they found after taking a ticket at the entrance barrier. The truck, although it had served them well, was a scrapper and they had no intention of returning for it. They continued on their way to the airport where Angus would start drinking to numb his fear of flying. He carried all the bags up the escalator like a pack mule. Vanessa looked around as the two of them juddered on up towards the shops and international terminals and security clearances.

Just then, a tall, willowy girl appeared holding a large coffee. She rushed over to Angus, dropping her near-empty paper cup with coffee in it and throwing her arms rounds her father.

"Isobel ma' lovely daughter!" Angus cried out.

Vanessa half smiled as Isobel stroked Angus's arm lovingly. She turned, still holding him around his neck and reaching out to shake Isobel's hand. Her cheekbones were high like those of an oriental princess, her lips were succulent and thick. She was twenty years younger than Vanessa who shook Isobel's hand in a very stiff unfriendly way.

"Darlin' we should try to clear security, we don't have much time before the flight to Madrid."

"Nonsense we've got lots of time," Isobel said, grinning daggers at Vanessa.

Angus wanted to shake them both. He could see what was happening. "Och both of ye', sit down over there, and I mean now!"

Vanessa and Isobel went over to the coffee shop plonking down on the seats outside of the steaming coffee dispensers. Angus followed them over.

"Both of ye' listen! I've spent hours neck-deep in Scottish shit and stone dust to get to this point!"

Vanessa cleared her throat, reddening with anger. "Darlin' it is not just about you, it's also about my brother as well, he's not dead. None of my family in Chile believes he's dead, not one of them!" She exclaimed thumping the table. "He is alive. A man like him with his special skills could survive forever in those seas."

"I lassie I canna' deny your conviction," Angus breathed deeply.

"Meanwhile, there's no official map or record which charts this place. No one knows about it, other than us, at the moment". But Angus knew that wasn't necessarily true. "Darlin' my spirit guides know? They told me this morning that Rodrigo lives."

Angus didn't like such talk, it unnerved him somehow.

From the other side of the table, Isobel stopped her dagger looks realising that antagonism was not the way forward. The start of a smile flashed across her face.

"Look, I am sorry," Isobel said. "I just want my dad back. And what are you both rambling about? It is really freaky. But wow, what an adventure, hey! Wait till my mother hears all about it and especially that jerk she's ready to marry with his dyed hair and manicured nails."

Angus sniggered, agreeing with his daughter's sentiment about Max Rothman. It hadn't quite dawned on him how far Max had gone with his greedy ambitions. Yet the stench of his connection to the New Babylonians and their agenda was ever-present. But this was a fear, he learnt not to vocalise in certain quarters. It was not just a passing thought. But who were the New Babylonian inner circle anyway? And where did they hang out? Perhaps as some had said, they were so-called world leaders who liked to call themselves elites? Angus considered the possibility that some kind of mass hysteria was occurring with humanity. So many weird things were happening on the planet. He'd had the premonitions of a major world disaster coming and he couldn't explain why. Sometimes he'd believed people when they said he was being delusional.

Angus chuckled making light of the situation. He'd always known that Max Rothman was a small wheel in the New Babylonian machine. "Aye, it's true, Rothman is nowt' but an old smoothie wi' dyed hair." Isobel knew that the break-up between him and her mother had been difficult for Angus. And Angus was slow to move on or turn the next page as Vanessa had prosaically described his prolonged sensitivities.

"Look come on bonnie lassies, you'll ha' to stop tha' bitch dialogue, you know how important this mission is, to have this kind of reality TV bullshit happening. It is getting like Glasgow housewives!"

"Mission you call it! You bunch of freaks, that's rich, alright then let's get on with it," Isobel said, actually excited about the prospect of a South American adventure.

Angus wandered over to the bar opposite the security terminus ordering another double single malt whisky as Vanessa and Isobel continued chatting, testing each other's boundaries. Angus had always known that Rosslyn Chapel was a storehouse for the greatest of all treasures and the greatest of all knowledge. But he hadn't joined up exactly how it could all be connected to a volcano in the middle of Chile, but then there's no smoke without fire.

Surrounded by other travellers, Vanessa and Isobel watched the flight departure monitor. Angus observed them grow friendly to each other in that unfathomable womanly way, after they'd ripped each other to shreds. Things mellowed now as the numbing vibe of the whisky kicked in. As with his previous flight to Chile, he remembered very little about it. Soon they were in Santiago airport again looking for their flight connection to Castro in the south of the country.

Castro, Chiloe, South America

It was mid-summer in the Southern Hemisphere. The aircraft banked round and descended to make its landing. Below in Castro, the air temperature was now pushing 70 degrees. The atmosphere buzzed with tension brought on by rising temperatures. Normally the climate is moderate, but a strange humid stillness had fallen across the lands and seas. Angus had a déjà vu feeling, remembering back to the atmosphere on Sinclair Bay Scotland as if everything was about to change, not just inside himself, but also in the reality around him.

The Island of Sailing Souls

Angus had something on his mind as the aircraft turned for its final descent. Below he saw the wild landscape of Lagos, through the mountains of Chiloe where a dark mound rose out of the dense savanna landscape surrounded by a halo of white mist. Angus gripped the seat in front of him. Vanessa understood his foreboding. She turned in the seat next to him and pulled down the screen on the plane window.

"That's the Calbunco volcanic crater. We have been having much trouble with strange magnetic occurrences down there."

"What do you mean?"

"Sometimes government expeditions are endeavouring to discover the source of its mystery. That's what happened to the Industrialist Don Miguel who was trying to exploit the natural resources. He was plundering in the forest again, assisted by New Babylonian traitors in the local government, you know how it works? That's how Rodrigo came into the equation," she tapped her back pocket to insinuate bribery.

"But how did ya' know he was involved in all this?" Angus was juggling information. "Most Special Forces operations are covert right?" Vanessa didn't reply.

Finally, the aircraft bumped down on the runway followed by the noise of screeching tyres and the whoosh of reversing jet engines. They collected their baggage after clearing Castro customs. Outside now the air was much cooler because Chiloe where Castro is situated is much closer to Antarctica than Santiago.

Sometimes in Chiloe bitter cold thermal currents blew the wind, burning the faces of the locals giving them the skin colour of Inuits. Southern Chile's climate is similar to Scotland in late spring. There were many similarities between Chile in the south of the country and Scotland, including the incessant rain. Great stone cities remained undiscovered in the Lagos region of Chile which had not made the news because they were so remote and uncharted. It was said that escaped Nazis had been the first to discover them releasing the information through their organisation called *'Die Freiheit'*, but people didn't care, obsessed with a faster and faster lifestyle pregnant with greed.

In Castro airport, people carried and pulled vast amounts of luggage whilst policemen wearing high peaked hats and side-arms watched them from behind mirrored sunglasses. Angus had done some research about Chile and was aware of the curious connection between renegade Nazis after World War 2 and the governance of emerging Chile with its vast amounts of natural resources and cheap labour. It was common knowledge that Chile as well as other Latin American states, concealed war renegades and escapees.

Some years before, Vanessa had been trekking in a forest overlooking the sea. She saw an old Germanic looking man slumped on his horse in full military uniform riding along the forest path. This lost soldier was carrying a rifle across his shoulder and a Luger pistol strapped to his withered leg. For this man, the war had not finished. It was the same for the secret Nazi organisation, *'Die Freiheit'*, which connected sympathisers to the New Babylonians, who assisted them in their exile in return for their knowledge and organisational influence over local officials easily bribed.

In Chile, it was common back then for young, idealistic women to take up revolutionary causes. In a way, it was another method of making a statement against the conservative status quo thought to be responsible for female emancipation. And so President Allende's cause had become the mule to carry not only the idea of greater autonomy and democracy but also neo-liberal values had jumped on its back as well. As a result many who'd experienced the revolution later became new age pagans, rejecting the right-wing faith of Roman Catholicism, drifting into unknown spiritual territory. Paganism was now thriving and this trend had been hijacked by the greedy New Babylonians, ever ready to cultivate the masses and to smear them with their own infernal influences.

When Angus thought about this, it bothered him. He'd maintained a belief in God and sometimes his Christian belief system clashed with Vanessa's new age nature worship. He believed that God was protecting him, for belief and faith had always been his anchors in desperate times.

The three of them were driven to a remote beach opposite Vanessa's Island in an airport taxi. In Chiloe people were always getting dropped off in remote areas. The taxi drivers here were experts at getting near to secret places. Their livelihood depended on it.

Vanessa's island was set like a tiny jewel in the azure sea. This was the place of sea legends, sea monsters, pirates and ghost ships which vanished mysteriously, for it was on the periphery of a magical inland sea. Nearby were uniquely coloured wooden houses built on stilts lifting them high into the air. Those who lived nearby had no idea of the great mystery which lay close to them. Painted in their bright colours, these houses had been chosen to represent the beauty of southern Chile on holiday brochures and calendars.

There was once a little church on Vanessa's island built from wood in the local style by Jesuit priests. Later it was blown off its foundations in a typhoon. The painted blue church flew away, crumpling into the sea like a fallen seagull. Vanessa's island was called the 'Island of Sailing Souls'. It was said that the dead buried there, journeyed on a kind of ship sailing to heaven. Originally it had been torn away and birthed from the mainland in the great volcanic eruptions in the 1960's. The earthquake was the most powerful ever on the planet and so severe it killed six thousand people causing two million people to be homeless. A man had gone insane after witnessing the tide going out and not coming back in again. Nobody knew exactly what had made him go insane. But from an asylum in Valdivia, he mumbled on about dead sea monsters and lost cities.

Vanessa and her Island of Sailing Souls

After the time of the great volcanic eruptions separating it from the mainland, the Island of Sailing Souls was owned by an old Portuguese man, Ramirez De Vasconcellos. He developed a deep connection with the natives and built his house where the church had been. The Island had been left to Vanessa after the death of Ramirez, who had taken a liking to her. To his wife's dismay, he'd left the Island along with his writings, research and studies into the culture of Mapuche natives all to Vanessa. Alongside the little house, Vanessa had inherited a huge Mapuche graveyard. The keeper of it was destined to provide a service to the avenues of dead natives. Every day, she placed fresh wildflowers and pebbles on the graves. When she was not there, the Mapuche housekeeper Olga looked after the graves.

Olga was coming, rowing her boat across the seas towards them. The three weary adventurers waited on the shore to go to this place. The Island was cut off by the tide most of the time, requiring a short boat journey to get to it. The housekeeper lived in a small cottage performing certain tasks essential for the running of the Island. Olga, could do anything from clean and cook fish to gathering mussels and making fires that burst into life, even in the interminable damp climate, typical for the area. The fire maker was king here.

In the past, Chiloe had been infested with European and South American pirates. The Conquistador Spanish had built several small forts from stone and heavy timber, protected by cannon as a deterrent to the rebels. Yet the fort defence system had not worked. The pirates had intermarried with the natives and their combined legends had cultivated a hybrid of beliefs. If the natives were abused or murdered by the Spanish then the pirates would take revenge on them. There was also the legend of the great civilisation which rose from the water like some South American Brigadoon somewhere amongst its miles and miles of seas, islands, and outlets. Angus knew something strange was happening, he believed that there was 'no smoke without fire'. Whatever the unseen mystery was, it was connected to Angus's life force now and previously to the coordinates they'd discovered in Scotland at Rosslyn and the nearby ancient Knights Templar HQ, in some supernatural way.

Glancing at Vanessa he put his arm around Isobel who was so tired she just dropped her bags onto the muddy sand. Oystercatchers darted from the rolling waves of the inland seas nearby. In the distance, blubbery bull sea lions boomed out guttural cries asserting their territory from the fishing platforms on the sea.

The boat was coming for them from the Island of Sailing Souls. Olga steered the boat as close to the beach as she could, where they could all get into it without getting wet. Angus picked up Isobel's bags first and passed them to Olga, who greeted Vanessa in Spanish.

"Como esta tu hermana."

"Estoy bien pero un poco de problemas aqui con su hija," Vanessa replied.

"Och' aye lassie do ya' not want me to row that boat. I'll have us back to the Island in nay' time."

"No darlin'. Olga is a great woman of the sea, it would be an insult to her if you rowed us back."

Angus looked crestfallen. But he didn't want to get into a fight about the rowing. He scanned the horizon and saw that things were looking ominous and heavy. Yet he'd imagined himself spending time fishing and rowing around the Island for exercise. He wanted to collect various shellfish for their meals so he could make a type of Paella. His prospective recipe had been adapted from its original Spanish origin to assimilate the reflections of other cultures like the native Mapuche Indians. It was just his way of trying to respect another culture.

There'd been much trouble with these Mapuche natives who fought against the erosion of their lands being carried out by mining and logging companies. The peculiar twist, if one could call it that, was that the man behind the profiteering corporations was the Argentine Industrialist Don Miguel del Monte. But he'd gone missing on his superyacht in Chiloe amongst the mysterious sea myths, legends, and magic. People were blaming the Mapuche again. The incident had developed into a national embarrassment as Don Miguel was bringing valuable commerce into an area ripe for exploitation, where copper ore and timber could be easily ripped ruthlessly out of the Earth. He simply bribed a few politicians to turn a blind eye to the rape of the land. Don Miguel was being sponsored by the New Babylonians.

There was the added contradiction about Rodrigo, Vanessa's brother. Contrary to Vanessa's new age ethics her brother had gone missing suspected of being on board Don Miguel's yacht as part of a Special Forces protection team. Another curious connection was Don Miguel's link to the infamous Nazi, Walter Rife, who had invented the mobile gas Chamber. Walter Rife died in Argentina in 1984 surrounded by his sieg-heiling supporters after they'd fled Europe. It was yet another connection to the huge New Babylonian hydra with its tentacles of corruption spreading through local governments enabled by political affiliations throughout every country. Many Nazi scientists had been assimilated into bio and genetic engineering programmes of other countries, enabled by the New Babylonians. But the Mapuche natives resisted all who came to take their forests and lands in Chiloe.

The spring sun dulled over Chiloe. Angus and Vanessa had begun researching an earlier event that happened just after the Second World War. Angus couldn't be completely sure, but he thought he'd seen the large shadow of a Skull and Cross Bones in the darkening clouds. It worried him, as he'd read that people who see faces or human shapes in the rocks or clouds could be suffering from schizophrenia, he was told this when he went through his neurological problems as a result of his breakdown. The experts called the phenomenon, Pareidolia. He had since learnt that it was a facet of an awakening psychic ability. And curiously, what had happened around these Islands did indeed include acts of piracy by ships flying the Skull and Cross Bones as his fate would confirm extraordinarily.

The hard evidence came from a German U-boat which was one of the first modern vessels to document a very bloody and peculiar incident. The escaping Nazi submarine had been kept top secret. The hidden event concerned the capture of a German U-boat in the Chilean archipelago of Chiloe, close to Vanessa's Island. Many Nazis entered South America through Argentina and Chile. Angus and Vanessa had read the writings several times. The style of the narrated document was more like an extract from an intended novel rather than an official report. The submarine's Officer Secretary was Reiner Gorst. His main duties included keeping logs and doing administration work. Partly disabled, Reiner had volunteered to enlist in the German war effort as a non-combatant. He was also an aspiring novelist. Like the rest of the crew, Reiner was never seen again. There was very little wreckage and clues as to the fate of U-Boat 96 apart from the enclosed writing, which was found in a sailor's sealed mess tin along with some bits and pieces.

"Aye lassie there's no smoke without fire as I keep saying and it's well written, but I don't know if I can believe it though. But I have to admit whoever wrote it got all the U-boat crew names correct enough."

Vanessa said nothing.

U-BOAT 96, 1945, Chile

Captain Otto Von Straffon was pleased with the progress as his U-boat slipped through the oily waters. Not only had they eluded both the British and Americans, but they had also arrived at the river channel, ready to pick up their pilot on the coastal estuary known as Chiloetes, Chile. From here UB96 German navy submarine would motor ahead above the water to her secret landing zone. Below decks, several escaping high ranking Nazis were preparing to leave the vessel with their plunder, consisting of gold bullion, cash, and famous works of art plundered from Europe, particularly artworks from the Louvre Gallery, Paris. They each had enough money to set up estates and to buy favour whenever required. Their escape from justice had been engineered through the infamous ratlines created by both the Vatican and the Swiss banks already in operation. These men had first travelled to Italy where U-boats were waiting for them. They continued to South America after refuelling at strategic stations and Nazi outpost bases. Some of our SS officers had opted instead to take their own lives rather than be captured. There'd been rumours that the US Government had known that many Third Reich personnel would try to escape, especially those from the Nazi party with their ill gotten gains.

General Ralph Klein had finalised his army career after the Russian front as the camp Commandant of the infamous death camp of Troika in Poland. He had signed the extermination warrants of some 40 thousand men, women and children during his tenure with no more remorse than if he had been swatting flies. Also on board were others from various campaigns who had committed unmentionable cruelties in the name of war. Equally responsible, but in other ways were several non-combatants scientists and medical experimenters who mingled freely with the rest. They too were said to be attempting to join a corrupt new world power mechanism called the New Babylonians, had they not been intercepted by an unusual group of archaic people.

Captain Von Straffon steered his U-boat with typical Kreigsmarine precision and commitment, and what happened next was not on the scale of normal human comprehension.

An ancient pilot cutter with several ragtag oarsmen rowed out in front of the path of UB96. To all intent and purpose, they resembled a group of down and outs with unkempt beards and grimy faces grinning black or yellow teeth. The man at the tiller who kept the boat steady was different though. He, like the rest, was bearded yet strangely clad in a spotless white vest over his leather jacket. Emblazoned on it was the cross of a Knights Templar.

The cutter was hauling a rope attached to a massive chain, dragging it across the river entrance. Before Captain Von Straffon could think to blast this intruder out of the water, the ancient wooden boat along with its curious rowers then disappeared. It was understandable that Captain Von Straffon could not process the information nor could his second in command. It was as though they were looking at spectres of the fabled Pirates.

Then dressed in the same bizarre combination of clothing like the other rowers from the other boat these pirates marched purposefully over the marshes and behind UB96 hauling another chain towards a redwood tree. Some were tattooed with black pitch and soot depicting enigmatic symbols of the long lost days of piracy. Those in charge wore the same Templar cross as the man at the tiller in the other longboat. With chains in their hands, the men secured it to a metal band fastened around a huge redwood tree. They moved as if in some well-synchronised opera from the sea, securing shackles with their stained clamp-like fingers. They smiled and grimaced and spat out tobacco juice as they worked.

Confused, UB96 went into full astern. Captain Von Straffon had been concentrating on the events unfolding ahead of him and failed to notice what was happening astern. Unable to create any momentum ahead or astern, UB96 ran to a complete halt. Bewildered, Von Straffon looked at his men and then ordered a contingent of armed marines out of the bowels of the submarine. Rather than sit about even the Nazis armed up accordingly. Nobody was expecting this.

There was a crack and flash from the forest and a shot fired with deadly accuracy thudding into Lieutenant Krieger, a youngish man of stereotypical German proportions, who fell dead next to Captain Von Straffon, splattering a welter of blood and gore across him. The problem was he fell into the submarine turret entrance making it impossible for the other armed crew to get out onto the deck. Meanwhile, an organised contingent of pirates, clambering athletically aboard UB96, using both ropes and pilot ladders. They carried arms spanning a few hundred years, from flintlocks to Mauser pistols from WW1. All of their side arms had been immaculately maintained. Von Straffon began to fire off rounds from his Luger pistol into the middle of the motley crew. Two of the pirates dropped, one wounded, the other dead whilst another barked out orders in some ancient pirate patwa.

"Avast ye' dogs here be a great prize from the new world! Gold pieces to the man that captures her Lord."

Captain Von Straffon looked down to see if his man had been dragged clear. In the seconds it took him to look up again, he was confronted with large bearded faces with curiously humorous eyes. He remembered the crow's feet around them and the scars running across his cheek. Then, with expert precision, the man sliced off his ear. There was blinding pain and then there was the thud of the crack of a club knocking him unconscious. There was a loud cheer from the others. Captain Von Straffon still unconscious was lifted above them and rolled down onto the deck of the U boat below the observation tower deck. He bled out onto the deck from both the wound of his missing ear and from his split skull, but did not die. As his blood ran in lines down the camber of the submarine, dust from the day stuck to it. Carefully his ear was placed next to him on the deck. For this was the proof of the payment required for his capture indemnified into the articles of engagement from the Pirate Brethren of the Coast. One left ear for one gold piece payment.

The action above in the turret continued. Then the escape hatch of U-boat 96 opened squashing the fallen man against the side of the submarine's observation tower. And one by one German submariners emerged and began firing at will at the greater number of pirates on her deck. To start with they'd been taken by surprise, shots from different calibre arms rang out from the jungle and the German sailors went down under their fire. More pirates swarmed aboard and soon they were wrestling with the main observation hatch to stop it from being closed by those desperately pushing at it, below to escape.

All combatants on board who resisted had their throats cut or were shot. They had been lined up on the deck of the submarine to await inspection from the Pirate war leader. Three of the Nazis aboard seem to have been spared. They were bound together with coir ropes blinking and confused in the intense sun. All three bore the skull and crossbones insignia of the Gestapo on their peaked hats. Myself, Reiner Gorst will try to make my escape, but it is not looking good for …..

Here the writing stopped abruptly. The papers were splattered in blood.

Olga continued to row them back across the choppy sea to Vanessa's Island. Wafts of fish and salmon oil drifted across from the industrial fishing platforms, where the blubbery bull sea lions had made their harems. Their boat appeared tiny as it passed next to the platform. The fat docile occupants watched, rocking the platform as they moved. The bull sea lions were not dangerous, but they were big enough to squash small rowboats which they might inadvertently launch themselves onto. Olga kept an eye on them as their boat corkscrewed past.

Angus looked at Vanessa desiring her. Something came over him, he flushed crimson, realising his daughter was watching him looking at Vanessa. He was always taken by surprise by women, they knew about desire, they knew what was in a man's heart at the wrong times. Women understood desire like lion tamers understand their lions. Isobel snarled her father a disapproving look. The shoreline of the island suddenly appeared in the light sea mist indicating a change of air temperature. Olga pushed hard on the sculling oar forcing the rowboat to slide crunching up the sandy beach. Angus got out splashing in the sea and took the large bags up the beach to the main house. Vanessa and Isobel followed behind talking and carrying the smaller bags.

They went into the house. There was something on Isobel's mind. There had been from the start. Something personal. Angus knew that at some point he would have to acknowledge that his daughter had grown up.

In the wooden house, Isobel picked up a silver corkscrew like it was jewellery. There was wine on the kitchen table ready. She'd inherited the family weakness for the 'falling down water'. She uncorked a bottle and began drinking. She had a certain way of looking provocative when holding a glass. Angus knew she'd copied this pose from her mother. He watched Isobel looking at the wine label with typical fake intellectual curiosity which lush's exhibit when trying to draw attention away from their condition.

Scattered around them in the main house lay the objects and furniture of Vanessa's past life. Like wooden carvings of fish and painted cabinets full of old fishing gear. She'd bought the old sofa from a local antique shop, which originally came from Edwardian England. All of the papers and old maps were stacked in neat bundles tied with string placed out of the way as if she'd spent a lifetime gathering information. There was an old wood-burning stove with a maker's mark stamped into its cast Iron from Paris, France. There were jars of fruit preserved the previous year of apples and quinces.

Olga had been harvesting mussels on the beach. There was a metal dish full of them cooked with their shells open presenting their light orange flesh to eat. They'd been gathered locally, where they were farmed attached to long ropes. Isobel took another swig from the glass. Something was bothering her.

Angus had heard that some old British men and women remained in the area scattered around like refugees from another age. Some had arrived as farmers and shepherds and others as wanderers and misfits. They'd arrived before the troubles, settling at various times and mainly after the last World War. It was probable they'd had children as well and then like everyone else, their first language would become Spanish. Chile was a great country, despite the turbulent history.

Angus looked across towards the Spada Peninsula. He needed to talk with some of the veteran farmers, to find out about this strange feeling he was having. Perhaps it was an intuition that something wasn't quite right about the area, there was something sinister about the energy and his heart searched for kindred hearts from old Britain. He didn't know why though.

"Hey Vanessa, is that the farm where you said British people were living over there?" Angus pointed across to the island opposite.

"Yes, darlin' they farm sheep. I only know them as the Pooles, I guess they are very old. I've heard nothing about them for years."

Meanwhile, Isobel glugged her wine. Angus was beginning to regret her coming but he still wanted to get to the bottom of her problem.

"Hey! Steady with that Isobel."

"You can talk Dad, you've just sobered up!" Isobel looked over to see if Angus was paying attention. Angus was thinking about something else.

"Ok, I think I am going to take the boat to see if I can get to talk to Mr and Mrs Poole," Angus saw that Isobel's mood was changing. Vanessa took it in her stride bustling from one table to the next doing tasks. As Angus left the main cottage Isobel pushed past him on her way to the lodge.

"I am staying over in the out cabin tonight, so that you both have some peace, so if you'll excuse me, I am going now." She made Angus feel guilty.

Angus couldn't remember Vanessa explaining to Isobel that the guest cabin was available. But it looked like they'd had words. Angus simply imagined her being in the upstairs main bedroom, where he could keep an eye on her. He thought it would be nice for them to have breakfast together in the morning. Just as they did when they remembered back to their little life together when he was married. Isobel was just a teenager then. Isobel grabbed two bottles of wine, including the one she was drinking and waltzed out dramatically. She wanted to call Damon in private. She was missing her inappropriate lover. Vanessa was relieved that Isobel was going to the guest cabin. She and Angus could be alone in the main house tonight. So she busied herself brushing her thick roots of dark hair and applying Argan oil, as usual, oiling it up again.

"Yes, Angus I told Isobel about the cabin. I had Olga make it ready for her. Isobel is all grown up. So stop treating her like daddy's girl."

"Aye well ya' can say that again," he replied wanting to say more but knowing he'd come off worse.

The Spada Peninsula - Mr and Mrs Poole

It was colder in the early evening sea air. Angus had a sinking feeling in his gut. As he passed the lodge bedroom on the way to the boat, he could see his daughter's silhouette gesticulating like a Chinese theatre puppet in the window as he walked down to the beach.

He found some plastic boating boots and grabbed the oars for the little rowboat standing against the boat shed. It took him two minutes to crunch down to the beach where the boat was. The tide was just ebbing in the inland sea and there was no real momentum to the flow. He pushed off from the beach and rowed out over the sea towards the small farmstead where Mr and Mrs Poole lived. It was a typically spontaneous Angus move. Vanessa hadn't said much about them only indicating vaguely, that they were English sheep farmers. He thought an English speaking voice would be welcomed on their farmstead albeit, in his own Scottish accent. He had so many questions. He needed to get away from the politics of female territory on the Island, in fact, he'd wanted to do it since they'd arrived there. He'd mentioned it before to Vanessa but she skimmed over the question.

He let go of the anchor rope secured to a spigot on the beach. Heaving against the oars he propelled the boat over the short distance to the sheep farm. He was in his element rowing small boats, having been raised on the Pentland Firth and spending more time fishing than at school. Old school rowing had developed his superb boat handling skills. He put his weight behind the oars. Cold licks of waves splashed over her prow as the boat scudded towards the Spada Peninsula. He was ideally built for rowing heavy boats. He would have looked out of place on anything smaller.

"Nay long now!" He said aloud, turning about to face the approaching land. He could see Marino type sheep calmly grazing in the pasture near the tin shack homestead of Mr and Mrs Poole. Merino sheep were a favoured breed in South America on account of their good quality wool. In Argentina, the men liked to wear classy tango suits made from it. The Pooles, like many British sheep farmers, had grabbed the free land offers from Argentina and Chile just after the war. At the time it was policy to try to attract Europeans to South America, a policy of Chile's compliance with International Imperialism.

Angus reached out for the extended wooden pier where small boats could land. He turned the oars in their rowlocks, pointing them forward and taking hold of a greasy landing rope attached to the pier by an old tyre. Some of the wood around it began to splinter. The landing jetty was in bad repair. He looked back across to the Island of Sailing Souls and wondered why Vanessa had not come to visit the Pooles. It was such a quick journey taking him a short time to row over. But he kept an eye on the tidal flow he didn't want to be caught out.

He tied the boat up and clambered out onto the wooden decking. Treading along the stronger planks, he tiptoed over it towards the Poole's main house, if you could call it that. He didn't like the feeling of despair drifting down from the old tin shack. Perhaps the pier might only be safe for another few visits. Angus wondered how the Pooles would get their supplies. He thought about practicalities like that for other people. He walked up the wire fenced road towards the front door where an old man appeared holding a shotgun, grasping the top of the barrel as a handle, like it was a walking stick.

"Excuse me, what the hell are you doing?" The old man questioned.

"Hello Sir, I am just after some information," Angus exclaimed, stopping in his tracks. There was an immediate ex-pat understanding between them both. The old man softened as soon as he realised Angus wasn't local or German.

"What an incredible surprise. My God a Brit! What brings you to my door? Come on then, this demands a drink."

Old Mr Poole was lonely. Angus walked quickly towards the cabin's front door reaching out to shake his calloused hand caused by a lifetime of farming work.

"Ah, nice to meet you, Mr Poole yer' a hard man to find."

"Well, my very obvious Scottish friend, if you come inside you'll see exactly why. Come on, let's have a drink."

Angus entered directly into what could be described as a front room to see a large yellowing portrait of Queen Elizabeth II taken when she was about 30 years old. There was a ram's skull with spiralling horns underneath, pretending to be an ordinary fireplace ornament. The roof above them was dark coloured corrugated iron. A fire was crackling away in the hearth. Across from the fireplace there was a bedroom where the door was open and an old woman sat in bed dressed in a wool shawl looking curiously out.

"Don't worry, she can't speak, she hasn't been able to say a word since her stroke some eight years ago," Frank Poole explained in a matter of fact way. "The old lass can remember Christmas and English bank holidays. It's very strange because she still thinks she is back in Dorset. Which I suppose might be a blessing under the circumstances." Angus realised she was in a bad way.

"Sorry to see this Mr Poole."

"Less of the 'Mr' please, just call me Frank."

He figured that Mr Poole was in his eighties. It was a miracle he'd survived here for so long.

"Look, tell me a bit about yourself whilst I pour the whisky."

"Well, you might say, I am an opportunistic Scotsman or something like that."

Mr Poole laughed. "Aren't all the bloody Scots? I've not met one yet, that isn't an opportunist of some kind. I had many Scottish friends here mainly shepherds and farmers, but most of them have gone now."

"Gone where?" Angus questioned stupidly.

"Dead my dear boy, long since dead, where I should be. To tell you the truth, if it wasn't for Gloria in there, I'd be dead right now myself," he smiled, looking down at the shotgun.

"I am sticking around to look after her, but as soon as she's gone, then that will change."

Angus didn't want to think of the implications because it reminded him of his mentor Andrew Sinclair's recent death. A person was here one minute then gone the next. And now Frank was booking himself on the death conveyor. Angus was uncomfortable, but he wanted to know more. Frank shuffled over to the window and adjusted the lantern so it burned less brightly. From the cabinet on which the light was placed, he reached down for a bottle of whisky using the shotgun like a walking stick to steady himself.

"Luckily I managed to buy a cart-load of this stuff. I've been drinking it since God knows when. And at four pounds a bottle who could blame me." He brought out a fresh bottle of Johnnie Walker whisky. Angus smirked.

"Ah, my whisky of choice, seems I am named after it, and nay' tax on it here," Angus said, laughing.

"Don't think I am so trusting. I could've easily blown your head off, without a second thought. I've used the gun before you know on a couple of local robbers, wouldn't think twice." Angus believed him. A look of despair flashed over his puffy white face. He looked through the open tin-plated door to where his wife was propped up in bed. "I've been tempted a couple of times to finish her off, but can't seem to get the job done." Mrs Poole mumbled from her bed. Frank poured the whisky into a couple of metal cups, passing one to Angus.

"Look, old man, it's a good blended whisky, and it's Scottish. Well, bottoms up and perhaps you could tell me who the hell you are?"

"Not much to say Frank, I am staying over on the Island with Vanessa Bermodes. I met her in Scotland, I believe it was fate."

"Ah, that explains a lot. You're her lover then?" he said smirking.

"She's a wild woman that Chilote. You've heard of a Chilote have you? They are the locals here and very loyal to Chiloe. She's got some reputation. I mean there's a lot of politics you need to know before you decide to stay. There's been many a time I wished I'd returned to Britain. And then Gloria took her attack and we couldn't go anywhere."

"How do ya' manage with the farm Frank?" Both of them gulped their whisky at the same time. "I have help from another Scotsman Jamie Sinclair, well, he's half Scots anyway. His mother is local and his father was a shepherd from Caithness in Scotland." Angus was dumbfounded by the fact that Jamie was called Sinclair as well.

"Aye, ya' never know, maybe he's from near where I was born," Angus said, building up a picture of the situation. Now he knew why the Marino sheep were in such good condition. He was intrigued by the idea of Frank's helper coming from Scotland and being a Sinclair. It was yet another curious synchronicity. Frank was also intrigued by the arrival of Angus.

"So you were brought up the hard way, eh?"

"Well, I was originally raised at the top of Scotland overlooking the Orkneys, it is all Gunn country up there. I spent months rowing and living the hard life, going fishing with ma' Uncle Colin, instead of going to school."

"The Scots get everywhere. I think Jamie boy, has lost his Scottish language. He was very young when he arrived here. He uses Spanish as his main language now. And calls himself a 'pastora', which means shepherd. Although I caught him thumbing through an old copy of the Scottish Field Magazine last week after he'd finished butchering one of the sheep for me."

"I was just going to ask you about the area, a few weird things have happened since I came. I can't quite put my finger on it, but it's creepy. I was doing some research into the myths and legends of the area. As you say, there's a lot of magic stuff going on," Angus said.

"I am too long in the tooth for all that nonsense," Frank's instinct was to ignore information he considered controversial.

Angus was trying to open Frank up for information. "However a few rather boring things happen here, like black magic or something like that. The locals used this magic against their Spanish overlords," Frank explained, stoically hiding his fear with old school English bluster. "The Chilotes, never identified with the conquering Spanish. They were always more native than the Spanish and they've got other blood in their veins making for very intuitive people. Anyway, they seemed to be able to cause problems for their enemies."

"Aye, I've noticed the locals are very much against Europeans. And who could blame them," Angus said, thinking back to what Vanessa had said. But Angus knew there was a particular group of Europeans and their allies causing the planet's problem and Frank knew this also.

Frank continued, "many say that the local warlocks had some kind of ruling body in Santiago. They turned the lands sour after the Spanish stole it from them. And they also killed their Spanish overlords' animals through incantations and that sort of thing. Bloody nasty if you ask me!" Frank took another gulp of whisky rattling his worn-down teeth on the metal rim of the tin mug. "And we'd much trouble here some years ago! A couple of the local brothers here tried to rob me way back in 1980, and I had to shoot them. I used grit shot, so nothing lethal, I blew some skin off their arses."

Sweating profusely Frank wiped his forehead with an old rag, Angus understood now why Vanessa had not mentioned much about Mr and Mrs Poole because Frank could be dangerous.

"This old shotgun has seen a bit of action you know. It belonged to my father, he used it back on the farm in Dorset, especially during the last war, but not for shooting the enemy. Not much food you see, so he'd have to go out and bag a few rabbits or pheasants for the pot," Frank relaxed back and sat down on an old chair. "My family in the past were quite famous you know?"

"How's that Frank?"

"Well, originally we came from seafaring people, as did many folks from Dorset."

Angus had a feeling he knew what was coming next.

"We had this sea captain chap ancestor who got captured by some really bad pirates way back in the day." Angus listened intently. "Anyway, damn pirates were going to hang him on the mast of his own ship. Strangely, in peril of his own life, he recited his Knight's Code of Distress. He was in charge of a small charitable order of Knight Seafarers back on the shore. Anyway, the buggers let him go and they even presented his dog with a bone. And that bone was put in a glass case and is still in the Knight Seafarer's meeting house in Poole to this day. Turned out that bloody pirate captain was in the same organisation as himself."

Angus was dumbfounded as he'd researched the exact event several times with Vanessa, which was more than coincidental. But then he knew about the important laws of synchronicity and how everything was interconnected.

"But what happened then with the witchcraft stuff?" Angus asked.

"Not witchcraft, it was a peculiar form of monovalent warlock magic, apparently this group of desperados are known as the 'Cave Committee'."

"Sounds a bit nasty to me," said Angus.

"Well, I think it's a lot of old rubbish, but I have to admit Gloria succumbed to a heart attack directly after the event. And it turned out those two robber brothers, I shot, were connected to it all somehow."

Angus decided to use his ace card. "Did you ever hear anything about the ghost ship?"

"Oh, you mean like the local native ship which appears and disappears at will?"

"What's that then?" Angus asked almost knowing the answer.

"It's called the Calueche, it's a sort of supernatural sailing vessel. It kidnaps people and sings some strange hymn in the night, it also lights up, and it can sail underwater, they say."

Angus sat back in astonishment. The first thing he thought about was Nazi U-boats. For some reason, he thought about the escaping Nazi U-boats said to have operated in the area just as WW2 was ending. He'd read the writings of Reiner Gorst supposedly the officer secretary of U-Boat 96. Nazis had escaped from Germany with vast amounts of gold and precious works of art. Angus and Vanessa were investigating the occurrence where it happened, near the Calbunco volcanic crater.

"The ghost ship was supposed to be owned by the Cave Committee. They are the same scoundrels in charge of all this black magic mumbo jumbo."

"Aye damn them, and fear God," Angus replied.

Old Frank began to tire of his recollections. He was getting too old for psychological disturbances. But he hadn't finished. "It was a nasty business and a lot of people went missing. And there was talk of a Nazi U-boat skulking around. I thought about it and figured this ridiculous ghost ship could well have been an excuse for the submarine going about kidnapping folk. It was detestable and better left alone though." Frank gulped back his whisky. "You probably haven't heard yet, but a large ship went missing belonging to an Argentinian despot. It happened some months back. Many ships and vessels go missing around these parts and some said this phantom ship was responsible for it."

But the real reason was much more interesting and relevant. Angus was getting to the end of his investigations. Frank continued making his point.

"I know this area was once infested by the pirates, some of them English. And that's how it is. If I were you I'd be thinking about going home to Britain. They are strange people around here you know. I'd have returned home years ago, but you know how life speeds on." Frank slipped grabbing at the arm of his old chair and stopping himself from staggering along the wooden floorboards. "I'll be ok in a minute, feeling a bit dizzy, that's all. I haven't been able to get my medication from the mainland over the last few months since Gloria deteriorated.

And they won't give it to Jamie, he's likely to take it himself!" Frank took a couple of deep breaths, grinning. "The whole bloody world is on drugs or medication these days." Frank knew more about the world than he was letting on. "They say the whisky keeps yer' blood thin, and I've still got 100 bottles to get through. It would be disgraceful to croak before finishing them," he added stoically.

"Look Frank, it's been great to meet you. I will tell Vanessa we spoke, and if there's anything I can do to help, I will."

"That's bloody decent of you. And you haven't told me your full name yet?"

"It's Angus, Angus MacWilliam. I hope to be around on the Island of Sailing Souls for some time," he replied pointing out over the water dramatically.

From the bedroom, Gloria's mumbling progressed into a gurgle. She was going downhill rapidly. He escorted Angus to the rotten front door with its mottled lead-based paint and its verdigris brass fox's head knocker. Angus was pleased to get the extra information about the disappearance of the Argentine Industrialist curiously linked to his ex-wife. Frank was getting ready to tell Angus some hard truth before he went.

"Goodbye, Frank I hope all goes well for you," Angus said.

"Look, can I tell you something, old man?" Frank said, steadying himself. "Things are going to change here. I might be old, but far from stupid. They're going to start ramping up the logging and using the land for factory farming and those mutant GMO crops. Because something is going on behind the scenes. The Mapuche won't like what they are doing and they will oppose them anyway. And you can blame that damned Argentinian. He might have been kidnapped or killed or whatever, but believe me, there's a basket load of bastards following."

Frank stood up straight as he could. "My time is just about finished here, my advice is to try another country before the shit hits the fan. You seem to be a resourceful sort of chap." Frank looked at Angus with some kind of stoic affection. "Look you will probably be aware by now there's something bad happening in the world, one might say contrary to the laws of God. I've never been a man for church and all, but I am a believer. You know as well as me, the hand of Satan seems to be squeezing the world. And the thing is we can all feel it. Those in power are behaving very strangely and they have been for some time. So watch out my boy!"

Old Frank wasn't one for long goodbyes. But before he shut the door, he stopped in his tracks. Leaning on his shotgun he turned to face Angus. "Angus my boy I've got something which might be useful for you." Frank lifted the shotgun whilst holding the door with his other hand. "Take this with you, you might need it, I have others."

"Och' man ya' should na," Angus replied, reaching out and grasping it. "Right Frank it may come in very useful where we are going." Already Angus was thinking about modifying the shotgun into a sawn-off version.

Angus looked back across the sea to Vanessa's Island. He thought about the Caleuche ghost ship and the disappearances of so many vessels he was researching with her. Angus knew there was something peculiar happening in the area. The black magic stuff which Frank Poole had described as 'mumbo jumbo' was in fact a smokescreen for something real going on, and far more interesting. It was becoming clear that the Caleuche the legendary underwater sailing ship, was, in reality, one of the German U-boats which had escaped into South America with Nazi criminals and their stolen gold.

The tide was about to turn. Angus went back to the boat and climbed down into it, the rickety mooring pier creaked under his weight. It was getting darker and he was careful not to drop the shotgun. He thought he'd timed his little voyage perfectly, but he was wrong. Rowing back was going to be hard work for the calm sea was changing, catching up with the rolls of thunder rumbling in the background. Already white flecks of spray began to appear and flick over the bows of the rowboat. Leaning further back and pulling on the oars for extra purchase, he put his strength into the work. Rowing against the surging outgoing tide invigorated Angus. Small charges of fork lightning lit up the evergreen forest further away. The foreboding sky made the seascape stand out as though it was lit from underwater caves. The newly arrived prevailing wind made the sea heavy and turgid and it surged against the rowboat. Sweating Angus realised why there were no boats on the waters. Even the bellowing sea lions on their pontoon harems had quietened down in the magnetically charged air. A flotilla of squid propelled themselves under the boat through the transparent sea, as if they were also fleeing from something foreboding. Angus pulled hard on the oars. As the tide turned he could feel the power under the boat. Gulping in the heavy storm laden air he pulled harder on the oars. He was just in time. A solitary gull took to the air like it was late for something and was blown away like a white rag. Angus realised there was some kind of magnetic changes happening, disturbing birds, fish and animals.

He turned around and looked up to see the beach of Vanessa's Island. He pulled harder against the oars and the boat ploughed forward up the beach crunching the sand underneath. He took the oars out of the rowlocks and jumped over the side up to his knees in the sea. After hauling the rowboat up the beach and securing its anchor rope, he crunched up the short climb to the main house, to see how things were going. He brought the shotgun with him. The trees around the house were swaying with small branches being shaken off.

He saw Olga the housekeeper carrying a suitcase. Something worried Angus about her. It was like she was carrying the revengeful sword for the Mapuche natives in her heart. Like she was avenging the historical abuse they'd suffered as well as protecting Vanessa. It seemed that caring for the graves of her ancestors had fermented hatred of all Europeans and what they tried to do to her country folk. He was wrong because she had developed loyalty to something far more profound.

Tonight the moon would be as large as it could be. Perhaps the dolphins would visit again. Angus and Vanessa were exhausted and she knew Angus didn't trust Olga anyway. She expected this dynamic between a European and a Chiloe native. It had always been like this between the Mapuche and Europeans, perhaps rightly so. But it was obvious there was more going on with Olga.

Sacred Love on the Island

He approached the main house, walking back through the roosts of the vultures compelled in the wind to soar on the thermal currents. They had also been spooked into action by the active magnetic energies. The vultures were not as innovative as the famed Chilean falcon officially labelled 'opportunistic', as Frank Poole had called most Scotsman. Chilean falcons would feed on the beach from dead fish and shellfish, consequently, time had bestowed a beak on this bird of prey somewhere between a parrot and a falcon. Sometimes they would wait outside fish or mussel factories waiting for the entrails and scraps. Sometimes they would hunt properly like a falcon. And later Angus would feed them ham slices from the end of a stick. Face to face with his bird totem!

He could see Vanessa had changed into her green satin dress which he'd first admired back in Santiago. She appeared on the wooden deck of the veranda in the dress, looking like a handmaiden at the court of King Arthur. He loved her wearing it. He loved it because he could see her female form underneath, gently brushing against the lining. He forgot about his duties to his daughter and went to Vanessa as the night began to pour in around the Island like fog. And even though the moon was showing full in the background, it could not penetrate the darkness that surrounded the island.

Now was not the time to plan their mission, because Vanessa was moving instinctively to him and he wanted her. The evening blurred with romance, he touched her neck under her ear. She lay her head on his chest, letting him stroke under her hair on the back of her neck where it was softest. She reached behind and handed him a glass of Chilean wine which moved like the turgid inland sea in the glass. He felt himself stooping to kiss her throat like an amorous wolf. He worked his way round to the back of her neck and bit her ever so gently. Vanessa shivered. He tried to make visual contact with her, but she wouldn't look directly into his eyes. Still, he could see other worlds in her every blink feeling every raised hair on her neck tickling his cheek. Vanessa began to moan with mutterings of love. Angus smelled her scent in some animalistic way around her neck, where the rush of blood flushed her flesh pink. He wanted that charge of energy from her, it made him feel happy and alive when they held each other. It was as if this had brought him back from the dank grave of a Grail Knight. Angus pushed her dress down past her breasts. The dress slipped down, though defiantly halted on her nipples, so she helped it. The Arthurian dress flowed down her onto the floor where it lay around her brown legs and feet. She'd asked Angus what style of dress she should wear for him more than once and now she was stepping out of it. She began to unbutton his shirt. He wanted his flesh to touch her flesh to experience the electric union like before. She helped him off with it and they began to kiss. They felt everything in this kiss. It was an ancestral enabling of the genetic memory of their past life together. The castle from Seville appeared again, the stone arched window looking over the Moorish villas of the Islamic Caliphate. Their past lives collided when she'd come to him back then in 1300. The Moors like the New Babylonians also wanted the great Christian treasure.

Angus took her in prolonged ecstasy. It was happening again as he remembered everything the centuries had blacked out. She pulled him onto her, dragging him down onto the bed. Vanessa had become his wife back then in Moorish Seville in Spain. And they died together only to be reunited again back in each other's arms. Angus remembered all, through the giving and receiving of ecstatic love. He grasped her hair, holding her head down on the pillow and she smiled gloriously back writhing beneath him. She was excited to be in this love, through their eternal sacred union. And then it happened, and as she accepted him once more, Vanessa relived the beautiful words of Heloise to Abelard.

"God knows that I never wanted anything from you, but yourself; desiring not what was yours, but you alone. I did not look for the bonds of marriage nor any dowry, nor did I even consider my wishes or desires, but I endeavoured to satisfy yours, as you well know."

Their coupling began as a passionate embrace, growing into a prolonged athletic ecstasy of love, their bodies locked, their eyes flooding into each other. It was true that during this climactic moment, even God was wary, as it was the time when lover's considerations were away from him when only their passion mattered. Opposite to this was the moment of death when nothing was relevant anymore. Angus although God-fearing had overstepped the mark as he usually did during his high passion for Vanessa briefly letting go of the golden thread attached to his final purpose. Unfortunately he was about to learn a very hard lesson.

From their bedroom, he saw shadows darker than the moonlit night over the fathomless sea. Distracted by ecstasy, neither of them could see what was happening outside on the beach, perhaps it was better that way.

Purposefully the pirates moved up the beach towards the cabin where Isobel was. They were dressed from other periods of time, carrying weapons such as swords to recently captured Browning 9 mm pistols. The pirate's eyes glinted in the darkness like 6 tiny moons sparkling in orbit around each other. As they moved, they made hand signals in secret sign language. Below them on the beach was their ancient rowing boat with leather fitted to the hull to muffle the sound as they dragged it up the beach. A lady dressed in black with a dull red cross on her hat sat holding the tiller in the aft of the boat. She was armed with an AK47 assault rifle, yet she wore a knight's mantle with a Templar cross.

In the blackness, the men crept silently past the bedroom window of the lovers. They wore the same simplistic cap, but on their caps was the 'Memento Mori' known also as the skull and crossbones. The design had not changed since the symbol was used on the escaping Templar ships coming from La Rochelle, France.

Angus and Vanessa's love reached its explosive climax, both reaching complete victory, crying out together in the silence of the night. The last man to pass the window was listening, smiling to himself. The men from the sea entered the cabin where Angus's troubled daughter Isobel lay, in her drunken slumber. She didn't get a chance to scream and was quickly wrapped in a large sack and gagged. She was naked in the sack apart from her King Robert the Bruce pendant holding his axe, slung onto a pirate's shoulder in her delirious state. As they left one of the pirates took the one full bottle of wine left on the table and drained it. The men walked quietly back to the boat where the woman with the red cross on her cloak waited. Isobel was placed carefully in the boat. Somehow she managed to drop her pendant onto the sand. The men clambered into the boat and silently pushed off from the beach back into the sea, under the full moon. The Templar Lady made a sign across her mouth and the men fell silent. Olga the housekeeper simultaneously extinguished the small night light. For this dim candle had guided the modern-day pirates to the Island of Sailing Souls. Yet Vanessa and Angus lay lathered in sweat, exposed to the cooling air. They held hands happy in their moment and unaware of what had happened.

Angus's death recollection of being the knight under the tombstone at Balantrodoch disappeared during their ecstasy. He wanted to tell her about it, as it was ever-present in his mind. He nudged her. "Wake up!" he cried, but she was asleep, sound asleep, breathing gently, her chest rising as the dawn approached.

Meanwhile, the pirates rowed back silently across the darkness towards their mother ship with Angus's daughter. He pulled Vanessa on top of him holding her. He slept wrapped in her beautiful form as if she were a winter coat.

When they both woke, they felt guilty. Something was wrong. Olga, her housekeeper hadn't been up to light the fire and she was usually up at 5am. Angus had wanted to light it, for some reason, Vanessa preferred Olga to light it. Lighting the fire had always been Olga's work, but where was she? Vanessa went into the bathroom and started to run the shower whilst Angus went over to the lodge not expecting Isobel to be up. Perhaps Isobel would be stumbling to the bathroom or giving him dagger looks for coming into her domain as she'd done when she was a teenager. As a father, he felt responsible after his marriage collapsed. But what could he have done? His wife had preferred the financial security of a wealthy American when he hadn't even got a pot to piss in. The door to the lodge was open leading to silence. He went in. He knew something was wrong all along. But still he went through the motions as if somehow punishing himself for his moment of ecstasy.

"Isobel darling, where have you gone, lassie? Come on we're starting breakfast."

Nothing, no answer. He thudded up the wooden stairs, everything was wooden here in South Chiloe, all the churches were wooden, like a puppet stage set, from Pinocchio he thought. The Jesuits had been involved in building magnificent churches in these parts and it wasn't long after, the locals were building them better, but at least wood was a change from the stone of Scotland. It was a simple premise but one which would soon be cancelled out by a momentous discovery.

"Isobel love, come on let's go! We've got some stuff we ha' to do today?"

Still no answer. In his mind he'd gone back to the time when Isobel was a teenager. He went to the top of the stairs expecting to see her lying drunk across the bed. She wasn't there. His heart began to pound and his breathing quickened, he panicked.

"Oh God Isobel, where are you?" he muttered under his breath. He looked around the bedroom seeing the empty wine glass and bottles laying on the floorboards next to her mobile phone. He wondered how he'd miss the noise of the bottles clattering down by her bed. And then he remembered his ecstasy with Vanessa. And now he was regretting asking Isobel to come join him over from the USA perhaps he wasn't capable of the responsibility. Perhaps she'd gone for a walk, perhaps she was blowing out the cobwebs walking around the Island. He moved his large frame as fast as it would go, stumbling back down the stairs and out into the cool light of early morning. He went back over his time listening to Mr Poole telling him about the Caleuche ghost ship. There had to be a link.

"Isobel! Love where are you?"

The returned vultures with their crooked necks, broke branches from their roost above, flapping away over to the sea. Still there was nothing. He noticed Vanessa's makeshift new age altar, outside with flowers and stones on it. Isobel had been curious about it too.

"For God sake where are ye?" he shouted. Vanessa appeared from the bathroom in her dressing gown.

"Angus what's wrong, where's Isobel?"

"I don't know she must be walking somewhere."

Vanessa was no stranger to trauma.

"Something's wrong. Olga's not in her cottage either, there's been trouble down there. I feel violated. My spirit guides say something is wrong!"

Already Angus was thinking of preparing the launch, maybe she'd gone off rowing by herself. They looked out down to the beach and saw the rowing boat still there attached to the chain. Angus jogged down to the beach and blundered around it. More birds darted back to the safety of the sea flying low wheeling and screeching. Angus clawed at his own neck panicking.

"For Christ sake, what's happening?" he screamed, looking up, questioning God.

Then he noticed a long channel flattened out in the sand leading to the sea. It was like one of the local bull sea lions had been floundering there overnight. The other marks in the sand were boot imprints and scuffles. He knew immediately it was the memory of the much larger boat and its crew who'd taken his daughter. He looked closer falling onto to his knees looking for more clues. Nearby something glinted from the sand. There was a neck charm on a chain. He reached down and picked it up and then broke down. It was the charm he'd bought Isobel in the Edinburgh Grass Market some years ago. It was a silver pendant of King Robert the Bruce, riding a horse holding his axe. He wept like a child, blubbering.

"Aye for God's sake, she left this! She dropped it for us," Angus said gutted.

Isobel rarely took the pendant off. She'd always worn it. It was round her neck in every photo she'd ever sent him from New York. She knew how much Angus revered King Robert the Bruce.

Vanessa knew now her housekeeper had disappeared. There was no sign of Olga or her bags. But then Olga had been behaving strangely. Vanessa had gone to see Olga's cottage right next to the sea, she returned with a heavy heart.

A man had been walking back across the sands from the yacht marina. Angus had seen him earlier from the cottage window. Vanessa knew him.

"It's that German from the yacht club. He said there was a strange boat here last night without the correct navigation lights," Vanessa said.

Angus realised it was the guy who owned the yacht club across the sands. Only a German would have noticed and reported such an incident. No one else gave a damn round here. There were lots of Germans round these parts and whole towns which only spoke German and Heinrich was the type of guy who would have documented a fart and that was a good thing in this situation.

"He said it was a strange looking cigar shaped vessel more like a submarine than anything else," Vanessa said.

Angus recalled why he'd had the premonition about the Caleuche ghost ship. But Vanessa knew more than she was letting on.

"Ok, let's get back up to the house and plan," Vanessa asserted. There would be testing times ahead. But like Angus, she was beginning to sense that their expedition to the Calbunco crater archipelago micro-climate was approaching. She was satisfied that Angus had experienced how she'd felt about the disappearance of her beloved brother Rodrigo. Now they were even. Now they were both feeling the same hurt. Now they bled equally. And now Angus would be more than motivated to find where she'd gone, which in turn, as Vanessa suspected, would lead them to Rodrigo. The only thing she had resented about Angus was that he seemed unconcerned about her brother. Now he would learn the hard way. The reality of the pain was here for them both now.

It would be useless to call the authorities, what the hell could they do? One could do almost anything in Chile on account of the vast amounts of uninhabited natural space, that's why so many renegades, rebels and escapees had gone there for another chance to live again.

"Darlin' the great South American explorer Pizarro hadn't discovered Peru at this point, so how did Piri Reis know about the Andes in 1513?

Now Angus felt she wasn't paying enough attention to the disappearance of his daughter.

"Aye, alright Vanessa. I've got other things to think about."

"Exactly" she replied.

Vanessa was trying to get Angus to think about something else. He'd listened to Vanessa's words and empathised with the torment she'd carried, worrying about the fate of Rodrigo her brother. It was the real reason she'd gone to Rosslyn Chapel and by chance, if you could call it that, found Angus.

"In Charles Hapgood's book, *Earth's Shifting Crust* endorsed by Albert Einstein, it explains that the earth's surface is constantly moving, and yes the Calbunco volcanic crater was on the map then. But it somehow shifted or time changed."

Vanessa listened intently. She realised Angus had been studying the book she'd previously recommended to him. "Clever darling, you never mentioned you'd studied Hapgood's book. You are very foxy." Angus winked at her. So she brought out the big guns.

"The Calbunco volcano crater and its location could be likened to a floating island because it moves almost like some kind of a revolving door. But when it's closed all is well and its position remains constant. The location shifts though when it is open. I think this could have something to do with extraordinary lunar influence over the Earth. It is like the moon at certain times exerts magnetic power over the tectonic plates here."

The full moon was still visible. Angus had been told by a musician who lived in the Templar village of Balantrodoch back in Scotland, that when a full moon appeared, accompanied by a halo, strange things happened underground. Angus had been interested in the Templar tombstones there discovering that one of them had been his own.

Famous musicians, who visited the Templar HQ, went there to hear a loud trumpet sound that reverberated through the ground when the moon displayed the halo effect as a horn sounding in a cavernous chamber. His heart quickened, knowing that more powerful cycles of the full moon were due here soon. When Angus thought back to the moon from the previous evening he knew it was no coincidence that whoever had come for his daughter had arrived purposefully during that particular moon phase. It was common knowledge that during the lunar cycles, some cultures try to influence how things happen, even making supernatural things happen. Lord Reay had done the same in matters of the politics of men.

Angus walked over to the cupboard in the study where the gun was. It might be wise under the circumstances to bring it with them. Vanessa had told him about the old British war pistol in a black leather holster, which had been around for as long as Vanessa could remember. But they also had the shot gun which Angus preferred 'sawn off'. He brought some ammunition stacked in a metal box. They packed enough food for a week along with enough freshwater. And then they heard El Nino barking again from the beach.

"One more thing to do love, " Angus proclaimed handling the ancient pistol like it was toxic. "I am gonna have to saw Mr Poole's shotgun off, much more direct shall we say."

Vanessa was pleased with Angus's ingenuity. "Ok darlin' I am going to get the launch-ready."

"What are we going to do with El Nino, I thought you said he'd run off again up to Castro?" But Vanessa had gone to the boat shed.

El Nino was a bull terrier cross that wandered around as he pleased. He'd been Olga's dog officially, although Vanessa had rescued him on the streets in Santiago. She'd had to leave her island again to continue her work in the Atacama Desert in Northern Chile. She often worked in Peru as well with the Chilean Government as the borders between Peru and Chile were still being debated. The well-muscled dog appeared panting and swishing his tail. He must have heard their voices. He lay down in the sand to cool himself.

"Ok I don't know why boy, looks like you're coming with us" Angus said to the dog.

Vanessa had pulled strings with Rodrigo to get the launch from the Chilean navy well before his disappearance. The vessel had been motored down from Valdivia further up the coast by Rodrigo. It was ready for action.

"El Nino, here boy! Get in, we are going." Wagging his tail the dog ran across the sand and jumped into the launch and sat there like a gargoyle waiting for Angus who appeared brandishing the sawn off shotgun and the pistol and other things. Angus put everything he'd been carrying over the side into the launch and climbed aboard. From amidships Angus turned the wheel away from the jetty as Vanessa cast off the launch's head rope. El Nino banked balancing against the launch. Angus eased the throttle forward more and they sped away, gliding across the mirror sea in the direction of the Calbunco Volcanic crater. They went past the fishing platforms where the sea lions lived. Angus and Vanessa watched the little Island of Sailing Souls growing smaller and smaller until it disappeared. Angus thought about Frank Poole and his sick wife Gloria as they motored past the Spada Peninsula where they lived. They'd had a good interesting life, but it couldn't guarantee he'd see them again. He thought about his daughter, handling her King Robert the Bruce pendant he'd put round his own neck. Isobel was taking precedence over everything.

The dog sheltered under the bulwarks from the wind. Vanessa began to sing a native song about her search for her brother. The song she sang came from the natives who had lost loved ones, slaughtered and abused by the Spanish. The Mapuche had many songs of mourning about their lost and murdered kinfolk which Vanessa carried in her heart. Angus couldn't stop wondering about the darkness over this land where thousands of ritual sacrifices had diabolically fed the soil with the living blood to please their gods, which to him was equally as horrible.

He couldn't explain it. There was a curious alternative dimensionality to it all. Still, he steered the launch out into the inland sea until neither the Spada Peninsula, or Island of Sailing Souls could be seen. Further out to sea, there was no land from which to take a reckoning and the compass was misbehaving. It flickered inconclusively from north to south.

"Aw Vanny' ye' have fallen asleep lassie."

Exhausted after recent events Vanessa had crashed out. El Nino nestled in round her legs, wagging his tail gently in expectation. Angus let them sleep for a while steering towards the volcano. Even though the sun shone, Angus felt the sea breeze acutely. He slowed the launch down and put on a shirt. He wanted to be ready for the next moon cycle, it was coming and he was ready for it and what it would bring.

The tombstone he discovered at the Templar headquarters in Scotland had unnerved him because it represented further evidence of his past life after he'd realised he'd excavated his own grave under a Templar tombstone. Still, he avoided thinking about it seriously. He'd been unsettled by his continuing past-life flashbacks to medieval times in Seville, Spain as a rebel Templar. The key, however, to the portal into this place was his sacred love for Vanessa. Sacred love seemed to be the key to the transition. After all, it was all because of his love for Vanessa in Seville in those medieval days, that he was with her again now. God had allowed them to unite one more time and to continue the Quest.

It was revealed to him, that he'd been part of the medieval excavation team, discovering the greatest treasure from the Temple of Solomon. Yet he'd assigned that knowledge to his subconscious. The poet

Wordsworth had called it 'intimations of immortality'. Angus tried to rationalise it by remembering his investigation into Quantum Physics and how this highlighted the idea that people's thoughts can control life on a molecular level. He'd considered that somehow he was creating all that was happening in his own mind like a hyper-real dream.

He rammed the lever throttle to speed up the launch surging towards the periphery of the Calbunco crater. The satellite navigation system was still misbehaving. Angus tapped it gently.

"Och' shite man, it's cutting out on me."

He could see the Calbunco Volcano on the horizon. Vanessa stirred holding her hand over her face even though the sun had gone for there was a brightness around which was a mystery. El Nino responded by stretching in anticipation. Angus looked at the compass reading, it was spinning uncontrollably. The launch surged on towards the large volcano mound in the distance.

"Wake up Vanessa, I need those coordinates now. I think I can see Calbunco."

"I put them on the whiteboard, next to the wheel, let me rest darlin'."

Sure enough, the coordinates were there, in big black felt tip letters.

"I see, sorry," he said entering the coordinates into the satellite system which in turn activated the automatic pilot despite the previous erratic behaviour of the compass.

Angus drifted back in his mind to a previous expedition to a Neolithic lunar observatory above the deepest sea Loch Eriboll near Tongue at the top of Scotland. He'd gone on a winter expedition with a lady friend called Angela. Angela was supposedly tuned into earth energy, she'd fainted as they both walked through what felt like a band of vibrating force field. He remembered the moment just before she slumped to the ground. Disorientated he'd almost passed out himself. He never believed it until it happened to him.

The moon observatory was also where Lord Reay the seventh son of a seventh son went to practice a form of occult manipulation of people involved in politics in north Scotland three hundred years ago. Angus wondered if Lord Reay had somehow tapped into lunar powers with his knowledge of how the moon cycles affected them psychologically. Lord Reay used this knowledge if he wanted political support or was raising soldiers for a mercenary war. He'd always gone to that remote lunar observation tower at certain times according to the cycles of the moon. For this occult Lord was able to predict the reactions and moods of men and women, by how the moon affected them. It seemed no different to the computerised predictions, political scientists use today to predict how people will react to the New Babylonian social experiments designed to control them. Both methods were abhorrent to Angus. But in many ways, he realised that both Lord Reay's manipulation of people through his knowledge of the moon and modern computerised predictions were the same evil.

Now he was feeling the same sense of disorientation he'd experienced near the Neolithic moon observatory near Tongue in Scotland as the Calbunco volcano loomed near. Suddenly the automatic satellite navigation aid restored itself and his trusted old compass did the same. They'd travelled through some kind of energy band width, losing several hours of real-time. He checked the fuel tanks realising they were two thirds full. But surely they couldn't have been travelling at their current speed for 4 hours? His watch was telling him the same. The boat couldn't have got so far in real-time. And now the sea colour had changed to dark blue. Beneath the launch, the tidal flow was moving in a circular motion like a slowly turning whirlpool. They motored over great swathes of an underwater forest of seaweed which swayed with beckoning frond-like hands in a circular motion and he saw the shadows of unknown creatures moving amongst it.

What really happened at the Calbunco Volcano 1320 AD

A huge large swan-like galley glided down a South American sea estuary. Pegasus remained undefeated by her enemies. She was said to be the biggest medieval warship ever launched in the Mediterranean Sea. Painted in her black and red war colours, she had arrived with her sacred treasure to this secret hidden place. Near them were the other eighteen vessels and the lost Templar fleet, which remained in the safety of the glades until the unbreakable Pegasus had ventured further into the caves. The Templars aboard the fleet came out and cheered as the Pegasus glided past. The crew and knights on the Templar fleet had remained patiently waiting for the arrival of the mother ship with the temple builders aboard.

The knights stood watching on the deck as seafarers went about their business tidying ropes and tightening the sails to maximize the power of the diminishing wind. On port and starboard, two men were casting a rope with a weight on it, into the sea estuary, sounding for depth as the Pegasus slipped through the oily waters. Sometimes the dense green bush along the river banks brushed against the vessel slowing her down. Small birds fell on the decks, clinging to branches as Pegasus scudded against the undergrowth. Guards were posted bearing flaming torches in the diminished light. Below teams of rowers propelled the sombre vessel towards her final destination with the beat of a booming drum.

It was not by chance that the knights and pirates would share their symbols. For the Skull and Crossbones or Memento Mori carved into the tombstones of long-dead knights marked their confederation. Vanan Petri was the Templar Master of the Pegasus. His Marshal, Milo, had returned from his watch in the crow's nest aloft on the mainmast.

"There is no sign of any ship on the horizon, and no sign of anything, not even whales spouting."

"Good Milo please join the boarding party and make ready to start our fortifications. We must wait to see our brothers and sisters from the lost fleet, then we will build our base camp."

For this purpose, the Templars brought with them a team of stonemasons and labourers to begin the arduous task of building a pirate settlement beyond the caves. They carried with them all that was required to build both a settlement and a sepulchre to contain the treasure on-board the Pegasus. Vanan Petri was one of many refugee Templars who would follow the lost Templar fleet through the ages to the City of Light. He called for his navigator to come forward with the maps. Many believed that there'd once been an advanced civilisation on the Earth first mentioned by the Greek philosopher Plato. Many thought that the volcano had previously been a base for surviving Atlanteans after the great deluge also known as the great flood of Noah. The original Atlantis civilisation ground plan was created in the shape of several concentric circles diminishing to an inner sanctum like a Labyrinth. The connections to this mysterious civilization had long been known by the Templars who, like the Atlanteans, were great seafarers as well as geophysical explorers. Now the knowledge of their legacy was being carried by both the Knights Hospitaller and what remained of the illustrious Templars. According to the proven testimony of Jean de Chalons, Templar treasures of great magnitude had been loaded aboard several Templar ships at the port of La Rochelle. But this had been stowed aboard the Pegasus known to be the largest and greatest war galley ever built.

Native Chilean Mapuche

Soon one of the natives came forward and stood in anticipation. The navigators of the Pegasus knew the sea and changeable river as it ran towards the mountainous cave entrance. He gestured to them to change the course of the Pegasus and to stream their sea anchors to slow the vessel down in the waters, as they entered the sea cave opening. The crew laboured going about their duties. The knights went below and cried out to the slaves to stop rowing. Then came the great splash of the sea anchors being released and Pegasus began to slow quickly. Men at arms poured out of the vessel and stood ready around the bulwarks with shields bearing their various crosses. It was synchronised chaos as Pegasus neared her destination. As she rounded the estuary flow, the sea cave entrance was visible. The tidal flow disappeared in controlled plumes of white foam around the cathedral-like cave opening which Pegasus floated silently towards. The mouth of the cave had risen upwards during a previous volcanic eruption, creating another basin after the rock twisted, fusing with the volcano to create a unique micro-climate, where many prehistoric plants and creatures remained.

Sailors began to turn the great windlass. They hauled two sea anchors back onto the ship. Juan the Mapuche elder talked with Master Vanan and ordered the helmsman to turn gently. Juan smiled knowingly and the vessel stabilised perfectly in the dark flat calm. No man would have dared enter a cave like this without prior knowledge of what lay after the entrance. The men on the windlass drew up the second sea anchor at the same time. It was a perfect manoeuvre of coordinated seamanship. They sailed into the cave, stopping before the turbulent waters in anticipation.

Then a macabre voice echoed over the water to the vessel. There was a war canoe bearing a fierce carved head in its stem. Another native cried out. Juan called back and the war canoe was paddled over the dark flat water towards the Pegasus. Several well-muscled natives clambered up a rope ladder onto her main deck. The Sentinels instinctively tightened their grip on their swords despite knowing the natives were friends. The Pegasus floated gently down onto a secondary tributary where the current of another river carried her further down towards the cave's opening.

The natives stood with their clansman as the Pegasus descended on the current like they were riding a leaf down a river. Above them, great cave stalactites pointed down like the spears of descending angels. Courageously they entered the caves with its legends of sea witches and monsters. The gallant refugees risked their lives to take their mighty ship to its sanctuary where they would be reunited with their brethren. Above, great pterodactyls with membranous wings circled the exit on thermal currents. These flying dinosaurs were thought to be long gone. But like other anomalous birds and creatures, they survived in this unknown land presenting both an interest and a challenge for all who dwelt in the cave. As yet these monsters had proven no danger to the natives, but there was always going to be an exception to the rule.

Soldiers stood ready behind primitive swivel canons. Crossbowmen watched with their powerful weapons capable of sending a short armour piercing bolt through the body of an enemy.

Pegasus turned in the second river. Soon she was floating through the fathomless depths towards the Volcano basin. Here once molten rock poured forth, now thick green flora and fauna covered the soft pumice from which the body of the basin was created. There was a great flat red meteorite situated across the water. Van Petri bellowed the order to row on and the Pegasus glided onto the meteorite. Already twenty knights and one hundred men at arms were bustling about on the main deck in preparation. The natives had already disembarked over the side and paddled their canoe ahead of the Pegasus, transporting stonemasons and blacksmiths. The leather-clad workers carried great steel pins and rings with which to fasten Pegasus to its temporary meteorite mooring. They clambered up the great stone and hammered home the steel spigots. The thudding of the hammers rang out over the stillness, alerting jungle birds to sing in alarm. The ship's crew then tied Pegasus up fastening her to the red rock. The knights and their allies were home, ready to start building their settlement and the Temple once again. But further into the side of the volcano, it was clear that the Templars and Hospitallers had not been the first visitors to this cavernous volcano. A huge entrance had already been cut into the living rock by another race. There was a Skull and Crossbones carved into a panel above the cave where it grinned at the new adventurers. This vanguard had rediscovered the settlement previously only known about by the Templars. Old maps had brought them home to join their Brethren. Soon more ships of Knights and Pirates would follow.

The lost Templar fleet re-appears 2020

Latitude: S 41° 19' 57.9396 Longitude: W 72° 36' 39.9312

All the time the Calbunco Volcano crater loomed nearer as the great expanse of the sea shrank to an estuary outlet where small clumps of the forest began to appear. The launch motored on down a channel of greenery which grew denser under the sea where the banks on either side were naturally woven of old branches. Fast-growing kelp had attached itself forming a natural barrier. Even nature seemed to be conspiring to hide something.

Vanessa woke bewildered. A dolphin broke the surface of the sea ahead of the launch. El Nino jumped up whining and scrambling to the prow to look out at the unexpected visitor wagging his tail. Angus reached down for his old war pistol holstered on his thigh. He also had his preferred weapon of the sawn-off shot gun standing by. Birds sang in the trees as chattering monkeys swung through the branches, but something wasn't real about the situation. Angus could tell.

"Er' darlin' those monkeys should not be here. This is Chile we don't have them, we don't have monkeys."

"Aye lassie, I noticed that as well."

Then a supernaturally large membranous bird with a saw-like beak, soared over them and descended into the forest screeching as it went. It was close enough for them to feel the down draught from its membranous wings. The stench of rotting flesh was overpowering, instinctively El Nino ducked down.

"I think it's a particular type of dinosaur that should not be here in Chile." Yet Angus knew there'd been many records of these flying dinosaurs in modern times. He'd seen the photographs of giant flying insects shot by Argentinean troops over the years just across the border.

"It's a Pterodactyl or some kind of similar membranous winged lizard," he said, nursing the revolver and knew giant flying lizards were being discovered in uncharted areas of South America all the time. "Such monsters still exist. I am not a Darwinist or anything like that. I know things can go wrong in the food chain of the living and the dead, especially in the uncharted places near Patagonia."

"Darlin' calm down if you can," Vanessa said with a motherly tone.

There was a disturbance from the trees, branches thrashed and snapped whilst birds scattered. The Pterodactyl had caught its prey. The monstrous flying lizard rose into the air grasping a large mammal struggling from its bloody claws. El Nino looked up barking at it.

"My God, it's killed a sloth, that's a sloth, not a monkey."

"We don't have sloths in Chile either darlin'."

In front of them over the channel of seawater, the Calbunco volcanic crater loomed before them.

"I feel disorientated. I thought I was back in our previous life with Arab minarets and the prayer towers above our captured castle. I tell you lassie I could smell the spices and the oils! There was such a sense of blessed finality to it all back then."

Vanessa brushed her dark hair back into a clump and slipped a band around it. "There was nothing I could do about the bleeding from your leg back then in Seville. The silken sheets were red with your life force. It was sticking to my hands!"

Angus always had problems with his left knee and thigh. Nobody could get to the root of the matter. He visualised that deep sword gash cutting his artery. Even the Moorish physicians couldn't stop the blood flow and Angus had slowly lost his life force under the castle battlements of old Seville. They'd been laid out together on their previous marital bed back then, but now they lived again all be it in a semi-fiction world.

Angus thought back to the stones of Rosslyn having both repaired and examined the elaborate carving when he was a stonemason there.

"Aye, lass! There's more to it all than we could possibly know. Remember that TV history channel documentary on the magnetic qualities of stone? They examined at Rosslyn, the voices of thousands of people singing and talking through time accompanied by an orchestra of harps, emanating from Rosslyn's magnetic stones."

The flying creature soared round above, gripping the sloth with its razor beak while it wriggled tormented in slow motion.

"Darlin' watch out! Until this monster has finished its business. Whatever it is, I don't want you or me to be its next meal."

El Nino barked in a frenzy, looking up at the flying monster.

"Och lassie, it's not that large, perhaps no bigger than a condor."

"Yes, darlin', but we do have the Condors in Chile," she replied, trying to make light of their situation.

The flying monster's display continued higher into the sky. Then they saw the moon beyond in broad daylight. It was like a silver coin hanging on the horizon. Angus slowed the launch down in the sea estuary, cutting the noise of the engine, to take stock of the situation. Still, they didn't have a clear explanation of what was happening. Angus switched the engine off and let the vessel drift towards the volcano peacefully. Vanessa was happy to sit watching nature unfold around her. Shoals of fish swam under the waves, their tails flopping through the surface. Dolphins swept back and forth around the boat catching the fish, whilst the enigmatic monkeys chattered on. Vanessa got the main map out and started taking readings, writing the figures in pencil on the map.

"Darlin'! Admiral Piri Reis must have been here, he must have known about this place. Yet somehow this whole area shifted with the landmass more like Madagascar than Chile. We are in a different reality. Perhaps the clue is how Admiral Piri Reis charted the landmass under the ice of Antarctica. Perhaps there's something hidden within the Calbunco volcanic crater?"

"Aye, it's like we are between the edges of the tectonic plates in an unknown quadrant, a forgotten world," Angus said.

Angus recounted their voyage from the launch. They'd travelled through an anomalous field of energy disorientating them both, bringing on the visions of their past life in Seville. This phenomenon had previously only happened when Angus made love to Vanessa or whilst he was dreaming. Now he was starting to question the nature of reality. He considered his own ability to be able to influence reality with positive thoughts to make things happen. But then this was like a prayer to him anyway. Scientists had formulated opinions that somehow we can change bad things for good which was poorly labelled by scientists as Quantum Physics. This was the point where many atheist scientists involved in such experiments, turned to God. Both Angus and Vanessa knew that there was an unseen world beyond. And those who became enlightened or awakened began to experience other versions of events as though they had put their hand through the veil.

With a sense of relief, Angus began to understand why Rosslyn Chapel back in Scotland had been built to encode critical geophysical information, for the proof was looming in front of them. And he'd just seen what was probably a pterodactyl soaring on the thermal currents above. How could this be happening when they died out 1 million years ago? Suddenly Angus slammed the engine throttle into reverse. Sea birds followed the launch clapping their wings flying out of the way. He was struggling again, getting upset.

"Whoa' stop Angus, what's wrong", Vanessa screamed.

"Listen, Vanessa, we need to pray." Vanessa knew what he meant. She was aware of the supernatural predicament.

He slumped over the wheel of the launch as it turned gently. Putting his hands together, he began praying. "Father, protect our loved ones, Isobel and Rodrigo, as we come to know our purpose and do not forget ta' protect us, oh Lord."

El Nino crouched shivering now. Further ahead a forest of ship masts appeared, they saw a flag pennant high up in a clearing in the greenery. At first, it looked like a flag had been tied to a tall tree branch. Then another and another appeared. As they drifted nearer it became clear that it was a flotilla of ancient-looking ships, creaking and moaning rope fenders rubbed against each other. The trees seethed behind as if they housed an army of monkeys preparing for war. But bold as they were, they kept away from the living museum of medieval vessels.

"Jesus Christ protects us!", Angus exclaimed.

Restarting the boat, he opened the launch throttle propelling on towards the masts below the hill of greenery. Vanessa watched open-mouthed as the full extent of the medieval fleet became clear. The vessels were well preserved as if created for a film set.

"Ah, it's a film set, that's it, they must be filming. It's got to be a film set. Aye! TV has gone crazy for films and documentaries on the Templars."

All the time he knew exactly what he was looking at, preferring to accept the impossible solution rather than the supernatural one. Even so, it was like viewing a living Renaissance painting of the lost Templar fleet. There was no sign of any living thing near the medieval type lateen sailed cargo vessels. It was as if the ships were protected by a powerful force field illustrated by thousands of tiny golden orbs around.

As the launch came nearer to the vessels, it was clear they'd been methodically maintained. One might say worshipped. Their hulls had been oiled and their ropes perfectly tended. The smell of seasoned wood drifted upon the light breeze and their copper plated hulls glinted through the clear seas below. They groaned melodiously rocking back and forth. Angus began to count them.

"I think there's eighteen of them, eighteen of them."

Vanessa knew about the Templar's eighteen vessels.

"That was how many Templar vessels left from La Rochelle, France in 1307 after their dissolution wasn't it?"

Angus worked through the information, quoting the words of another Templar who had observed their great escape, which he'd memorised.

'On the evening before the raid, Thursday, October 12th 1307, I myself saw three carts loaded with straw, which left the Paris Temple shortly before nightfall, also Gerard de Villiers and Hugo de Chalons, at the head of fifty horsemen. There were chests hidden on the carts, which contained the entire treasure of the visitor Hugo de Pairaud. They took the road for the coast, where they were to be taken aboard in eighteen of the Order's ships.'

"Supernatural!" Angus's words echoed out over the water. Then the truth came.

"It's the lost Templar fleet." Angus flashed Vanessa a haunted look. "Look at their flags, they fly the Skull and Cross Bones. When the

Templars left La Rochelle their ships were flying the Skull and Cross Bones."

"Why are they so well preserved? And look they still have their original pirate flags. The most astounding thing ever was that the original 18 Templar vessels which left La Rochelle in France, all of them flew the Skull and Cross Bones thought to be only flown by pirate ships. And I'd often wondered why the Templars carved Skull and Cross Bones over their tombstones."

"Aye, lass, it's remarkable a lot is coming together now, no doubt we are going to find out the truth."

"We are just about on our target coordinates", Vanessa said, looking past the Templar fleet cross towards the Calbunco crater in the distance.

"My spirit guides are telling me that we are in another place, perhaps a lost quadrant like a portal area in a parallel existence," Vanessa said.

Vanessa's channelling was sometimes right on the mark. Angus had been taught that divination was dangerous. Sometimes it went wrong, presenting the wrong path on which to travel. Angus decided to investigate further. "Hey lassie, I am gonna' take a look, I need to know how real this is."

"No, don't go! It's dangerous! Maybe there are people on them?"

Angus moved with an underlying feeling of foreboding. "Aye, that'll be right."

Angus discovers his sword in the lost Templar fleet

They steered the launch alongside the first ship which was the largest. He pushed the throttle forward steering toward a large wooden post previously used to support a gin wheel for hauling up supplies and merchandise. A rope with a neatly spliced end dangled down above the launch. Grasping it, he pulled himself up, climbing the wooden planks onto the deck of the ghost ship. The planks had been so well oiled he found it hard work getting his footing. Vanessa slowed the engine down. She stayed at the wheel, steering the launch hard alongside the vessel. El Nino began to skitter up and down anxiously. The rope climb was hard work for Angus, he wasn't built to be a circus performer. He lumbered onto the deck disappearing from Vanessa's sight. She could still hear him swearing though, blundering about the decks.

"Not going to be a long time up here!" He shouted down at her. As he turned around on the ship, he could see the decks had been maintained perfectly. But he dare not think by whom. Treading carefully, he headed towards the vessel's main cabin, where there was an ancient door with a carved Skull and Crossbones above it. He crept past the neatly coiled ropes and squares of canvas previously used to repair her sails, all neatly laid out, ship-shape and Bristol fashion, as the nautical saying went.

"I am taking a look in the main cabin! There's a Skull and Cross Bones on the door," he shouted. He could still see her with the dog barking below, but they couldn't see him.

He lifted the latch on the cabin door and pushed it avoiding, looking directly at the Skull and Cross Bones motive carved in wood. The door opened silently on well-oiled hinges into the darkness. He switched on his micro torch illuminating the interior. Something glinted in front of him. There was a cross fashioned from copper, reflecting the light. The

Crucifixion scene was on a table, carved elaborately into the wood beneath. Under that was the cross of the Knights Templar. Angus approached the makeshift altar. He went behind it where he'd seen something else glinting. There was a large medieval-type sword presented on two wooden holders. The sword's scabbard was hung on a hook next to it.

"My God, it's a Viking pommelled Templar Sword." He'd noticed the Templar cross on the pommel. Something else was on his mind though. For he knew the sword was his own. He picked it up. It was heavy in the hand but well balanced. It sent a tingle through his body. He saw primitive carved letters cut into the sword's blade. The lettered sword was strictly northern European, but the techniques for smelting this famous Damascus type steel probably originated in Syria and developed in Spain. Angus's forehead creased with concentration. The lettering on the blade was the brand of the legendary Viking steel Ulfberht. This type of sword was rare and prized by the Templars. The sword felt familiar. He swung it in an arc, it sang. He guided its tip within a hair's breadth near the wooden bulkhead ceiling of the little cabin with a supernatural premonition of timing. It whirred and flexed in his hand, and through the blood it had shed, he remembered it like a long lost friend.

"I have you back again," Angus said, without knowing why. And thus his words of the declaration were signed, sealed and delivered before the altar of some long lost soldier of God. But then he remembered who he'd been. He saw the shadows of battles raging around him, Templar flags and the Lamb of God, the screaming of men and horses. And then he saw himself in an underground vault with other knights. He was inside the Temple of Solomon stood looking at the golden aura around the Holy Ark of God and he held the sword. He was overwhelmed.

Looking out to sea, away from the huddle of masts in the forest of green, Angus stumbled out of the cabin panting for oxygen, sucking in deep gulps of the ion charged air. Still, the monkeys, which should not be there crashed about in the trees. It was like the scene was happening on another channel.

The vessel smelt like spices, but there was another aroma like rotting flesh permeating the spices. He'd smelt the same thing when he'd excavated his own grave back in Scotland. Angus felt at home on the deck of the ancient vessel. He walked towards the seaboard side of the vessel and looked down at Vanessa in the launch from the bulwarks. The sword was like an extension of himself. It seemed like the whole situation had been set up for him to find the sword. He passed it down to Vanessa after placing it back in the scabbard. Vanessa grasped it, cradling it like a baby. He climbed back down the thick hemp rope dropping into the launch. Suddenly the forest of ships began to rock on the sea. A strange tidal wake rocked the vessels as if something forceful was coming over the sea.

"What's that in the distance just under the crater?" Angus said, raising his binoculars to the horizon. Several dark wedge shapes oscillated there in the azure light.

"Come on, we must go, those boats are coming darlin' look how the galleons are dancing on the sea." She'd a pleasant way of downgrading a critical situation. El Nino was scenting in the direction of the threat on the horizon, growling.

"But where can we go?" All of his preparation and readiness seemed worthless now.

"Darling, wait, be calm, I think this is the source of our Quest." Angus sensed she was thinking about her brother. He thought about the Viking Templar Sword. Vanessa stepped out of the way. Both of them listened to the creaking timbers from the lost Templar vessels as the other small boats glided nearer over the waves.

Vanessa began to stroke the beautiful yet deadly blade tracing her fingers over the rough writing of the Ulfrabecht inscription engraved into the steel under the hilt.

"Ya' like that sword lassie, ya' almost stroking it," Angus remarked.

"You know darlin' I think this was your sword. I seem to remember the engraved Viking text on it" she said, looking towards the boats on the horizon. "There's trouble here now. They are coming for us!" For both of them knew their redemption had arrived.

It was too late. A huge dark cloud descended over the bay where the vessels were moored. There was a swooshing in the air like a sudden flock of homing pigeons had flown over at high speed, then the splashing noise like the dolphins they'd seen earlier jumping out of the water. And then a large black net fell on them, across the boat. The men from the sea were back, moving shadow-like about the launch. One stood brazenly on the launch's stern like an apparition from a lost kingdom. There was a stench from them as well. It was the same as the stench of rotting flesh and spices he'd smelt earlier. Pirates were here, moving as one, they swarmed over into the launch. Angus and Vanessa were helpless. El Nino barked fearfully under the weight of the net. Angus prayed that they wouldn't be killed as he reached for his revolver. Vanessa could see his old leather boots typically focussing on the small detail of how well the boots had been repaired. Each stitch exquisitely threaded from the boots of a 17th Century Pirate Captain. The men said nothing. The sea boot squashed Angus's hand, preventing him from properly gripping the gun. The men operated with indescribable signs and gestures. Angus tried to move, but it was useless. Both were trussed up with plastic ties. They even hogtied El Nino.

"Who the hell are you?" Angus mumbled, his face pushed into the bilges of the launch. The pirate in charge gestured to another with a sign which they all recognised. It meant they knew who Angus was because they were acknowledging that their mission had been accomplished.

El Nino whimpered as the giant net was removed. Angus stretched his leg out to touch Vanessa. Another man started the launch whilst another fixed a skull and crossbones pendant to mini ensign mast. Then they opened up the throttle and the launch lifted dramatically upon the sea, scudding towards the Calbunco crater. Angus turned to see the lost Templar fleet now knowing the ships were real. He peeped out as one of the men covered the medieval sword with a leather sheet, he made a hand gesture which Angus recognised as a Templar sign. The pirate drew his hand across his neck, whilst another drew his hand across his arm in acknowledgement.

His head throbbed in the bilges of the launch, now he was a reluctant prisoner of these mysterious sea people. He struggled to focus. The buzzing intensified in his ears and he pulled at his collar in panic. He would fight this feeling, he must for Vanessa, she needed him like never before. His mind was overloaded with information, swollen with psychic awakening. Perhaps his pumping adrenaline was the trigger, switching his mind into meltdown. Another vision came now and this time he saw standards illuminated in a golden light. Gathered around them was a squadron of knights in their white mantles with red crosses over their hearts. Then there was nothingness, as he passed out.

The next thing, he was being roused. Cradled above him in the mist was the great Calbunco volcanic crater. He smelt the stench of old flesh and spices. It was the smell of the sea and death. Angus and Vanessa and the dog were being transferred by the men from their launch into a cart drawn by horses as he struggled to process the information from the recent events. Angus felt Isobel was safe. Curiously Vanessa was thinking the same about her brother Rodrigo. It was logical that if their kidnappers wanted them dead, they would have been killed back on the island when they had kidnapped Isobel. Angus and Vanessa were certain these were the same people.

Angus was sure about the flying lizards in the sky, circling on the thermal currents around the volcano.

"They are not dinosaurs darlin', they are Condors, as you well know, they are my soaring sacred bird of choice."

Angus touched her shoulder. She touched him back reassuringly. After trundling along in the cart they came to an old harbour wall with marks cut into the stone to mark various tide levels. The horse drawn cart was driven by three pirates who sat across the seat. El Nino whimpered. But then from the blackness of the volcano crater, a huge medieval galley was rowing towards the harbour wall built from its magma rock. He remembered seeing a similar building technique used on the Sinclair Templar sea fortress, woven into the cliffs in Scotland.

It appeared they were on the outskirts of a huge stone city where castle battlements and a Temple looked down at them from inside the volcano. The dense jungle had been neatly pruned back to make way for a complex fortified stone settlement. Angus began to see more ships of various types. He realised he was looking at many of the lost vessels he'd been researching with Vanessa. And in the middle of the huddle of masts, a large luxury yacht with a bright plastic funnel moored amongst them. It had been locked from moving with sheathed anchor chain. Angus recognised it as being the Argentinean Industrialist's superyacht. The yacht had been all over the television when Don Miguel had gone missing. Well, here she was captured by these anomalous pirates and knights. And now the boat was being looked after by these curious archaic people. And another thing, further down the harbour tied up against the wall was U-Boat 96, the same one Reiner Gorst had written about. All the vessels the pirates and knights had captured over hundreds of years were here in various shapes and sizes and all had been maintained and looked after by an unknown army.

Pegasus's ship's figurehead was a wooden winged horse nosing upwards as if flying into the sky on its carved wings. This was the famed symbol of both the Templars and the Knights Hospitallers. This majestic symbol was overtly displayed outside the Law Courts near the Temple of London annexed to Fleet Street. From here the Templars had orchestrated Magna Carta pressuring King John to sign it, steering the nation towards the rule of the people by the people.

The galley slowly turned into the wall as one bank of oars held fast in the dark waters lapping around the foot of the volcano, as the Templar flag billowed from her stern in the breeze. All the sailors and pirates stationed saluted, holding their hands over their hearts as Pegasus turned under her own momentum towards the harbour wall.

Further into the depths of the volcano high-speed motorboats darted about in the sea's expanse under the mountain. In context to the immensity of the crater, everything else was tiny. Soon the oars of the galley had been pulled inboard and Pegasus was tied up against the harbour wall. A boarding ladder was rolled out along the dockside and tied into position by more men of the sea. Those who had driven the cart began urging their three captives out and onto the harbour wall. Angus felt privileged as they gestured in their sign language between each other. Then one of them cut the plastic cable ties binding their wrists. Angus winced as if the knife might cut him and he trembled. This caught the attention of one of the pirates. It was as though he was looking for signs of his fear. Angus held his hands out and looked away. The pirates had Skull and Crossbones tattoos wrapped like nooses around their thick necks. The man who had detested Angus, looked disdainfully down and spat out tobacco insolently, which splattered so close, Angus smelt its pungent aroma.

Vanessa was helped onto the harbour wall built from blocks of petrified volcanic ash. El Nino was brought out on a rope, he tugged at the rope straining and panting. They were pushed gently towards the waiting galley. Condors surged and glided above. It was a fair walk to the galley and Angus figured it would be an opportunity to observe his surroundings as they were ushered toward the boarding ladders where a tall cloaked figure waited. Under his mantle, his medieval sword was showing. Angus stumbled and the Templar moved forward as if to help him. It was then he realised they may well be guests rather than prisoners.

Vanessa was scanning the volcano crater's interior. There was a series of walls built under the surface of the dark waters, fashioned like a giant labyrinth similar to the carved images of spiral formations carved in rocks by unknown artisans. Angus discovered many of them in Scotland which started him thinking about Plato's description of Atlantis again. Plato had said that 'the lost city of Atlantis' had been formed by concentric circles reducing in size to an inner-sanctum. Could this Volcano settlement somehow have been based on Atlantis? And when he considered their nearness to Antarctica, he wondered if it was linked. In the bright sunlight, the men released the main ropes of Pegasus. Moving closer to Vanessa, Angus took her hand as the Great War galley slid through the sea away from the wall. Pegasus had huge auxiliary engines installed. El Nino instinctively turned quickly to face the oncoming mantled figures. Three ancient-looking cloaked men with white beards appeared. The Templar gave way, bowing. The three men wore different cloaks. Angus recognised their denomination as being Templar, Knights Hospitaller and Pirate Brethren.

The Templar spoke first.

"Hail Questers, this is not a usual situation for you, very sorry." He looked on with compassionate eyes. "I am the Grand Marshall here, here is the Grandmaster of the Knight Hospitallers and next to him is the Master of the Pirate Brethren." The three men lurched forward bowing. Behind him and taking notes was a very elderly man in a wheelchair. Angus knew immediately it was Reiner Gorst. The capture of the UB 96 looked like it had really happened.

"And all is good for you both. Your loved ones are safe for the moment." Vanessa began to cry out loud as El Nino stopped straining on the leash. "And Pegasus has been upgraded somewhat, she now has engines and much more. She remains the symbolic connection of our glorious past, although now, all her timbers have been replaced with high tensile armour plate. And we've added the most up to date weapon technology and perhaps a little more."

Pegasus turned on the still water of the stone harbour to face the Calbunco volcano looming above before them. The membranous winged flying lizards were still to be seen gliding on thermal currents.

"You're right, they're not condors, they are pterodactyls." The flying beasts were interested in something below them on a stone ledge.

The Templar spoke "As God knows, you will know the truth of the world soon. Perhaps you will come with us to the state cabin and we can explain. Prepare yourselves, you are very close to enlightenment and knowing the hidden history!"

There was something both ominous and liberating about his words. The three leaders walked slowly over the well-scrubbed decks towards the stern of the vessel. Angus and Vanessa held hands like bewitched children. Everywhere on the decks was plated by titanium armour. The pirates followed them down some wide wooden stairs into a large gallery space. The room was like a medieval lecture theatre where rows of seats were filled with mantled men and women. The great stateroom had a stained glass window with the Salvator Mundi painting by Leonardo da Vinci emblazoned on it. One could never have imagined the great size of the auditorium, compared to the size of Pegasus.

Amidships there was a large flat red meteorite stone where 'The Ark of the Covenant' was to be placed. Angus looked out over the emerging stone city, where the Pegasus was heading. Angus and Vanessa were ushered into the lecture auditorium space. As they entered all those present stood up. Here Knights and Dames colour coded in their respective cloaks and insignia sat waiting in their cinema-style seats circling the lecture auditorium.

Rising out of the middle of the auditorium on a raised platform, there was an architectural model of the City of Light under an exact modelled replication of the volcano. The first level showed the buildings on the surface under the shadow of the Calbunco crater. It was like the greatest of ancient cities where clearly they'd been trying to create a huge entrance under it. But to continue this excavation work, it was clear to Angus that they would need something like the Holy Ark to finish the work. Angus gazed at the model. Even miniature plastic pterodactyls and condors were flying attached by barely visible wires to the volcano. All the stone features of the walls and doorways along with their gargoyle carvings had been carved in miniature replicating the carvings of Rosslyn Chapel.

Models of high powered attack boats armed with sophisticated weapons were placed strategically around the harbour city. He was no expert, but he thought the weaponry looked like laser technology. Lurking in caves, submarines and sophisticated naval vessels were berthed. All over, model figures of both combatants and civilians were going about their daily business. There was even a hospital with patients. Strangely, wild animals stalked about above and away from the main hidden underground city. Then arranged in military formation were rows of Templar and Hospitaller foot soldiers with their respective crosses on their tunics. Behind them were Templars who sat astride their mounts close to the water's edge. And tucked away in the background merging amongst vessels, were the Pirate Brethren striding about bearing tiny cutlasses, carrying skull and cross bone flags, and rifles over their shoulders. It was a curious mixture of medieval and modern advancement which had developed as a secret.

Angus and Vanessa realised on what side they both stood now. The battle lines between good and evil were being drawn in the sand and in reality. Humanity would have to choose their sides, the end was coming. They were taken to their seats and given water and some refreshments. They'd been well treated by their pirate captors, except for the pirate who spat his tobacco out close to Angus's face. That incident was still in the back of Angus's mind, ribbed with malevolence which Angus could not forgive.

The Quester address against the New Babylonians

And so it started. Two knights and one pirate stepped up to the rostrum and took their places. The great host in the auditorium stood up, placing their hands over their hearts. Another ancient-looking man in a Templar cloak appeared walking up to the raised platform where the volcanic city model was. Angus and Vanessa stood up like the rest. A large screen monitor appeared and then the name of the last Grand Master of the Templars, Jacques De Molay flashed on to it. Along with the subheading, '**We were never finished in 1312, they lied**'.

The Templar waited for silence. "Greetings to all those who Quest." He looked straight over to Angus and Vanessa, El Nino settled down nuzzling in between Vanessa's feet. "Sorry it had to be this way, be not concerned, your family are safe with us, and you will see them soon."

Strangely Angus could feel the stare of the pirate who had taken an unnatural interest in him from the back of the cart. He looked around to see him smirking. It quickened Angus's heartbeat with anger the likes of which he thought he'd forgotten.

The screen enlarged, then the presentations began like a film production. There was silence in the auditorium. The Templar presenter raised his hand to begin.

"It was presumed that our Grand Master Jacques De Molay was burned by our most hateful persecutors."

A scene unfolded showing the Templar Grandmaster Jacques de Molay being smuggled out of his tower jail whilst a look-alike was smuggled into the jail taking his place.

"We are grateful to our penitent brother sacrificing himself. For De Molay did not die on that fateful day, he joined the Templar treasure train, after it passed near where he and the others had been wickedly incarcerated in Chinnon jail after we fled Paris." That moment was recalled in words as if it had just happened. "Our penitent brother willingly burned to death to be tested in the fires of atonement to protect the Grand Master. But he was given poison before the fire began to burn his flesh, saving him from the pain. And so De Molay sailed with the Templar fleet and its treasures to South America. Whilst our penitent brother sailed with a clear conscience to our saviour." Vanessa rolled her eyes again. "I told you they didn't kill him I told you", she said elbowing Angus.

The scene zoomed into the Templar sailing vessels berthed in the forest bay where Angus and Vanessa had been captured by the pirates.

"And with all the recent developments in genetic engineering, our last Grand Master's resurrection project was completed. Might I remind you, that we were in front of this development before the New Babylonians! And reluctantly."

Rhythmic clapping lifted into the air. Black and white film scenes followed from a 1945 genetic engineering of DNA strands being extracted from red body tissues. Captured Nazi scientists walked about in their white lab coats. Black and white images of their U boat being towed back to the City of Light. Angus noticed other dead men in German uniforms laid out the decking.

Vanessa murmured under her breath "God, they killed the Nazi".

"Yes, they killed some of the Nazis", Angus replied widening his eyes. "Look over there it's like a retirement home for them. And that Reiner Gorst fella is still working by the looks of it."

Sure enough, sitting in a small group were several ancient Nazis. They were dressed in the coats of Penitents. Never to be released from their service to mankind under pain of death.

Next came the Knights Hospitaller presenter in his dark brown cloak. On the screen, a huge stone fortress appeared rising next to the dark blue sea on the island of Rhodes which Angus recognised. The cameras panned onto images of tombstones of skull and crossbones scattered about like seeds ready for rebirth.

"Here the greatest defence against the enemy of the faith took place. If it had not been for the Pirate Brethren, things could have gone against us."

Images of pirate flags, skulls and crossbones, cutlasses with illustrations of various pirate captains, flashed on the screen. Those gathered stood up and began to clap in rhythmic unison. There were several thousand people in the auditorium. From the rear men and women from the pirate brethren of the coast began to stamp their feet, drumming. The atmosphere was rising hot now. The Templar presenter took over.

"Calm yourselves, brothers and sisters! We know some of the greatest treasures known came from God into the possession of the Templars. And contrary to the propaganda of conventional history, those treasures are safe with us, saved by the Sinclairs of Rosslyn."

There was another volley of cheers. Then two mantled assistants wheeled out a replica of the famous 'Ark of the Covenant' adorned with golden crouching cherubim angels on top. An incredulous gasp rose from the audience.

"This is very nearly real, yet still a replica of God's Holy Ark." Many crossed themselves. Others stood solemnly, heads bowed, right hands covering their hearts. The presentation on the screen rolled on with a great army of knights marching across unknown deserts. White mantled knights sat astride horses foaming at the bit, shields, and crucifixes, marching foot soldiers, black and white checked battle flags superimposed and fluttering ethereally in the background. Then marching in, came a host of Knights Hospitallers. Nearby upon the sea, pirates sailed in pursuit of enemy ships. It had all been choreographed like a fantastic opera to inspire. The presentation was coming to the point.

"During the dark years, we grew to understand who our enemies were. And although we fought the enemies of the faith, it appeared, there was another more deadly unseen enemy controlling the Earth, and the truth is that they are our true foe and the main enemy of God. They're an oligarchy of both spiritual and physical dimensions. For the Babylonians have been resurrected and we know them as the New Babylonians. No longer do they wear opulent clothes of gold spun thread, now they drive elite cars and wear designer brands with silk ties, supported by corrupt Corporate decadence and lust for power."

The Knight Hospitaller presenter took over.

"The New Babylonians have subverted everything they know about humanity. Through their commercial activity, they are purposefully destroying the Earth. It's clear for those who want to see. Through their agents, they desire and still want our Templar treasures as a source of power for themselves." Names of companies and corporations involved in logging and other commercial activity in Brazil's Amazonia flashed onto the screen. Corporations, oil giants, companies, governments, administrations and politicians whose families and connections had been meticulously researched. A combination of names, logos and countries combined to create a great picture of the New Babylonian seven-headed hydra as mentioned in Revelations. Above the hydra written in block letters was the title 'Enemy of God'.

The Templars had traced the enemies of the world back through their New Babylonian bloodlines. God knew them well also. And the head of the evil Hydra grinned from London, England along with the seven faces of the New Babylonian leaders leading the onslaught against humanity on planet Earth.

Images of man-made catastrophes flashed over the screen, images from the polar regions where the retreating ice was beginning to reveal the remains of unknown civilisations, images of starving animals and famine struck populations. Then came pictures of social unrest, riots, and marching populations followed by the identities of the company executives with their profit before the Earth agenda who were responsible for the assault on the planet. But the cry for a better world burned in the hearts and minds of everyone in the auditorium.

From the rear, a mantled Lady Knight rose from her seat.

"We must act before the Earth goes into cataclysm as it did 6,500 years during the great flood. The New Babylonians are accelerating their work against God and the planet, endeavouring to destroy it. They are ripping out the lungs of the planet and in our sacred forests and must be stopped."

The Knight Hospitaller presenter continued.

"We know the lost and ancient peoples of the earth are our allies, the Amazonian peoples, the American natives, the Inuit, and the Mapuche peoples here will help us as they have done many times, those native groups who hold the Earth sacred, as we now do. Their prophecies are exactly like ours."

Ye shall know them by their works

A picture of the Industrialist Don Miguel De Monte flashed up on the screen. He was eating rich food and drinking wine, whilst the chaos in South America that he'd organised smouldered with images of burning rain forests. Then came live transmissions from the industrialist's agents already arrived to take the spoils from the Mapuche forest and lands. A picture of Damon Shultz, Isobel's inappropriate lover flashed on the screen first, followed by Max Rothman and their colleagues along with the logos of their organisations carrying out the destruction of the Earth, alongside pictures of the complicit and those damned on the wrong side of history. As always the logos of the companies when viewed together formed a huge picture of the Hydra monster. Choreographed to counter the monster, the familiar stones of Rosslyn Chapel flashed up on the big screen followed by a jubilant cheer. The camera zoomed in on the remarkably ornate stone ceiling. Where stars in stone were carved in sequence behind a portrait of Jesus holding his hand up in a warning gesture. Further away on the carved barrel ceiling, there was a dove in flight like the one which returned to Noah after 40 days holding an olive branch in its beak signifying land was near. The carved giant stars disguised the fatal angle of the astronomical axial alignment of planet Earth. This encoded message could only be read by those who knew that the Earth would tilt and cataclysmic events would follow. Mankind was now so corrupted and vile, the planet couldn't be saved by God's Grace. Plato had inferred the same about the Atlanteans.

"As for those genealogies of yours which you have related to us, they are no better than the tales of children; for in the first place, you remember one deluge only, whereas there were a number of them. And in the next place there dwelt in your land, which you do not know, the fairest and noblest race of men that ever lived of which you are but a seed or remnant. And this was not known to you because for

many generations the survivors of that destruction made no records." Plato: Timaeus.

But still, the New Babylonians continued to subvert humanity, for they had always worshipped idols and demons and continued this practice in secret, deep underground, which God forbade. It was part of the great enlightenment, to know that all things on the Earth were connected to God. In fact, all was God. The Templar walked forward purposefully opening his arms to the audience and spoke.

"Rosslyn Chapel is aligned according to the Earth's cosmic coordinates and the chapel relates to the universe. This information is carved symbolically into the stone roof. And the message from Earl William Sinclair our prophet builder, is still the same today, if mankind deviates from God's purpose, then the Earth will fall away from its normal trajectory around the sun. Mankind would again fall from the Grace of God and a catastrophe would follow." The knight scanned the audience. "All this is known to us because of the knowledge passed down from people of Atlantis. William Sinclair the Architect of Rosslyn encoded this information for future generations to see in the form of stone carvings. Rosslyn was the last Temple to have this coded information carved into the precious stones. William Sinclair was not just the Architect of Rosslyn, he was also the last of the world's Temple guardians. His legacy connects the matrix of Temples and edifices worldwide.

Angus grasped Vanessa's hand squeezing it tightly. What was happening was incomprehensible.

The Pirate Brethren were typically silent. Uncommonly, one of them stood up and raised his hand from the front row. Like his colleagues, he was wearing a simple hat with a symbol of his rank and a strip of bullets wrapped around his chest.

"I beg permission to speak my illustrious brothers and sisters," he said springing to his feet.

"You've always had permission to speak Joshua, but you've always made a point of not addressing The Confederation of Knights and Pirates directly," the Templar presenter explained.

"Aye, tis' true, but now I shall say my piece on behalf of the Pirate Brethren".

Joshua Gartock their Master, walked along the front of the auditorium in front of the gathering. He was a tall, angular man with a dark complexion. He wore round-rimmed spectacles and carried the pirate articles under his arm. His persona was somewhere between a warrior and a scholar. It was his father who had captured the escaping U-Boat 96, just after WW2 along with the art treasures and a contingent of their scientists. He climbed the stairs to the platform.

"Greetings Questers. I salute you with the words of Sam Bellamy pirate and just to make these events authentic, we have a relative of Sam here. Stand up Laura Bellamy".

A dark-haired girl stood up and placed her hand over her heart in the official manner.

"Can you read out your ancestor's mantra please sister? For we can see the truth in his words now. Those words, count more today, than ever." Emboldened Laura read out Sam's words.

"*Damn ye altogether: damn them for a pack of crafty rascals, and you, who serve them, for a parcel of hen-hearted numbskulls. They vilify us, the scoundrels do, when there is only this difference, they rob the poor under the cover of law, forsooth, and we plunder the rich under the protection of our own courage; had you not better make one of us, than sneak after the asses of those villains for employment?*"

The Pirate Brethren had worked out the real balance of power in the world three hundred years before. Because they had also fought the New Babylonians alongside their allies the Templars and the Hospitallers on the high seas all over the world.

The Knight Presenter switched to another screen, where the last Grand Master of the Knights Templar was reclining in a leather chair.

"Welcome all. I am Jacques de Molay, the last Grandmaster of the Templars. And I did not die when the writer's of history removed my legacy. As you all know, I was recalibrated. Even today in an age of evil intent, I still have a few years to live and to help your coming battle, for the battle of the final days draws near. God has allowed me more time here. We are destined to fight. We are strong enough for that. As you all know we the Templars modified and rectified the sinful and maligned powers of New Babylonians back then. And now with the Holy Ark and our recalibrated army, we are nearing the point of conflict once more. But this time we are ready for them".

The Templar's last Grand Master was able to see through the screen and was staring directly at Angus and Vanessa at the back of the auditorium.

"Now to business brothers and sisters." De Molay rose from his seat, from where he lived in a simple dwelling with exotic plants in the background somewhere above, in the City of Light. Although aged he stood straight and carried himself like the King he still was.

"Glory be, for we have God's Ark here under the volcano for safekeeping. We built Rosslyn Chapel through our agents the Sinclairs. The chapel is a book in stone to those who can see the codes carved there by the stonemasons descended from those who built the great Temple. We knew and read the stars combining this information, with geophysical knowledge of the life span of the Earth and the key to God's Grace, and to live in harmony with that majesty on the Earth".

Murmurings of agreement rose into the replicated starry firmament of the auditorium where more carvings from Rosslyn had been reproduced under the barrel-vaulted ceiling of the auditorium. Vanessa nudged Angus in the ribs, rolling her eyes until he paid attention.

The Ark is revealed

"Finally, we now have the second activation stone, the Thummin stone, previously under the care of our High Priest Aaron. This is the key to activating God's Holy Ark."

All those present looked over at Angus and Vanessa, De Molay watched on. The Presenter continued walking to the side of the big screen. Angus still unaware he'd inadvertently led them to the Thummin stone.

"Angus you have earned many commendations, through Questus and what it means. All of you who remained to seek the truth of this world, we have watched you, as you developed your higher nature in the far north of Scotland. But we had to engineer certain situations so you would lead us to a tombstone at the old Templar HQ at Balantrodoch. This was your tombstone which was lost. And you will find out why, soon enough. Only you could have found it, as it was written. We have already traced your line back and we know who you are. For Angus, you were once David de Omar, a Grail Knight present at the last excavation of the Temple of Solomon. But the others who were with you are gone, only you remain inflicted with a supernatural love for Vanessa Bermodes." The knight looked down at the ground. "And you came back for the love of women first and foremost which God permitted because you have a higher purpose yet to complete."

Angus felt dizzy again, dragging himself through the self-doubt barrier, his destiny had been finally confirmed like cast iron. At that moment he remembered back and realised he'd discovered his own dead-white hand, stark against the dark soil in his own grave at Temple Balantrodoch and it shocked him.

"As David de Omar Gunn you found the original stones from Aaron's breastplate during the medieval excavation of the Temple of Solomon. It was you who originally found both stones the Urim and Thummim stones which would activate the Holy Ark of God. The first stone was stored according to a biblical protocol in a vessel made from cedars of Lebanon, wrapped in the wool of a mountain sheep and compacted with Frankincense oil. If you recall the Holy Ark was made in part from cedars of Lebanon," the knight looked solemn and continued.

"In death, you forgot where you'd hidden the second stone, yet this was not an irretrievable situation. It was your fate to stay on the Earth, you begged to return. It was your Islamic captors who saved the stone motivated by high honour. It was they who had your tombstone carved along with the compartment in which to hide the stone. Often in certain circumstances, magnanimous Islamic caliphates made sure dead knights of quality were furnished in death with the correct coded tombstones and you were once such a knight. Then they shipped your body and your tombstone back to Britain along with that stone. You were linked by an alliance to the Sinclairs revered by your Islamic jailers, you were shipped to Leith Port, Edinburgh, pickled in honey and beeswax and then buried by your brethren at the Templar HQ at Balantrodoch."

Angus was still confused because he still wondered who had carved the inscription of the geophysical coordinates that linked the numerals and symbols they'd found under the statue of Admiral Piri Reis. Somebody must have done. That was the burning question. The knight presenter knew.

"You see, your early Islamic captors were the ancestors of Admiral Piri Reis, the man that discovered the landmass under the Antarctic. This place was known by all of them," the knight pointed round the auditorium. "And it was they, who carved the sacred numbers and symbols onto your tombstone. That is why his statue adorned Rosslyn

Chapel. And so you will know where that statue went. Take a look over at the other end of the auditorium."

A light illuminated a column plinth. The sheet which covered the statue was pulled away to reveal the ancient statue first carved at Rosslyn in 1480. In 1700 it had been removed along with all the other 112 statues. Obviously, some of them had been taken and transported to the City of Light. The audience in auditorium stood again and clapped. "But know this Angus, we removed the statue so that you could find the numerals and carvings which have brought you here. Because it was the Piri Reis group who rediscovered the City of Light, his map enabled us to find it. It has always been here since the time of man started," the knight explained.

De Molay continued after the knight presenter in the auditorium gave way to the Grandmaster.

"It was Moses' brother, Aaron with his breastplate of gems who activated the Shamir the energised lance with tongues of fire. It can slice through diamonds and any stone known to man. We used it to cut the stone in the building of the First Temple so as not to defile the sanctity of it. Very soon we will use it again, but this time against our enemies. Even though the New Babylonians who fear its power are attempting to find it and use it for themselves."

Angus was still lost. He still couldn't recollect ever seeing the second stone known as the Thummim stone. He remembered the first stone the Urim stone wrapped in sheep's wool found inside the wooden Grail discovered by Andrew outside the vaults under Rosslyn. That was the stone Andrew had shown him at Ackergill Towers overlooking Orkney. But then suddenly Andrew had died. He remembered being so consumed with his own Quest, he'd even skimmed over the details of his obituary in the Times of London.

He recalled the news of the heritage council employee being shot at the Templar HQ on the TV. He remembered the cunning Sinclairs and how they stuck together. Then he remembered digging down to the tombstone at the Templar HQ not far away. He remembered obtaining the second set of numbers and symbols from the front of his own tombstone which had brought him to Rosslyn and nearby Temple Balantrodoch. Then he remembered something else. He remembered the small oblong cavity carved into the back of the tombstone. Along with the initials D.d.O.G which were his own initials, when he was a Grail Knight. Wait a minute! But how did the Templars and pirates, get the first stone, the Urim stone that Andrew had discovered inside the wooden Grail?

After learning that Andrew had died in London, he was naturally disorientated and demoralised. Angus took matters into his own hands regarding his research. He couldn't be tied forever to all aspects of Andrew's investigations and brinkmanship. But something wasn't adding up.

Angus's test to Seize the day

Boldly the pirate strode forth into the arena. There was always something nasty to get in the way.

"Forgive my intrusion brothers, but I have a right under pirate articles and brotherhood to speak my mind. I witnessed this man's cowardice back on the cart. He flinched under the slightest provocation and pain. Not the behaviour of a knight and I believe him to be a fraud." There seemed to be no reason behind the pirate's hatred of Angus. But that's often the case in most disputes.

Vanessa squeezed Angus's hand again. She could feel his grip tightening with rage. The pirate spoke again.

"There be no smoke without fire! I challenge this false knight, in the normal way."

The auditorium of knights said nothing in Angus's defence. The pirate had called out the 'Big Test' as it was known. Angus must meet the challenge or risk being cast out into the wilderness, which would impact on Vanessa's situation with her brother. She'd also thought that Angus had to remember now who he was and why, as time was running out. It was understandable that the rule of honour and blood oath was something that had been the bedrock of this lost civilisation.

"We know who you are but only raw courage will save you now." The Templar looked downwards. "But if, as our pirate brother says you are lacking metal, then you will be found out and everything will change."

Vanessa moved closer to Angus, she was frightened. Angus looked over at the wiry pirate with his welts and scars. This man was consumed with hate. Angus wanted to say something, it was getting personal. He knew that the pirate wanted to fight him and for no real reason or so it seemed.

The Templar stepped backwards. "Under the articles of our confederation, combat must follow in the pit."

A rush of fear rumbled through Angus's guts. He couldn't believe what he was hearing. And this particular pirate wanted to test him to death. But he was ready.

"And my choice as stated in the Pirate Brethren articles, describes that first blood drawn wins all including possessions taken directly from the dead body, including his wives or otherwise, dead or alive." Vanessa squirmed. Murmurs of appreciation and agreement lifted into the auditorium. Angus saw that the test might end in his death. But what could he do?

"Challengers prerogative upheld. Take them to the test pit." The Templar Presenter's cold expression said it all. There would be no negotiation. The Pirate Brethren articles would be upheld.

Angus was in trouble. This would be a trial by combat with sword or dagger. They dragged Angus away from Vanessa, he could not show any emotion, all eyes were on him, watching how he behaved. El Nino lunged at the guards.

"Come on laddie, I don't have a sword!" Angus cried, knowing he wanted his own sword.

"You will be given one!" replied the Templar.

"I have the right to choose my sword, I want my sword! Or don't you believe who I am?"

"What weapon?"

"You know damn well what weapon ya' shitebag, I want my bloody sword! I want my Viking Ulfberht, that's my damned sword!" The wiry pirate shrank back from his former forthrightness. They'd awakened a sleeping psycho. The group deliberated on the stairs above the combat pit. Meanwhile, Angus removed his leather jacket to reveal his Hibernian football shirt, green hoops and their crest. And on the back was written 'Made by Scottish Whisky'.

"You may use the Ulfberht, it is permitted. Bring the sword to him. And you reveal your colours it seems?"

"Aye ma' colours bonnie laddie. Permitted eh? You better stand back ma' dander's up, ya' cowardly tosspot." His pirate accuser backed away thinking again.

The pirate swaggered down the stairs in his sea-boots, followed by his supporters. Both went through the wooden door into the arena. Those gathered in the lecture auditorium had turned around in their seats to watch the events down below. The pirate accuser walked over to an attendant standing by holding a selection of weapons, including a cutlass and a short chopping sword used in close-quarter combat. The Templar gave Angus the Ulfbertht medieval sword. Determinedly Angus drew the sword, swirling it and swooshing through the air in his green hooped football shirt. Astonished the Templar and the others backed away as he became one with his sword again.

The pirate chose the cutlass rubbing his thumb gently down its honed blade. A lick of red slipped down its blade. The pirate grimaced a fearful look, hoping to demoralise Angus. But grasping the Ulfbertht transported Angus back to his forgotten battles. His hand felt comfortable gripping the hilt, and then all trepidation left him. He wanted to try the whip steel blade again, which could break the standard steel of normal weapons. The onlookers shuffled off across the sand in the arena, slamming the ornate wooden door shut behind them. The two curious adversaries faced off, Angus physically larger, with his medieval sword which could cut tables in half, whilst the wiry pirate, with his deadly cutlass capable of slicing Damascus Silk. As they walked to the line in the sand the pirate removed his hat and leather coat.

The referee stepped away. The pirate made the first move, skipping quickly forward lunging rapier-like with his cutlass. Angus watched the tip of the blade slice past his face. He slipped the attack. He brought his sword into the on-guard position striking out with a well-timed slicing cut. The spring steel of the sword sang through the air, but it missed the head of the pirate who after ducking low, stabbed at Angus below his waist. Angus was remembering now and with that came re-knowing instinctive battle moves from his life as a Grail Knight. But the pirate's cutlass point pierced through Angus's football shirt leaving it flapping, yet it failed to cut his flesh.

"Ya' blooter' ya' done for laddie" Angus said stepping backwards.

He swung his blade into the chest of the pirate with a bludgeoning force that cut the pirate down crumbling to his knees. But no blood was drawn. The pirate rose, frowning with doubt, regretting his actions.

Angus felt the force of his warrior past returning. He followed up returning a natural backhand swipe, narrowly missing the pirate's head. Silently above them the audience watched as if this type of combat was a normal daily activity. The pirate rushed back at him, circling with dagger drawn. He turned over his cutlass and dagger at the same time like a miniature windmill. Angus remembered his former battles. They all came back as heads were lopped from shoulders, bones cracked and men bled. Angus remembered who he was again.

Jumping forward, Angus halved the distance to the pirate and using the flat end of the hilt smashed into his scowling face. It was a blow that would have dropped an ox, but not the pirate. The Templar referee looked for the blood to stop the fight. The pirate's head began to swell, but his face was a welter of healing rips and tears anyway. A look of desperation flashed across his face. Throwing caution to the wind, he rushed Angus like a screaming demon slashing his cutlass scythe-like but missing again.

Angus stood back just out of reach. The auditorium of onlookers gasped with dismay. They knew what was coming next. He swung the medieval blade round the back of his head without thinking. It was as if David de Omar the Grail Knight had climbed into him as Angus's self-doubt climbed out. Throwing his head back with a mighty well-timed slice, he stepped away from the lunging attack, returning a chopping blow across the pirate's face.

"Angus stop!" shouting came from above the pit. "It is proven!" Angus had cut the forehead of the pirate inflicting a gashed wound. Blood blurted down his face. "First blood to the knight." The pirate lay in the sand moaning holding his head. Instinctively Angus followed up, levelling the sword blade across the neck of the downed pirate.

"Say the word you maniac and I'll finish it," Angus bellowed, recalling the pirate's tobacco spit. The others grabbed his arms, struggling to hold him back. And as if to make sure, he booted the head of the pirate uncharacteristically knocking him senseless.

"But wait!" Angus recognised the voice.

"Stop you bloody fool you've won. You don't have to kill him." Angus came to his senses dropping the sword whilst the bloodied pirate was attended by his seconds. Angus looked around for the person whose voice had ordered him to stop. He knew the voice well, but he was struggling, it was a voice too far.

The door of the wooden pit opened and an elderly figure stepped methodically down the stairs and entered with gentle applause from the audience. Vanessa was by his side. Angus wiped away the stinging sweat, which had clouded his vision. His breathing lessened and his mind steadied as he wiped his face.

"Well done Angus you proved who you are 'the once and future knight' to steal some of the words of the author T. H. White."

Angus turned round to view the familiar form of his mentor Andrew Sinclair. Angus gawped wide-eyed. He was staring at a man, returned from the dead.

"Well, I told you, but you had to find out for yourself eventually. You are David de Omar Gunn a Quester now and a past Grail Knight. Finally, you remembered and believed, defeating your worst enemy, self-doubt and fear. Angus fell to his knees. "

"Andrew man, God, you are still alive!" Angus was taken up from the pit followed by Vanessa and the dog.

Andrew looked at Angus's ashen face. "Well, you look like someone just walked over your grave. But the truth is knocking on the doors of those who Quest."

Angus remembered the second stone called the Thummin stone and the curious light which emanated from it. Of course, it was Andrew who had rediscovered the first stone the Urim stone in the little wooden Grail in the famous vaults at Rosslyn Chapel. Angus drifted back to the moment he held it, along with the golden clasp which encased it, shaped like a fire breathing serpent. The thing was Angus was the knight who had found both of the stones to start with, in the Temple of Solomon.

The last Grand Master of the Templars watched with satisfaction from his cell library, overlooking the City of Light. "Seize the day!" he said under his breath.

They all went back up the stairs to the auditorium. Jacques De Molay had promised God's revenge on his enemies. But nobody had expected that the Holy Ark would be brought out as a possible deterrent against the New Babylonians. The fact was they'd now got both the stones required to activate it.

Questus report from Andrew Sinclair

The Templar spoke. "We've prepared the podium accordingly. It's time to know the truth about the world, and what is coming, and what we must do."

They were taken to the front and Andrew climbed the steps to the rostrum to make his address. Vanessa smiled over at Angus, aware that the hand of God was playing its part. But first, they were treated to a film of their lost loved ones. Rodrigo Bermodes came onto the screen in his Chilean army uniform. He waved and then spoke in Spanish from the screen next to Andrew at the rostrum but there was a surprise coming.

"Fui salvado por los caballeros. Estoy muy agradecida de estar viva, mi hermana que he visto y aprendido a lo largo de los meses. Te veré pronto para abrazar".

Andrew watched Rodrigo's reaction on the screen.

"The knights and pirates saved me. I am very grateful to be still here sister, I've watched and learnt over the months. Soon we will embrace, there is much truth to know about these wonders of this world." But the knights and pirates had also extracted valuable information from him regarding the plans of the New Babylonians. Although they'd used him to extract information, they were able to release him from these chains of servitude. He too would be used as a penitent knight, although he was a warrior already against the New Babylonians now that he knew the truth.

Vanessa rushed over to the screen, pushing her hand against her brother's hand through it. Angus backed away. And then his daughter Isobel appeared next to Rodrigo in a hoodie. She waved out from behind the screen. Angus was uplifted to see her looking so happy. And she'd been given a pet monkey to look after, which ran up and down her arm tugging at her beautiful hair, making her smile. And true, monkeys were not supposed to be in Chile. Andrew acknowledged all with a quick nod of his head, from where he was speaking.

"We stand here in the calm of this place, hewn from the living rock from the Calbunco volcano crater, by our ancestors the Templars, Hospitallers, and Pirate Brethren and those who came before them. I bring you the respect of the Questers." Those gathered placed their hands over their hearts. "Unfortunately, I also bring news from the world of the New Babylonians." Simultaneously an image of the Industrialist and Earth enemy Don Miguel de Monte flashed up. He was sitting in a partially lit cell from where he'd been jailed. He held his head in his hands.

Andrew shuffled his notes, continuing "Angus or perhaps I should say D.d.O.G. the letters of which are carved on your tombstone meaning David de Omar Gunn, finally you remembered. You lead us to your tombstone, placed under the old Kirk wall at Temple Balantrodoch built over your body after it was returned from Seville by your Islamic captors, and purposefully I might add."

"Aye, this is true Andrew I was out of touch with so much, blinded to myself and by my own sensitivities. But better late than never."

"But you did not remember the small oblong cavity in the back of the Tombstone? Were you aware of it? Or were you still blinded by self-doubt? For in that cavity was where the Holy Ark's second activation stone known as the Thummin stone was placed. We knew you'd hid the stone inside it before you died or should I say was placed there by your captors. For you were a Grail Knight, David De Omar of Seville, adopted by the Gunns of Scotland, allies to the Sinclairs. It was you that found the Grail cup from the Temple of Solomon. As much in history is lost or forgotten, so was your tombstone. We have been waiting for you to return to find it. Only you could know with your supernatural sense activated through the process of your enlightenment," Andrew took a sip of wine, putting on his reading glasses.

"We eliminated the heritage officer at Balantrodoch, a New Babylonian agent. They've been watching the Templar HQ for some time. It seems everyone has been waiting for you to find your own tombstone!" Laughter lifted into the air. Andrew turned solemn. "And now we have both precious stones. We are ready to activate 'The Ark of the Covenant'," he said. "There's no easy way to say this. The New Babylonians are ramping up world destruction. They are destroying the animals, our freedom, our sea creatures, our hope, and the people's future. They're sending us all to damnation to come. Here are the names of those responsible."

The list of the New Babylonian destroyers went on and on and on. Family names, elite politicians, scientists, corporations, media and TV companies, all subverting and poisoning humanity endeavouring to install their own demons in the place of God.

Andrew held his earpiece looking out over the audience of those fated to protect the Earth. He was excited about something else and had more news. He held his earpiece waiting. "Ah, success! We have activated the Holy Ark. It appears that the Shamir is firing up and cutting through underground deposits of rock as we speak."

Andrew was interrupted again. Another progress bulletin flashed up on the screen showing the Holy Ark sparking into action at the foot of the Calbunco crater. The Ark had been set on the backboards of a simple cart. A pirate steadied the horses in front. The priests were clothed with a special mesh blanket developed in the City of Light by their scientists. A High Priest in robes girded in precious gems, directed events. Another priest attended to the Urim and Thummin stones which had activated the Ark. A bolt of electric blue light flashed and oscillated between two kneeling cherub angels where their wings touched forming an arch of golden feathers. A radiant yellow light flowed from the Ark pouring out around the priests, so they looked like they had a gold aura. They were abiding by the biblical codes of activation required to stay alive in the frantic light from the Ark.

"At this rate we shall have reached the inner City of light in 20 hours from the moment the Ark starts cutting the rock tunnel." Andrew looked over changing the seriousness of the situation. "Both of you better come up we've got your family to see again."

But no one present dared question, why they were excavating towards the underground City of Light.

Vanessa came out of the front row of the audience along with El Nino followed by Angus. Behind Andrew, a door in the screen opened and Isobel and Rodrigo appeared. Vanessa rushed over and embraced her brother. Angus hugged his daughter. As Vanessa pulled away from Rodrigo to say some words of encouragement and relief, she glanced down to see Rodrigo's hand releasing Isobel's hand. The audience stood and began to clap solemnly. Angus could see the new dynamic between his daughter and Rodrigo and was happy. It would solve a lot of his problems with Max Rothman and Damon Shultz. The host stood and clapped, for they lived with hope again. Angus was then led away to where he would receive his battle orders from the elders of the City of Light. They had already decided that Angus would become a leader as he always had been.

Andrew looked over at Angus with trepidation. "All that remains is for you to be given your war instructions."

The Templar Knight attendant next to Angus ushered him gently toward the centre of the auditorium knowing what would come next. Because it was time for the feast of all the days." Andrew looked around and nodded his head. De Molay raised his hand in agreement.

The auditorium changed from a place of business to a place of feast and celebration. Banquet tables were brought in as the great model of the City of Light descended through the floor. All those present left their seats and walked down to the newly created celebration space. The Templars sat together down one side of the room along with their Lady Knights. Opposite them sat the Pirate Brothers and Sisters and further along sat the Hospitallers. Ale was brought in as well as wine along with great wooden bowls containing fruit and chicken. And the feast began with them singing hymns and songs of God. They banged their tankards on the table intoxicated with life and what they were about.

There was a display of swordplay between Templars and pirates and their respective styles of combat. Sam Bellamy's ancestor Laura Bellamy fenced with a Knight of St John and the Mapuche natives performed a forest dance of celebration. Angus was reunited with his daughter Isobel. And Rodrigo was reunited with Vanessa. Vanessa and Angus sat watching the events with a beautiful love for the Earth in their hearts. All told there were over a thousand at the feast. Andrew and the leaders sat at the head of the feast waiting for the next set of orders. The whole event reminded Angus of the Pirate and Knight feast at Sinclair Castles back in Scotland. He began to realise now, from where that feast had evolved. Before the feast was over Angus was ushered towards the door of the auditorium on the Pegasus. A boat was waiting to take him to the outer wall of the City of Light to prepare for war.

Angus becomes a Knight Leader

Angus was growing naturally into his role as a war leader against the New Babylonians. In the cave of the bio-development sector, he'd been told that a New Babylonian drone attack was imminent. Yet he was still overwhelmed by the beauty of all around him. He loved the way that questers, knights, pirates and natives lived naturally with the animals and birds and insects they were working with. Even nature was also aware of what the real enemy was. A templar scientist watched Angus as a mongoose came over to him sniffing inquisitively.

"They do know what's happening, this was the main reason I came back to help because God is in everything. But there's a problem with the New Babylonians because they have chosen to become the enemies of God. It's a profound concept. God knows all we do and think, even before we have thought it. So these people are the enemies of everything on the Earth, everything."

A robin fluttered from one rock to the next. It flew so close, Angus thought it would land on his shoulder. It was like the robin was showing Angus that all nature is connected through the same divine spark to God. Angus felt this life force through the robin.

Meanwhile, New Babylonian drone technology had developed quickly over a short period. Billions of dollars had been stolen from the tax pots of many countries without accountability, to pay for the development of vile technologies including viruses and plagues to inflict humanity with. They had also replicated human beings, but they'd encountered fundamental problems with this from day one, for the human species had been programmed to break down and fail anyway. This was to protect the sanctity of the soul or inner being. So often all which was replicated was the malfunctioning outer shell of the human. Try as the New Babylonians might, they could never supersede

God. It was like the most beautiful Persian carpets explained in Islamic tradition. Their makers always left a mistake woven into the sequenced stitching somewhere. It was a way of illustrating God's intention of purposefully including the inherent fallibility of mankind.

The Questers had got their spies on the outside as well. Reports were coming back all the time via their untraceable carrier pigeons. The Questers had been developing counter biotechnology to combat the threat of the huge squadrons of New Babylonian drones as well as their other military assets and weapons. One female scientist from the Rosslyn Bio Institute had been kidnapped and re-educated about the world's enemy. Dr Carol Spencer had thus helped develop a type of Chilean falcon which instead of killing pigeons contrary to its nature, had been bred to protect them. When the carrier pigeons flew within their natural boundary in Chile they were protected from all kinds of natural predators, both pigeons and falcons had been reared to work in harmony with the knights.

The City of Light sent messages to the outside world via their low tech messenger pigeons. Lately, carrier pigeons had been flying into other countries protected by Chilean falcons. The incredible thing was both the messenger bird and its falcon protector flew within a force field of ether protection. Templar scientists were rapidly improving everything they were working on. Although this went against the rhythm of nature, it worked well. For the birds as well as all sentient beings were in their own way aware of the threat the New Babylonians posed to humanity and the planet. It was easier understood in people's comprehension of how a shepherd works with a dog in his daily life. God wanted humanity to work in conjunction with all beings since he had created humanity to look after them.

By using carrier pigeons, Questers could keep up to date on developments of the outside world without being monitored by New Babylonian technology. But this was not why Angus was being shown the science wing of the falcon development centre in the caves near the volcano. He was about to be shown the deadly locusts also created to protect the City of Light from enemy drone attacks. But first Angus would have to endure the test of his blood. The knight scientist stepped forward. Angus backed away warily.

"Angus let me show you the progress with the locusts. In Revelations, God unleashes millions of locusts for battle. They were like tiny warhorses with the teeth of lions and breastplates of bronze with hair like women. And riven on their armour was the Hebrew word for God." The Templar stood back. "We've been able to replicate them."

"Yes, I am remembering more and more now."

"Don't be wary Angus all that happens here is for your benefit so you can join us in the battles to come." The knight scientist was waiting for a sign from the locust pit.

Angus wanted to move out of the shadows to be next to the sparkling carved granite stone. Many hands had carved this sacred edifice from the living rock. He ran his hand over the surface of the stone as if feeling the energy.

"Aye laddie, you know the carvers of this granite had advanced skills and it's difficult to see any tool marks on the surface," Angus remarked.

"Ah thought you'd appreciate the stonework. It's not by chance we have with us, the descendants of the builders who constructed the Temple of Solomon. And actually, the descendants of the builders of Atlantis, same people, different time the common denominator being the deluge which finished the planet."

The knight looked up to the oriel window extending out of the living rock of the mountain next to the volcano. Screeching cries pierced the air above, the flying lizards were back.

"And that's where Grandmaster Jacques De Molay is, we re-birthed him a few years ago. But it wasn't as straightforward as many here thought as we had to repair the horrific tortures inflicted on him by the Inquisition."

"Hey, please tell me about those flying monsters, are ya' not living in fear with those giant aerial alligators above?"

The knight laughed. "Not really, but then pterodactyls are dangerous, we replicated them from the plentiful supply of dinosaur DNA available in Patagonia. Our knights range far and wide over this ancient land, gathering information about the Earth's shifting crust. The Templars had never just been about protecting pilgrims and defending the faith. We are the greatest explorers and documenters of all major geo-physical anomalies on the Earth. We know the history of all the lost civilisations, particularly the Atlanteans. God demanded we investigate it." The knight was deadly serious. "And this you should know yourself, Angus, for we are last of the Earth protectors."

The Templar scientist looked around the battlement tops of the City of Light above him.

"And what we discovered was that one entity, one force of design created this planet. But as you should know no man or woman can gaze upon the face of God and live. He works shadow-like through all organisms."

Then more robins appeared, scratching in the undergrowth around the large outer foundation stones. It was as though they understood his words. It made Angus think about the connectivity of all living beings on the planet. It was a moment of enlightenment, allowing him to see the spark of intelligent design was also within himself. The Templar looked at Angus with compassion recognising Angus's empathy with nature and continued.

"The nearest you got to the truth was your discovery of the symbols under where the statue of Admiral Piri Reis once stood at Rosslyn, along with the ancient directions to get here to the City of Light. When the knights came here to the outermost city limits, it was empty with no signs of life. Apart from the robins and there are thousands of them down here." The knight winked at Angus and continued. "After the dissolution of the Templars, we had a problem. Because we still held 'The Holy Ark of the Covenant', but both the activation stones, the Urim and Thummin were lost."

Andrew had known about the lost Templar fleet and the City of Light and about the New Babylonian agenda to destroy the Earth all along.

Through their media agents, the New Babylonians were brain-washing and subverting world populations, indoctrinating them to accept the coming empire of evil, contrary to the will of God. Their ultimate plan was to become immortal, living on through artificial intelligence and robotics known as transhumanism. But, God had already cast them out.

"Come on Angus, you wanted to see what we've got down in this cavern?"

"Not so much, I'd sooner be having a large whisky."

The knight laughed pushing a brass button, suddenly a metal roof started to retract into the stone. As the partition rolled back, a glass roof appeared under it.

The Locust Pit

"It's ok, move closer to see them. They can't harm you. They will only harm the New Babylonians and their helpers. That's their purpose. And I'll show you why."

Locusts bigger than fruit bats began to hover up from the bottom of the pit landing upside down sticking under the glass. Angus was astonished. They had unusual heads similar to the biblical description of those unleashed as a plague, with small jags of teeth and seemingly a bronze girdled chest and hair like women. They watched with their beady yellow eyes. As one moved so did they all, like they were of one mind.

"Now look closely, don't be scared, wait till you see their leaders. They are much bigger." Up they came, thudding against the glass window covering the pit. "We've developed them with a scorpion sting just like in the bible, which instantly congeals their victim's blood causing complete organ failure. We've enlarged their leaders to 5 times the size of a normal locust, enabling them to attack the New Babylonian drones as well. Their venom is powerful enough to melt metal and chips in drone electronics." The Templar scientist smiled as if it were all in a day's work. "We've developed a swarm of over 50 million." Angus drew away from the probing antennas and inquisitive eyes still watching him from their upside-down position, stuck to the glass.

"And will ye' release them to attack the enemy drones?"

"Yes, we will Angus, don't forget we've got our specially adapted falcons. Originally they were designed to protect our carrier pigeons and take out the drones. The locusts will not touch the falcons, they discern the blood of all animals and so know what to attack. The New

Babylonians better watch out. For we know Don Miguel's associates are in league with them."

Angus stood back with a questioning expression. "I saw that you captured his superyacht as well. I saw it moored with the other boats."

"Actually Angus their vessel nearly sank. We had to pump her bilges to get her back to the City of Light's harbour."

"Are the New Babylonians here?"

"Yes, unfortunately, Angus they've arrived and have started to make their bases in the Mapuche sacred forests. They have started clearing the forests, selling the wood and preparing the land for factory farming and genetically modified food." The knight stopped and closed his eyes. "And then they will install their false god belief system to capture the souls of those who have followed the growing trend of moving away from God, not just here but also all over the world. They've been working on that for some years." The Templar looked on expectantly holding his headpiece in his ear.

"This is where the battle starts. The feast of all days has finished and now the Pirate Brethren are preparing to attack," he said, pointing his finger at the granite mountain. A hologram appeared showing squadrons of pirate attack boats, preparing ready for the coming war in the Calbunco crater. "One of their numbers, however, is missing." The knight looked at Angus. "It appears the pirate you defeated in combat was working with the New Babylonians. He was a traitor, he provided them with the information to get here." Angus scowled, but said nothing, remembering the affront on his integrity.

"You know we've replicated ancient technology, which we've weaponised in the launches. It's quite spectacular. We can easily reduce a man to a pillar of salt, exactly like it happened to Lot's wife as she turned back to look at God's destruction of the City of Sodom and Gomorrah." Angus was astounded.

"We understand that you know of this man." The knight pointed at the granite wall and another hologram popped up showing Max Rothman."

Angus stepped back with a sickening expression.

"Yes, I know of him, he was the man who my ex-wife married."

"He is now a New Babylonian without a doubt. And he's got some interesting political connections with those who put profit before the planet. They profit by economically destabilising local peoples when their real goal is to replace local belief systems with those of the New Babylonian cult of their gods. So everything starts here. They think it will be easier to control humanity by installing a new god of their choosing, supported by their infernal evil."

"But what are you going to do about that I da' na' want to be fighting this by myself bonnie lad!"

"We all fight the battle against this evil by ourselves Angus, and in a way, this situation is just an extension of that. But know this now, that De Molay and our leaders have ordered that we release some of the weaponised locusts against them, not all of them, that won't be required just yet. To start with we will send out a smaller army, led by a few of the locust chiefs."

Now all aspects of Angus's previous life began synchronising with his present life. Events were progressing rapidly. The knight stood back. A projected image appeared on the granite wall of the last Grand Master of the Templars, Jacques De Molay, wearing his robes of office and his Templar beret.

Urgently the Templar looked at Angus. "We must act now before they destroy the forests, they've brought in their machines to tear up the Earth. They've started, now Angus you will see all. Stand back, please."

He marched over and cranked the pit lever button twice. All was silent, but beneath the glass roof shadows flickered like a wheat field of moving insect antenna down in the pit. Then the whirring of their wings began to beat as a host of the locust leaders flew up from the depths responding to the order to assemble. A hundred of the locust chiefs with shining breastplates and jags of teeth gathered in lines ready for war as the glass roof disappeared into the rock. Together they lifted into the air sounding like charging chariot wheels. Angus could feel the draft of their wings on his face, he covered his ears from the dreadful din. Their beady yellow eyes twinkled in anticipation of the next order. Then thousands of the regular-sized locust poured out over the side of the pit ready for war. The knight pulled Angus out of the way as they started to take an unnatural interest in him.

"Look!" said the knight pointing, "they move as if directed by God almighty." He wanted to show Angus something else. "I will call in their overall chief. It will be good for you to see this." The knight rolled up his leather sleeve and pricked his skin with the tip of his dagger. Immediately one of the locust chiefs left the rest and flew over landing with its twitching tail on his arm, it was as long as his forearm. It tilted its head towards where the spot of blood was, scenting it. Twisting round it peered at Angus. "Now stretch out your arm, Angus it is your turn!" The knight pricked Angus's outstretched forearm. Angus pulled away saying, "och' for pity sake man, is there any need for this?"

Yes, Angus, it is your turn now."

The locust rose from the knight and dropped with flashing wings onto Angus's outstretched forearm just in front of the red dot of blood, but looking directly at him with bug eyes. Angus could feel its sticky straw-like legs. He could see the locust's incredible hair like that of women with its jags of lion's teeth. The infernal insect wore a bronze breastplate with the name of God inscribed into it. Then it lifted back into the air, circling the pit once and joining the rest.

"If you'd had one drop of New Babylonian blood in your veins, you'd be dead before you hit the floor."

"Ma' God, man, how the hell do they do that?"

The locusts as like one entity turned away from Angus.

"Well, we reversed the New Babylonian bioengineering. They had already developed a genetic modification programme for which they'd created a serum which they then injected into those people with a belief gene, to turn it off. They were attempting to change their genetics. But as with many of their actions, they often failed. They'd previously carried out tests on what they termed religious fanatics, but in essence, those people were just better connected to God. And guess what?" The knight looked over to check that the locusts were out of the pit. "By smelling their blood, the locusts can identify the New Babylonians by the fact that they lack this gene, for they have removed themselves from the Grace of God. Our engineers developed the locusts to smell them out. As you know we work with nature rather than against it. In some curious way, the animal kingdom seems to know what's happening, because they also face the same enemy. If you can imagine everything there is we know, and everything we do not know, every speck of dust, every molecule everything as jigsaw pieces, then the combined picture is God, just as each piece is him also." Angus gawped open-mouthed.

"What do ya' mean 'Him'?"

"Ah yes, good point Angus, it's just a phrase, as we don't know what the power of God is. It's just convenient to call the power Him."

The dark cloud of locusts swarmed around the pit as their leaders emerged. They came out, springing off the walls, swarming in front of the rest in a V formation.

"Stay back! They have the scent of the New Babylonian's blood, nothing can stop them now."

"Ma' God, I feel the wind of their beating wings," said Angus, pushing against the granite walls trying to escape into it.

A trumpet sounded and the locusts swarmed out above the sea around the harbour of the City of Light. The locusts flew to war towards the sacred forests of the Mapuche natives, ready to attack those who were attempting to destroy them.

"One more thing Angus or should I say, Grail Knight," said the Templar scientist. It is time to restore your rightful rank. "Kneel" he ordered, pushing Angus's shoulder down. Angus stooped onto one knee. The Templar drew his sword and dubbed Angus on his right shoulder. "Rise, Knight Commander Angus MacWilliam now tested, and fit to take his place at battle stations once again." The Templar handed Angus a small dirk with a coin bearing two knights on one horse set into the handle. Angus kissed its razor edge with a sense of relief. "And Angus, know that you will be honoured in the Temple in London. The knights have ordered that we create your effigy in stone to be there for eternity. And I have to tell you there's more to this situation than meets the eye. Perhaps for another adventure, for this is one of many."

"Och laddie I da' na' need such opulence!"

"Knight Commander, it will be not for your benefit. It's a portal for something far greater. Now say no more about it. It is done! And the war is here."

The New Babylonians cometh

Max Rothman had arrived in the Mapuche sacred forests along with local men and women he'd paid off to start extracting timber from the forests. They'd worshipped and bowed down before their infernal gods dedicating black offerings and sacrifices, carrying out corruption and bringing death as usual. But their blood was marked, changed in some unfathomable way, damning them. All of nature knew this.

Already the logging companies had started to rip up trees, scattering wildlife further into the sacred forests. Great trucks rumbled down, ripping the ground and striping mud tracks into it as excavators began disembowelling the forest. Max was striding about as usual smoking his cigar and talking on his mobile phone. Soon the locusts descended through the clouds scenting their enemies. Angus and the knight scientist could see everything filmed from cameras attached to the locust leaders flying above the logging camp. They forged onward and then started to descend steeply.

Angus was shocked to see how well armed the New Babylonian camp was. They'd even got industrial flame throwers standing by as if they'd anticipated the day the locust swarm would come. Now the locusts with their flickering wings began to form into a humanoid shape during their descent. They'd created a giant animated and alive avenging angel and in this formation, they attacked the camp. The larger locust leaders formed the head and wings. It appeared as if the angel was holding an oscillating sword. Men fell away before the plague of locusts, holding their faces away from their stinging scorpion tails. As the locust moved they sounded like rolling iron wheels grating over the glass. Max ran away, trying to hide pursued by three of the giant locust chiefs, but there was no place for him to go. He stumbled over the body of a digger driver already stiff with death, Max's cigar crumpled over his cheek with sparks smouldering his hair as he fell to the floor.

"What the hell, get the flame throwers out?"

With twitching antennae the locusts attacked. A larger leader crawled up his chest amongst the terrible whirring of their wings, gripping Max's silk shirt with its barbed feet. More locust leaders joined in and began to sting Max with their scorpion tales. Max gurgled some unfathomable curse and tried in vain to dig himself into the mud. He screamed, gaping mouthed, as the locust retracted their barb stings from his flesh, filling him with poison. His tongue swelled choking him.

"Look away if you want Angus, it's a nasty business, but it will be more terrible than you can imagine if we let them continue with this destruction of the planet."

The rest of them began to fumble about the flame throwers. But they could only burn those locusts directly in front of them. Bursts of flames squirted out, igniting some of the locusts. Some of them sacrificed themselves, falling smoking to the ground. Others flitted behind the men operating the flame throwers. And with their sticky probing feet, they attached themselves to their clothing and began to sting them. Like Max, they died quickly falling forward with rolling eyes and swelling tongues. The locust army stung to death all the New Babylonian agents in the Mapuche forest within minutes. Those non-New Babylonians who remained, stood holding their hands over their eyes watching the locusts form up again, lifting into the air. None of the survivors had New Babylonian blood. For if they had, the locusts would have scented it and killed them. The oscillating locust angel rose into the air and flickered off with intent.

The City of Light was making ready for war. The pirate launches were ready with their crews standing by. The Pegasus was already sailing out, patrolling its territory, soon to return for the purpose she had been built which was to carry the Holy Ark of God.

Caroline Agostini fell to the floor raging, hammering the floor. As she cursed God, spittle and tears blurred her make-up.

"I swear I will kill whoever it was responsible for this!"

Somehow during her time with Max, she'd become drastically desensitised to the reality of their destruction of the planet. Pulling herself together, she started to make phone calls to friends of friends. That didn't take much. As you will see the New Babylonians abysmal rituals had always been designed for those participating in evil to recover from any emotional trauma speedily through mind manipulation techniques. Caroline picked up the phone.

"Hi, Damon can you get a message through to the Senators?"

"Hey, Caroline how are you? Senators are at the Gates of Ishtar, they've got urgent business to sort out. They have finished the artificial intelligence manifesto. In fact, it's going to be deployed shortly." He said like an arrogant schoolboy.

Damon had already witnessed what had happened in the Mapuche forest.

"Sorry about Max. We never saw it coming, did we? We never knew who that bastard Angus MacWilliam was either. Don't worry about Max he will be revenged soon by one of us. We are commanding the drone fleet to attack and much more. We must take the Mapuche forests, there are riches there. And my Max found the gold deposits! And then you'll get your share."

"Damon, I am not bothered about Isobel, we know she's with the God enemy. It was always going to happen based on her father."

"Well, he's back, and he's with the remaining Templars. I guess they were here for the gold as well then?" questioned Damon.

"I am done with Isobel, we were done long ago. She's been calling me from Southern Chile. The problem was we couldn't get an exact read on her location. The readings kept changing, scrambled by some kind of force field surrounding it. The Island kept appearing and disappearing. I don't know what's happening there? And she didn't seem to know anything. And as for the gold, and yes, you guessed it, it belongs to the Templars. They brought it from the Temple of Solomon."

"The Senators have been informed, that the drone squadrons are on the way along with our forces. All that remains is to dedicate the bodies of our dead to Baal. I've issued the order for the robot army to clean up. We can burn them as an offering."

But as the New Babylonians began to clear up in the forest thousands of Mapuche natives watched silently from the darkness of the forest. Angus had wondered what had happened to Vanessa's Island housekeeper Olga. His question was answered, for she appeared there, at the head of the native host holding an axe.

The attack of the mice and rats

Often in nature the smallest creature can be the most deadly. Soon frenzied forest mice emerged from their cover. They formed up into a seething mass moving as one like a giant blanket lit with a million eyes. As the robots stomped through the undergrowth the plague of mice wheeled round to face them. God often uses the smallest creations to defeat the most formidable of his enemies. The thing was, there was a mineral compound within the hydraulic oil in the pipes of the robots that the mice were attracted to and it was a specific mineral that they needed. As soon as they got its scent the mass of mice stopped in their tracks. The attack on the robots started with several mice scampering up them fearlessly and bobbing in and out of their mechanical joints looking for the pipes. Like arteries, which carried blood, the hydraulic pipes of the robots carried a life force for them also. Although the robots knew nothing about their status as 'being alive', even though mad scientists had tried to cobble together living flesh with microchips, these machines blundered on 'dead' on their mechanical feet. And such men that had financed this emerging technology were hoping that somehow it would allow them to live longer than their allotted time.

Frenzied, the plague of mice ran up and into the robots and began to gnaw into their plastic piping. Despite the infestation of mice inside them, they lumbered forward through the forest. The mice scampered behind their brazen masked heads, making them appear as though they were expressing multiple emotions behind their hollow eyes. Then one just stopped dead, and out of it poured the mineral hydraulic fluid. The mask it wore dropped and fell to the floor. There were now thousands of seething mice feeding off the oil. More robots cranked to a halt. The other robots clanking down into the forest glades simply slumped, covered with the swarming mice. Soon they had all cranked to a halt in various stages of seizure, done to death by the attacking plague of mice.

The New Babylonian senators controlling the operation with their agents, could do nothing but look on in dismay. The rats followed up the attack not only eating any dead mice but also feasting on the mineral oil from the pipes. As quickly as they'd come, they went, leaving the robots twisted in obscene angles and the forest was quiet again.

The drone Assets of Babylon

From the New Babylonian HQ, another order was given to deploy the drone fleet from nearby Argentina armed with all the latest death weapons their designers could drag from the pits of hell. They whirred up into the sky on mass from a redundant airfield. These drones were a faceless technology designed to kill without mercy. Wherever the New Babylonian destroyers went for blood profits they were protected by their drones. Their destructive capacity had already been tested over numerous worldwide wars.

The Templar scientist held his earpiece listening and looking at Angus.

"I wish ta' hell I knew what was happening, how all this started," Angus said searching.

"Firstly Angus this is not your concern, God sees everything, even before it happens. The New Babylonians can just switch off to any amount of distress. They've conditioned themselves to be base and unenlightened. They'd cultivated the downward spiral and they have a very low vibrational frequency. And as their souls shrink, the more material things they want, and so the more they age, endeavouring to fill the gaping spiritual hole inside of them. Death comes quicker for them than any others this is why they seek immortality."

Angus wanted to say something. He wanted to explain that he felt there was a battle going on inside himself. He knew the Templar would know exactly what he meant. It was a battle that had raged inside of himself, as it had raged around him.

"Well, as suspected the New Babylonians have released their drone army. De Molay, our Templar Grandmaster has countered it. Now is time to release all locusts from the pit. The war commences."

The New Babylonian Senate had been watching political developments in Chiloe, Southern Chile. Here the New Babylonians had been previously working with escaped renegade Nazis in many South American countries in fact they'd sponsored them. Many of the V1 and V2 rocket scientists had developed this technology which bombed Britain. They in turn were commandeered to create early drone technology for the New Babylonians, becoming in that process, New Babylonian themselves. And now another product of their evil was on its way whirring across the Argentinian border into Chile. "You see they operate by consolidating evil from any time in the world's weary history," said the Templar scientist pressing a lever embedded in the stone. He grimaced, turning to Angus. "Your boat is arriving Angus prepare yourself, brother."

"Let all the locusts rise from the pit Angus, their time has come," the knight scientist said.

"Och' man alive, keep them stick monsters away from me!" Angus replied.

"The New Babylonians have searched to destroy all that is good for a long time. We are not quite sure if they know what they are doing. But that's why it's so hard to do good at any level now through any system of governments. They've infested all the world Angus, all of it. And the first thing they use to identify a person by, is how good they are. They are attempting to get rid of the good people as these are the people who can see them for what they are, more so than others. The age-old battle between good and evil persists."

"Aye ya' right, I know many people that think the same thing. Ya' know you would think that a proper government would ha' a department for the greater good of the people or a good ideas department. Och' but na', seems governments intend to do wrong but make it look like they are doing good to fool the dumbed-down masses."

The Templar scientist looked weary. "Oh dear Angus, you know how it works, it's in every man or woman's capacity to become one of them, even you Angus." The knight looked to the heavens with a grimace. "But sometimes Angus, God sets the reset button and brings it all to an end."

"Will we win? Do we have a chance?" Angus replied, watching the monitor.

The Templar scientist held his hand over his eyes because of the intense sunlight. "Here they come, look at them, look at them! They've protected our messenger pigeons for years and now they will attack the enemy drones". But before he'd finished crossing himself, Angus climbed down into the pirate war launch which was crammed with knights, ready for war.

"Will we win, will we win?"

The Templar looked down at Angus in the boat. "Angus, that's not the point. God decides who wins. You see the lesson to learn in all of this, is that the New Babylonians are always near to us. They might be family members or lovers or employers. They might be good people who have lost their way, trying to survive in the world. Many people think that God has abandoned them. And so they will grasp the poisoned hand of the enemy under this or any other delusion and then they will be enticed to serve them. The battle on the main is inside ourselves, it happens in us all Angus."

Angus knew this story because his ex-wife had gone the same way. He knew how the New Babylonian cult had infiltrated all levels of world governments, heightened by the manipulation of people's weakness and insecurity by bribing them. And then evil became their purposeful policy.

The Templars learnt that the people who'd ignored God in their daily lives had unwittingly become the slaves to the New Babylonians, compliant to their propaganda of fear through media outlets. It was a familiar picture. They infiltrate host countries till they'd drained them dry of all of their assets, resulting in another soulless husk country for the New Babylonian empire.

"You know Angus you can never tell who will join the Babylonians. It's a supernatural dimensional mystery, Just like God." The Templar looked at Angus down in the launch listening to his orders from the City of Light. Make ready for the fight Angus your time is here."

"Aye, yer' right, but there's still good knights left, I am ready!" Angus replied.

More boats appeared under the granite harbour wall steered by pirates. Laura Bellamy was at the wheel of one of them. She waved at Angus in the next boat along on the harbour wall. The launches were gathering ready for the charge over the sea.

"Aye, well, my man, we're ready now," Angus said, tightening his grip on his famous Viking sword. It was clear to Angus, that the battle was as much spiritual as it was physical. And that the battle inside each good human to turn bad was as real as the sun now shining in the sky like an anthem for the City of Light. Angus could see Vanessa and her brother Rodrigo in another boat coming towards the harbour wall which worried him. The Templar could see Angus's trepidation. "Don't worry, there's more to Vanessa than you ever thought Angus. Do you know Angus that even your daughter wanted to fight the New Babylonians?"

Angus said nothing, but his heart was filled with pride.

El Nino leads the stray dogs

"And Vanessa would not remain at the City of Light saying she had a right to fight them the same as her brother, and to tell you the truth, both of them have remarkable skills." Angus looked over through the fine mist that the boats had generated and could see them both waving at him. From the harbour wall, the Templar spoke on. "Did you ever realise why you brought that white bulldog with you Angus? Did you ever understand it was all planned?"

"Och' man, tell me, El Nino is a law unto himself. Aye, balls of steel. Like a Hibee supporter," Angus replied, smiling.

The knight presenter looked bemused. "Exactly! he was chosen to lead all the wild dogs here against the robot dogs as their mission is as great as ours. For this is a conflict between all the protectors of planet Earth and the New Babylonians. Look across over there in the forest!"

The knight pointed to the scrub shoreline next to the walls of the City of Light. Sure enough, El Nino appeared leading thousands of dogs, he bounded ahead of every stray dog from miles around and they were heading towards the robot attack dogs clunking through the forests with lasers positioned between their eyes, burning anything that came in their way. Until that is they were attacked by the thousands of stray dogs.

"The thing is Angus the robot dogs have been programmed to only kill other humans and not dogs." He looked up to heaven exclaiming, "game, set and match".

A defeat of terrible proportions was taking place as the wild dogs disembowelled the robot dogs. On the main, they ripped out hardware and machine components, but sometimes there were traces of blood from real dog body tissue the New Babylonians had connected into them. El Nino had searched out the robot dog leader and was gripping onto to his jugular pipe. The lead robot dog clanked on with El Nino hanging onto him dangling from its plastic throat pipe.

More launches full of knights and pirates came to the wall. Rodrigo had taken command of a launch and Vanessa had helped him prepare. Both were excellent in small boats. There were by now some 50 launches gathered at the harbour wall.

Then the Templar scientist released the rest of the locust army and they flew upwards with flickering wings like huge swathes of fields of barley following the rest. For a moment the locust angel darkened the sun and as they went Angus could see their mask-like faces staring down. They gathered into their war formation, of the Archangel Michael. The Templar scientist pointed into the sky. The great locust angel was moving to war as a new aerial phenomenon was occurring. Angus remembered the Chilean falcons curiously following him whilst living on the Island of Sailing Souls. Now the sky was filling up with them again, thousands, flying in waves of irregular lines like the scrawling writing of a giant in the sky.

"Don't forget this strange weapon," said a knight handing Angus his sawn-off shotgun with a full cartridge belt.

Now Angus was ready for war in the launch. The vanguard of Templar leaders and Pirates who were with him were all armed to the teeth with a multitude of weapons. There was a telescopic laser fixed near the boat's high powered engine which propelled the launch without moving parts. Above squadrons of falcons whooshed with their beating wings over them through the skies. Angus thought back to the curious phenomenon of small garden birds attacking the latest Wi-Fi technology towers back in Scotland. He recalled footage of birds pecking wires and shorting them out. The birds were supernaturally aware that high powered magnetic waves were dangerous to them. This was indeed military technology, which had been designed to subdue humanity. Some said that the towers were in fact weapons designed to work in conjunction with bio-engineered plagues. In some instances, the Wi-Fi masts burst into flames. It was all adding up now as nature in some unfathomable way was aware of what the enemies of God were attempting to do to mankind. But these murmurings of defiance meant nothing to what was coming.

Even the Templar scientist put on his helmet. "We are ready to start, let battle commence." Enemy drones appeared and began firing randomly into the jungle around the City of Light. The New Babylonian HQ and their Senators had also anticipated such a day. Not only had they created swarms of computer microchipped mosquitoes, they'd also created artificial robot locusts to attack their biological opposites, now swarming to war in the shape of St Michael. So much money had been stolen from taxpayers over the years to pay for New Babylonian robotic's development. These black programmes had grown malevolently. And now these computerised New Babylonian robotic locusts formed up in the shape of the enemy of St Michael. They formed into the dark angel Lucifer, who God had cast out of heaven. This was another reflection of biblical predictions, but worse was still to come.

As the skies blackened, missiles appeared speeding towards the City of Light. De Molay had anticipated the attack and immediately neutralised them by beams of intense sunlight. Templar laser technology had been adapted to melt their missiles like they were made of chocolate, rendering them useless. They fell from the skies into the seas, sizzling as they sank. Angus donned his Quester mantle and helmet and pulled up the hood to keep the sea breeze off him. From the forbidden area where 'The Ark of the Covenant' was hidden, there was a great activity as Templars and female Levi priests in purple robes circled it. Then Andrew Sinclair appeared standing well back from the proceedings. He was part of the team activating the Holy Ark. Above and around them, all manner of birds and flying lizards circled on the thermal currents. Nature was also preparing for war bathed in the strange blue light that emanated from the Holy Ark.

Below on the sea the flotilla of launches crewed by both pirates and knights scudded towards the enemy. Two hundred launches in V formation scudded towards the enemy kicking up spray as they went. The spray formed a mist making it appear as if the launches were levitating. The enemy appeared in their strange craft being directed remotely by tech experts from their Gates of Ishtar, New Babylonian HQ in California. The whole battlescape had already been programmed just like their latest reality gaming technology. Already the bright young men and women sat at their gaming consoles in their headphones, directing the battle for Earth, all in hyper-reality mode. They already calculated the speeds of the knights and pirates in their launches. Providentially the Templars and the Questers had kidnapped several of the most famous video gaming experts and converted them for the good. They also had a bank of computer technology experts working out their enemy's next move.

Meanwhile, De Molay had received information giving him the exact reading as to where the Gates of Ishtar were. He'd received this from messenger pigeons who had returned in relays across the world. The New Babylonian drones who attacked the carrier pigeons had been attacked and destroyed by the Chilean falcons protecting them. De Molay had a plan up his sleeve as usual, and it wasn't going to end nicely.

Most of the enemy soldiers manning this strange craft were mercenaries, already genetically modified to eradicate pity or mercy. Augmented Intelligence was how the enemy liked to describe their humanoids and their boats were manned by them. They stood impassively balancing as they scudded over the seas stabilising with advanced gyroscopes, chipped into their part-brain augmented by electronic circuits.

Undeterred the army of knights and pirates raced towards their enemies. Above in the air, the Chilean falcons had started to attack the New Babylonian drones. Some of them were fired upon, bursting them open in explosions of feathers. But mainly, the falcons smashed the lightweight drones into plastic waste. And in this fashion, they went from one to the other mangling their propellers. Sometimes before they fell to the ground they misfired upon their own drones causing more destruction.

Angus stood in the lead launch moving over the waves like a surfboard. The greater mass of enemy hover-boats came against them. The charge of the sea launches opened fire with their sun rays against the New Babylonian boats. Some of them exploded in a mass of flying bits of plastic technology melting and twisting in heaps mingling microchips with blood and real tissue as the part machines exploded. But more of them came. Now in the lead boat, Angus stood brandishing his Viking sword crying, "Charge! Onward, ever onward!" Their knight's swords protected them by an unknown force field. Soon all the launches had smashed into the enemy boats, and hand to hand combat ensued.

Although outnumbered the knights and pirates were better warriors than the part machine Babylonians. The thing was these augmented intelligence beings were being controlled remotely and as such, there was always a slight delay from when a New Babylonian operator back at the Gates of Ishtar, pressed the button and the machine warrior responded in the boat. This critical one-second delay was their Achilles heel. "They are weak on the uptake," cried Angus as he turned to face the seven feet high enemy raising a sword ready to smash down on him. Quickly with his light razor-sharp Viking sword, he plunged it into the monster through its neck severing all its circuits. It just stopped, locked in that position.

And so the battle raged Templars and pirates and the Knights of St John raging against the New Babylonian part human, part machines. Vanessa and her brother worked together as a team firing bullets of light at them with high powered machine guns. Angus sliced away at the robots with his famous sword and if anything got away from him he fired at them with the shotgun which had a devastating effect on them at close range. He clicked out the spent cartridges and loaded up again.

The Battle of the Mosquitoes

Mosquitoes from miles and miles around lifted from dank swamps all around forming the darkest of clouds. It was something that happened from time to time anyway. But this time they were reacting to the miniature robotic replicas of themselves swarming into Chile released from anomalous New Babylonian military aircraft. It was a similar phenomenon to what happened in nature, when a relatively tame caged bird like a parrot is released into the wild. Quite often the other indigenous birds will attempt to kill it. The mosquitoes outnumbered their robotic counterparts and attacked them on mass and in this fashion destroyed every single one of them.

The Levi priest attendants to 'The Ark of the Covenant' had arrived. Andrew Sinclair was with them. Every ten seconds a grumbling voice emanated from the Ark and it shook as if trying to raise itself from the cart. Andrew raised his hands to the purple-robed priests. They pulled the Ark of God from the back of the cart. It seemed weightless. Each priest grasped the end of the Ark's carrying poles, which levitated intermittently, lifting the carriers off their feet. Andrew was fine-tuning the Thummin and Urim stones in conjunction with the High Priest and his breastplate of precious gems. Every so often Andrew banged the stones together and a welter of blue energy boomed around them in his endeavour to start up the Holy Ark. The Ark was followed by the other attendants carrying the Shamir or ancient stone cutting technology previously used to create the tunnels under the City of Light. For the moment that part of its job had been done. But there was now another more deadly task for it to undertake protecting the City of Light from the enemies of God. There was a sound from the skies like the trumpet of an angel. Red and orange light illuminated the City of Light.

The Templar's flagship Pegasus and De Molay had returned to collect the Holy Ark. Pegasus waited for it at the landing stage. The great steel galley slowed down on her approach to the Calbunco jetty. Astoundingly the aged Jacques De Molay was sat propped on a wooden chair next to the ship's wheel, still reciting biblical scripture. A New Babylonian surveillance drone was relaying pictures of him bound to his chair back to their headquarters. The New Babylonian Senate asked for close-up shots. The senate was made up of different types of so-called elite operators comprising of politicians and scientists to bankers and actors to social media presenters. They watched impassively as De Molay recited biblical tracks. They so wanted him gone.

De Molay spoke. "There comes a point in the history of mankind when God makes harsh judgements for their future. I feel that time is getting closer. Bring the Holy Ark aboard. We will take God's Ark into battle." The Levi priest turned around to face the Pegasus and lifted it again with its carrying poles. But that was not required. The Ark raised itself off the ground and the priests hung from its carrying poles, the Ark travelled itself onboard the Pegasus lifting up its carriers. De Molay who had not lost his humour in such dire times smiled.

The New Babylonians smirked at each other as if they controlled the entire world from their Gates of Ishtar HQ. Then, as if they came out of the sea, a cloud of mosquitos rose up over the bulwarks of Pegasus. They swarmed at De Molay. But they could get no further to him than two feet. They fired charges at him, exploding and flashing in the protective force field surrounding him. He appeared as if under a glass shell which was a shielding force of vibrating energy. As the insects got near they simply burst into flames in the intense energy. Templars fired their mounted swivel cannon adapted to use laser technology at the bulk of electronic mosquitoes frying them on mass.

The Ark landed softly onto the red meteorite stone on the forward deck of the Pegasus like the one in the crypt at Rosslyn Chapel. Andrew Sinclair followed walking solemnly with his hands behind his back. De

Molay met God's Ark speaking Holy Scripture and begging forgiveness. Then the Ark spoke to them.

"Take the Ark and tell all those of God to go to the new stone chamber at the City of Light and wait. Take all the animals and every living being with you even the insects, summon all your forces back there and wait". The Ark waited silently on the flat meteorite stone, as something was about to happen.

The Deluge comes

It started with an eerie light appearing in the East. The exhausted host of knights and pirates lay down their blood-splattered weapons and watched from their launches in the sea whilst the New Babylonians regrouped for another attack against them. Angus was aware that although they had battled bravely the New Babylonians had many more resources as another wave of New Babylonian hover boats appeared on the horizon. He knew this because now the Templar scientists had summoned the pterodactyls or 'flying alligators' as Angus had described them in this situation. They launched off, descending to attack the second wave of hover boats manned by yet more artificial intelligence beings. They caused much destruction amongst the boats of the knights and pirates and many of the pterodactyls were blown out of the sky in bloody bits.

De Molay and the Holy Ark priests stopped in their tracks and stared in that direction as if looking for a sign. Vanessa and Angus waited in their boats reunited with Isobel and Rodrigo. El Nino had returned a hero and sat there proudly waiting like all the other animals for the final command. The warriors and their vessels were now all pointing towards the Calbunco volcano having been turned by the sea in that direction like compass pointers. The Calbunco volcano above the City of Light was about to open. The Earth shuddered and the reflection from the eerie eastern light flashed across the surface of the sea, then the sea started to rise proportionately, lifting all the vessels and Pegasus in the huge swell.

The entrance opened fully into the Calbuco volcano where the Holy Ark had cut the rock to the inner sanctum of the City of Light. It opened like a door and the flow of the sea began to pour into it. The Earth shuddered again as it began to change direction. The great stone citadel which had been built so strongly moved over its rollers and then stabilised. Its masonry structures had been adapted to withstand earthquakes and catastrophes. Each interlocking stone slides in such a way, so as not to compromise its structural integrity. De Molay fell to his knees and prayed to God, all of them hunched over praying. And on the swirling seas, the launches and boats with Pegasus began to slowly move towards the opening in the volcano as a huge whirlpool began to spiral. As the seas rose beneath them it did the same in other areas, exposing great structures from the other civilisations through the conflicting forces at play. The seas began to wash onto the land where the battles had taken place against the New Babylonians.

Soon there would be no traces of the New Babylonian forces not just in the ongoing battle, but also in all their bases worldwide. Nothing could stop this deluge as it gently engulfed the land and the people who had not taken heed of the signs lay drowning looking like millions of midges on the surface. Buildings in all the world's cities began to collapse before the rising seas. Flashes of light and thunder emanated not from around the Earth, seemingly from inside it. The liquid magma of its core had awoken and was pouring out, creating unnatural thermal currents in the world's oceans. At the same time, the Earth tilted again realigning to a previous pattern of the procession around the sun. The cries of despair from humanity were quickly silenced by the seas as they mercifully engulfed their screams. Those who remained near the City of Light flowed down with the surging waters. Angus, Vanessa, Isobel and Rodrigo held onto their boat as the surge of the sea picked them up and lifted the launch on the white surf towards the rock door which had opened in the side of Calbunco. Angus could see the Templars, Knights and Pirates ahead beckoning them and lifting up their arms crying out to God. All of them flowed through the huge door in the stone into the City of Light seemingly built for such a day of the Deluge. When all the forces of good had gone through the great stone door, it began to close, grinding against the walls and booming shut.

The Last Tango dance

There was a gentle breeze now comforting the fallen man on the ground lying on a mound of the earth like it was a pillow on the perimeter of the famous chapel. But their dance would take place in the sacred stone crypt of Rosslyn Chapel. Warm fingers of wind brushed his face. It was touch and go if the man lived. But then he breathed drawing in the air like it was an elixir of life. He'd chosen life over death and the blood began to flow through his veins.

A promised Tango

The man down, Angus MacWilliam had once promised his girlfriend that he'd dance an exotic Milonga Tango with her. She expected that. And good to the letter of her word, she'd arrived in a slinky dark dress shaking out her gipsy hair. He'd toned his body for this moment cutting a fine figure in an Argentine double-breasted lounge suit. It was a big moment for them both. Everything had to be just right. Both of them wore brown patent leather dancing shoes, hers with a sculpted lady's Cuban heal clicking as she walked towards him over the stone-flagged floor. He'd chosen old fashioned tango shoes from Buenos Aries. The struggles over the past months had finished for now. There was no more pain. Together they'd overcome and resisted the hold of the New Babylonians, becoming enlightened through some remarkable portal that had changed their reality. Finally, now, they could just dance.

As Vanessa took hold of Angus's hand the light on her pearls glinted in his eyes. Angus slid his hand down into her waist. Holding her waist, his hand spanned round from her navel to her spine. He lifted her other hand into the air. Just how Don Carlos had taught him. There was a clear gap between their bodies as the protocol of the Milonga dance demanded. Their passion was erotically regulated yet enhanced by the disciplined tango. There was a heavy aroma in Rosslyn's crypt like it had absorbed all the passionate energy and sweat of other dancers over the years and which breathed back at Vanessa and Angus. She nodded to Don Carlos and he placed the needle onto the old vinyl record. It crackled into life ignited by the echoing voice of Miguel Zoto accompanied by the Spanish accordion. They began to circle each other with deft gliding movements. Angus had learnt well from Don Carlos the expert tango teacher back in Chile, his eyes were moist with admiration as Angus and Vanessa moved together. Occasionally, their faces touched and Don Carlos smiled in a way denouncing their flesh on flesh as a crime of passion. The two dancers continued through the ages gliding over the mountains of Chile and Scotland together. The stones down in Rosslyn's crypt absorbed them both as it had done with other dancers, who had arrived in this place for one reason or another. The dance continued, but eventually, the two dancers faded into a patch of light in the darkness and disappeared. The crypt of Rosslyn was empty again. A fresh red rose lay on the altar.

Outside the atmosphere freshened as Angus felt a full breeze on his face now. He remembered the sun shining on a spring day in Scotland. Early morning birds were singing. Rosslyn was here again now reflecting nature's green. All the carvings and sculptures had turned into a small forest representing the life force of nature. Her arching buttresses bowed like trees and all the animals and birds were animated. Here religion, spirit and life force fused together. He saw the stone birds and plants transform into real-life pulsating energy. A robin moved close to him and watched inquisitively tilting its head at him. Just as one had done on the outskirts of the City of Light. Now it was spring outside and he was back where it had all started outside Rosslyn Chapel. Hundreds of robins were strutting about in the undergrowth near where he was, they flew low under the undergrowth with purpose. For nature's smallest warriors had as much courage as lions.

Then an old lady came through the gate in the Rosslyn perimeter wall. She looked at Angus on the earth as though she knew him.

"Are you alright son?"

"Aye Mam, thank you, I just feel a bit woozy," Angus couldn't be exactly sure, but he seemed to recognise the slight accented Spanish voice but different from say Bolivian or Argentinean Spanish.

"Do you want me to get help, Angus?"

Angus began to sit up. It was such an iridescent morning. He thought he heard her mention his name."Nay lassie there's no need, I think I am going to be ok now."

The old lady looked compassionately down at him. In a way, she reminded him of an old version of Vanessa. But he didn't want to indulge in that thought for he didn't want to acknowledge what he might have lost or what he'd experienced or if it had really happened.

"It will all be alright now. I know exactly what you're thinking. It's like something changed in the world recently, isn't it?" Choked with a sudden burst of emotion Angus with his dry mouth, knew what she meant, but he was too emotional to answer.

"And don't forget your silver charm, over there, the little man on the horse, It looks like King Robert the Bruce brandishing his axe." Angus looked over into the grass as the old lady went over and picked it up.

"I feel I know this symbol," she said with half a smile, putting it in his outstretched hand.

"Aye ma'm it is King Robert the Bruce, but I canna' tell you how it got to be here." But actually, he knew. He knew fine well because he had forgotten to return it to Isobel.

Angus watched as the old lady moved back to a gap in the perimeter wall. It seemed that even with her stick she moved panther-like through it. But it wasn't clear where she was going.

The sun lifted gently over Rosslyn illuminating the glen and making the chapel stand out like a lost island in a sea of nature. Angus got to his feet feeling cleared of something. He looked over to where the old lady had disappeared. He couldn't see any sign of her, as one more time, he got up from the ground enveloped in the light of the sun. But somehow he knew he would see her face again.

And so it continues....

www.ingramcontent.com/pod-product-compliance
Lightning Source LLC
Chambersburg PA
CBHW030602310726
48979CB00003B/543

* 9 7 8 1 7 3 9 1 0 1 9 1 6 *